SANTA FE DECEPTION

A SCOTT HUNTER MYSTERY

SANTA FE DECEPTION

A Scott Hunter Mystery

MYRON BEARD

SUNSTONE
PRESS

SANTA FE

Sunstone books may be purchased for educational, business, or sales promotional use.
For information please write: Special Markets Department, Sunstone Press,
P.O. Box 2321, Santa Fe, New Mexico 87504-2321.

Book and cover design › R. Ahl
Printed on acid-free paper
∞
eBook 978-1-61139-663-8

Library of Congress Cataloging-in-Publication Data

Names: Beard, Myron, 1947- author. | Beard, Myron, 1947- Scott Hunter
  mystery.
Title: Santa Fe deception / by Myron Beard.
Description: Santa Fe, NM : Sunstone Press, 2022. | Series: A Scott Hunter
  mystery | Summary: "Psychologist Scott Hunter returns to his hometown,
  Santa Fe, at the request of his ex-wife to help solve the murder of the
  man for whom she left him, and his agreement to help her leads to
  surprising changes in his life"-- Provided by publisher.
Identifiers: LCCN 2022019569 | ISBN 9781632933775 (paperback) | ISBN
  9781611396638 (epub)
Subjects: LCSH: Hunter, Scott (Fictitious character) |
  Murder--Investigation--Fiction. | Santa Fe (N.M.)--Fiction. | LCGFT:
  Detective and mystery fiction. | Novels.
Classification: LCC PS3602.E2515 S26 2022 | DDC 813/.6--dc23/eng/20220513
LC record available at https://lccn.loc.gov/2022019569

WWW.SUNSTONEPRESS.COM
SUNSTONE PRESS / POST OFFICE BOX 2321 / SANTA FE, NM 87504-2321 /USA
(505) 988-4418 / FAX (505) 988-1025

DEDICATION

I dedicate this book to my grandparents, Lutie and Earl Beard, and to my parents, Ava and Joe Beard. They gave me a deep appreciation of Santa Fe and the wonderful diversity of culture, people, and perspectives in the community. I am forever grateful for having my view of the world enlarged through their lives.

PREFACE

I grew up in Santa Fe where my grandfather homesteaded in 1919, arriving from Illinois mostly by train hopping. Growing up, I came to appreciate the diversity of the three cultures (Native American, Hispanic, and Anglo) and the potential for the richness of relationships as well as the possibility for tension and conflict between them. The history of the region coupled with the intersecting cultures provides a very interesting, and complex, backdrop for mystery and intrigue. My interest in the cultures, and human behavior, has been deepened through my studies in psychology. Having received my doctorate in counseling psychology, I developed a deeper understanding of human motivation, particularly in extreme narcissists and their incredible ability to deceive and manipulate. This book is a product of my ongoing curiosity of the criminal mind in the context of the city, and people, I love so much.

In *Santa Fe Deception*, the first of my Scott Hunter mysteries, we learn that psychologist Scott departed Santa Fe eleven years earlier, totally humiliated with his life torn asunder by the betrayal of his ex-wife, Rebecca. Now after years with no communication, Rebecca calls him to assist her with a very serious problem, Scott must decide whether or not he will return to the scene of her betrayal to help solve the murder of the man with whom she cheated, her husband, Blake Martin. Scott vacillates between being intrigued by Rebecca's request and questioning his own state of mind for getting involved.

Serendipitously, Scott is able to reconnect with an old friend, Miguel Montez, now lead investigator for the Santa Fe Police Department. Following an impressive career managing a field office for the FBI, Miguel has returned to his hometown police force. In an unofficial capacity, Miguel asks Scott to interact with persons of interest who had possible motives for murdering Blake. Using his psychological training, Scott is often able to detect the kind of behaviors that are deceptive, thus helping narrow the field of suspects. Scott's journey takes him face-to-face with his own demons as well as with the underbelly of the art world, the illegal drug scene, and police corruption. Helping to solve this case shakes up Scott's world and causes him to redirect his priorities.

Those readers who already have an affection for Santa Fe because of its diverse culture, its wide-ranging artists and art galleries, its amazing culinary offerings, and its uniquely beautiful architecture, will feel as if they are visiting this charming city again. Those unfamiliar with Santa Fe will find themselves intrigued and drawn into the richness of the people and culture. In addition, mystery enthusiasts will experience a deep satisfaction trying to figure out the who, what, and why of this mystery. This book will take the reader through many twists and turns along the way. The twists and turns even surprised me as I was writing! I found myself so intrigued with the plot, and what might happen, that I often woke up in the middle of the night and unable to sleep, went to my study and continued writing. While I have written, and published, three non-fiction business books, none gave me the same enjoyment or pleasure as writing this piece of work.

This book would not have happened without the support and great assistance of my publisher, Sunstone Press. I am particularly grateful for the great editing of Jim Smith and the encouragement of Carl Condit. As with my previous books, my wife Ann, has not only been an amazing supporter and partner, but was greatly helpful in the early editing of the book. Without her encouragement and nudging the book may not have seen the light of day. I am also grateful to my friend, Tom Beam, for his insights into the legal system.

I hope you enjoy reading the book as much as I did in writing it.

SANTA FE
THE PRESENT

1

The flight to Santa Fe did not feel familiar until I could see the sage brushed landscape below and the Sangre de Cristo mountains to the north. Sitting at seven thousand feet above sea level, Santa Fe is in a semi-arid steppe with three hundred days of sunshine and cold winters. The barren, dry backdrop does not hint at the unique specialness of the area. Locals know that it is the intersection of three cultures—the Native Americans, the Spanish primarily from Mexico and the latter-day Anglo-Americans who began arriving about 1850 on the Santa Fe Trail. The high altitude and clear dry air create a deep blue sky, perfect for the kind of light contrasts loved by artists. No wonder it is called the land of enchantment. I had known this area all too well for many years before leaving my native state.

It had been eleven years since I was last in Santa Fe. I had left in disgrace, humiliated, and embarrassed by my own ineptitude. Being a psychologist, all of my friends thought that I should have seen what had been obvious to them—my wife (now ex) Rebecca was having an affair. Worse yet, she was having it under my nose, almost it seemed, flaunting it. Having specialized in marriage therapy, the irony was not lost on me that my own marriage was in shambles. Well doctor, heal thyself! When they say love is blind they also should also say love is dumb! Following a tumultuous and very painful divorce, I left Santa Fe with my tail between my legs and the expectation that I would never return.

I had vanquished myself to a place where I knew no one and no one knew me—Bozeman, Montana. Bozeman was remote enough for me to hide but, with a university, just large enough to feel connected to the world. I spent three years in my own intensive therapy focusing on my gullibility and issues regarding my continuing need to please. In the intervening years, I asked myself if I had matured and come to terms with the demons that had haunted me and if I was ready to confront the past? I would find out soon enough. I was returning to comfort and console the very woman that had so publicly humiliated me.

As the plane made its final mid-afternoon approach to the Santa Fe Regional Airport, I felt some of the same dread I had felt all those years back when I had left. Landing on the bumpy tarmac, the thumping of the wheels served to accentuate my already queasy stomach. Having grown up here, the very small, adobe building they called their airport was still familiar. It had not changed over the years. At one time, my uncle had been responsible for maintaining the small facility and airstrip; but that was before the passing of my parents and the loss of a need to ever return again. Ironically, the city that was at the top of so many travel lists, including *Conde Nast Traveler*, was the same place I could not get away from fast enough and had vowed never to return.

The runway at the Santa Fe airport was too small for larger planes and the airport was only busy seasonally. Deplaning was always right at the tarmac entrance to the small building. There are no jet bridges from the plane to the entrance, just the stairs from the plane to the entrance gate. Larger airplanes flew into the Albuquerque International Sunport, one hour south. As the airplane came to a halt and the propellers began to wind down, I looked out of my small window searching for Rebecca.

It had been just four days ago since I had received a frantic, nearly incoherent, call from her. I could not believe I was seeing her name on my caller ID. We had not spoken since my leaving. In fact, Rebecca had gone on to marry the very person with whom she was having the affair, Blake Martin. Even then, Blake was known as an entrepreneurial and, sometimes, ruthless businessman. He owned interest in a major art gallery, a jewelry store, and a number of retail shops in the center of Santa Fe and was then planning to duplicate his art galleries in New York and Los Angeles. By then, he had already been twice divorced and considered quite a philanderer. Because of his wealth, his influence had spread, and he rubbed shoulders with politicians and other national celebrities with connections to Santa Fe. I was perplexed that after eleven years, and with all of Blake's network, there was no one there to help her through this besides me. I had to wonder again, what the hell was I doing here?

At that moment I sighted her there in the shadows of the portal waiting for me to deplane. She had a scarf over her pulled back chestnut hair. She had on dark glasses and a red shawl draped over her shoulders, white blouse, blue jeans, and stylish boots. She was still trim and attractive. The years had been very kind to her. As I noted this to myself, I slapped my own face. How could I even begin to go down a path of thinking about anything but how badly she had hurt me?

As I deplaned, I looked around to see if there was anyone else there who might recognize me. My humiliation apparently still ran deep. Immediately after I made my way down the steps from the plane and through the entrance gate, Rebecca ran up, embraced me, and began to sob.

Through her tears she kept saying, "Oh Scott, thank you, thank you, thank you. I so hoped you would come."

After a longer embrace than I was comfortable with, we picked up my luggage and proceeded to her car, a red BMW convertible. Rebecca was never afraid to be noticed. She asked me to drive saying that she was too nervous to focus!

The Santa Fe airport was about fifteen miles from the center of the city known as the Plaza. Rebecca and I had previously decided that I would stay at the La Fonda hotel, adjacent to the Plaza. Rebecca and Blake were good friends with the owners, and they had graciously provided me a suite, *gratis*, for my time in town. Leaving the Santa Fe airport, there is a choice of two routes to get to the Plaza. When I had previously lived there, the most popular route was driving right through the center of the city on Cerrillos Road. Since I left, Cerrillos Road had become more congested with the development of chain stores, local shopping, restaurants, and malls. Except for the backdrop of the mountains, the route was indistinguishable from similarly crowded thoroughfares in other cities. Rebecca suggested a second route, NM-599, also known as Veteran's Memorial Highway. It is a loop, so to speak, going around the west end of the city and culminating at US-285 headed north, and just a short distance from the Plaza. Before leaving, I suggested we put the top of the BMW back up so we could talk without wind noise. So we pulled out from the adobe airport, turned right on Aviation Drive, and then left onto Veteran's Memorial Highway.

The loop had been created when I had previously lived in Santa Fe but not yet developed with retail and neighborhoods. Still, the only thing in the loop was a relatively new, and controversial, development called Las Vistas. It was branded as Santa Fe's only luxury master-planned community with high end homes and mostly out of state owners. One of the controversies was that the developers had created a sweetheart deal with the Santa Fe City Council to take a percentage of their water from the Rio Grande. In a land where water is a scarce commodity, the general population pointed to this arrangement as yet another way that the wealthy took advantage of the locals.

The route was moderately traffic free. We could talk and I could concentrate without having to worry about interference. Immediately after getting on our route, Rebecca began her tale of woe, no prodding necessary. Never one to hold back, Rebecca jumped into her dilemma.

Five days earlier, Rebecca had been at home in their own gated estate, just blocks off Canyon Road. She was to meet Blake, who was still at their gallery, for dinner at the restaurant. Canyon Road is known in the art world as the center of Santa Fe's art district. Santa Fe has over three hundred galleries and is always considered one of the most vibrant art centers in the country. Canyon Road is a narrow, very walkable, winding one-way road filled with art galleries, charming restaurants, and coffee shops. Property near Canyon Road is always considered premium. It was confirmed as Rebecca talked that Blake had not been just a mediocre art dealer.

Rebecca said that she and Blake had reservations at Geronimo, an upscale restaurant in a repurposed adobe home on Canyon Road built in 1756 by Geronimo Lopez. The house had been through several iterations and had been the home of Geronimo restaurant for some time and the restaurant had been the winner of numerous national awards for fine dining. As agreed upon, Rebecca went ahead to Geronimo to meet Blake at their seven thirty reservation time.

Rebecca said that she had been seated at the restaurant at about seven forty and ordered a glass of Chardonnay as she waited for Blake to arrive. When Blake had not arrived by eight and Rebecca was on her second glass of Chardonnay, she began to be concerned. She tried his mobile phone, but it went to voice mail. By eight-thirty, after having exhausted all her attempts to locate Blake, Rebecca decided that she would go to the gallery to check on him.

The gallery that Blake owned and ran, cleverly known as the Blake Martin Gallery, was a standalone house on East Palace Avenue, not far from the Cathedral Basilica of St. Francis of Assisi (known to locals simply as the Cathedral) and within walking distance to the Plaza. Blake had purchased the house over twenty years ago when its occupants had decided to sell as they moved into a local retirement center, El Castillo. Blake had the vision to see the house as a place that was only a slight distance from the plaza and, most importantly, had its own parking spaces. The house gave Blake the option of expanding and creating a unique art space.

Upon arriving at the gallery, Rebecca noted that Blake's black Range Rover HSE was in the parking lot. Her initial relief turned to apprehension when she found the back door, the one they always used closest to the parking lot, ajar. This was unusual because they always kept it locked after hours. Rebecca proceeded into the gallery calling out Blake's name, but the house was eerily silent, no response. She proceeded into the main room of the gallery and there, in the middle of the floor, was Blake's body lying in a pool of blood. She ran to Blake, thinking that somehow he must have had an accidental fall. She called his name, "Blake, Blake." But no response. After her unsuccessful attempts to shake him to life, she dialed 911. Now Blake was dead, apparently murdered, and Rebecca said she had nowhere else to turn.

2

While the route was new to me it was fairly straight, uncomplicated, and fast. We were at the Plaza twenty minutes after having left the airport. Rebecca had my attention now as I continued our journey to the plaza, and I was shocked and more than a little bit dazed. The woman to whom I had been married, who left me for another, was now asking me to console her for the loss of the very one that took her away from me. It was more than just a little confusing. You really could not make this shit up! At the same time, to be honest, I was already beginning to feel exhausted. The apprehension of coming back to Santa Fe and seeing Rebecca, along with hearing her incredible tale had initially given me an adrenalin rush followed by the inevitable crash. I knew that I was here to help her through this, but I also knew I needed some time to check-in and recover. Upon arriving at the hotel, we agreed that I would meet her at her house for dinner and further discussion at eight o'clock.

We pulled up to the La Fonda hotel at four forty-five. I found a short-term parking space, got my luggage and, again, gave Rebecca a short hug as she moved into the driver's seat. I had her address and volunteered to grab a taxi to get to her house at eight. As we parted, I noted that Rebecca had again rotated the convertible top back so that she would be driving in open air. I could only smile to myself recalling how she never shied away from the limelight.

La Fonda is a true Santa Fe landmark known as "the Inn at the end of the Santa Fe trail." Its history goes back to 1821 when it became a preferred stopping off place for soldiers, gold seekers, and trappers. Later, it was purchased by Fred Harvey and became one of several of the Harvey House inns, strategically located near railroad stops throughout the western United States. In 1968 it had then been purchased by a local family and, just recently, by a local investment group. It has the appearance of a pueblo with its multi-story stairstep adobe structure. It takes up an entire block and is a gathering place for locals at the inside bars and restaurants.

Walking into the lobby brought back a flood of memories. The terrazzo floors, original Southwestern art on the walls, and glazed and brightly painted and decorated stucco walls recalled an era of former elegance. I can still remember having our high school prom in one of the large ballrooms at the hotel. Later, Rebecca and I would come here for New Year's Eve parties and meet for an after-work drink. It is located within walking distance to my old office in Sena Plaza. Shortly before my father's passing, he and I had a special dinner in the *La Plazuela* restaurant. I could not help but feel a strong sense of nostalgia as I stepped up to the front desk to check in. There to greet me was a lively, and lovely, young woman.

"Good afternoon," she greeted. "May I help you?"

"Yes," I replied. "I think you have a reservation for Doctor Scott Hunter."

"Oh, yes Doctor Hunter. We have been expecting you," she said.

"What personal or credit card information can I provide you," I inquired.

"Nothing required, Doctor Hunter. Your entire visit has already been taken care of. Let me get your room key," she replied.

She handed me the key and a small map of the facility with my room circled. I then took leave of her and took the elevator to the private Concierge Floor. It was a floor with only ten suites and required the key to get onto the floor. My room was actually a two-room suite with a spacious living room and a large bedroom with an Ensuite bathroom and king size bed. The room had the touches of Santa Fe including a corner fireplace, Native American designed rugs, Southwestern art, and diamond plastered walls. In addition, the Concierge Floor had a private lounge available only to guests on the Concierge Floor, complete with a stocked bar and an assortment of handheld hors d'oeuvres from five o'clock to seven-thirty. It was clear that either Rebecca had spared no expense or, that in some measure, the current manager was in Rebecca's debt.

While I was tempted to make my way to the private lounge for a drink, I was exhausted. I unpacked my bag, set my phone alarm for seven fifteen and lay down. I was out in a flash.

The beep-beep-beep of my phone alarm brought me to a rude awakening. I was momentarily disoriented before realizing where I was. I roused myself, got up and freshened up with a new shirt and pair of jeans and called down to the desk for a taxi to Rebecca's house. I was instructed to be in the lobby in twenty minutes.

I was now fully engaged and began processing again what Rebecca had told me. Rebecca, my ex-wife had found Blake, the man for whom she had left me, dead on the floor of their posh art gallery. She had been identified as a person of interest but, because of Blake's standing in the community, she was temporarily released on her own recognizance. She had called me because, even eleven years after our divorce, there was no one here whom she could rely on to help her. Made perfect sense to me. What the hell had I gotten myself into?

3

The taxi was ready and waiting outside the front door of La Fonda. I gave the driver the address and we were off. Santa Fe is often known as a big little city. It is the third largest art community in the United States but has a population of under 150,000 in the entire county. By car, and under normal conditions, you can get to anywhere in Santa Fe in twenty to thirty minutes. It is truly a big little city.

Rebecca and Blake had a gated estate in the foothills near St. John's College. The foothills are dotted with Chamisa plants, scrub evergreens, pinon trees and sage brush. For an outsider, the beauty of the landscape is sometimes an acquired taste. I loved it. In the taxi, we took the route up Canyon Road to Camino del Monte Sol and to their front gate. On the way, we passed Geronimo restaurant that Rebecca had referenced in her recount of events. When we arrived, I pushed the button on the microphone box to the gate entrance and the taxi was quickly buzzed in. The driver drove me into a large circular gravel driveway. There was a main house and two additional guest casitas. Before getting out of the taxi, I got the driver's cell number and told him I would call him in a couple of hours for the return trip. The location of their estate is in the foothills of Santa Fe. Homes here are typically on small acreage and secluded. There are some additional estates with larger acreage, but typically under five acres. The homes are high end and people in this area are the very wealthy and value their privacy.

From the driveway, there was a well-lit flagstone walk to the front door. The house was traditional adobe with a dark brown tint. The front porch had a high ceiling and two large entry doors. I pushed the doorbell and Rebecca opened the front door with a flair. She had changed from her earlier attire into a beautiful long sleeve turquoise silk blouse with a coral squash blossom necklace, dark slim fit jeans with silver Conchos down the side and black boots with a slight heel. Her hair was now down to her shoulders. She looked stunning. Rebecca did not look like a grieving widow. For a moment, I forgot everything that had happened and why I was really here. My heart raced and I began to feel my neck redden. For God's sake man, get a grip! I hoped that she had not noticed my flight into temporary insanity.

"Right on time," she said. "Come into my humble abode."

I noticed that she said, "*my* humble abode," not "our (meaning Blake) humble abode."

The interior was half art gallery, half Architectural Digest. The main room exuded both elegance and warmth. A large fireplace with a well-lit fire was against one wall. The furniture was all high end with ample leather and glass features. The floor was what appeared to be dark reclaimed farmhouse planks, a bit rustic and understated, while still screaming expensive. The ceiling was high and supported with large round wooden beams called vigas. Expensive looking art placed at museum height, tastefully lined diamond plastered walls. Bronze Southwest sculptures stood tastefully on tables with one large stand-alone modern abstract sculpture in one corner of the room. The lighting was muted and mostly indirect. It was all very inviting.

As I sat taking in the surroundings, I mused just how far Rebecca had come. She had moved to Santa Fe in high school because of a transfer her father, Robert Miller, had been given. Like many in Santa Fe, he was a government worker. The government had a Bureau of Land Management office in the foothills responsible for managing public land in New Mexico. Rebecca had grown up in a strict, but secure, middle-class family. She loathed her parents attempt to control her life and worked hard to individuate. Once she left for college, the contact with her parents became less and less frequent. Upon retirement, her parents had moved to their family farm back East where they continued to live. Rebecca, however, rarely had contact with them and when she did it was by phone and mostly on holidays. She wanted to escape any remnants of her upbringing.

Rebecca was a year behind me in high school and we barely knew each other. She was the youngest of three in her family and seemed to be somewhat of a free spirit. Her two sisters had gone out of state to college and had both settled into their own family lives on the West Coast. They had both resented, and admired, Rebecca's independence and courage to separate from her parents in ways they had not. Like her parents, Rebecca had not really kept up with her sisters nor was she involved in the lives of their children. Both Rebecca and I went to the University of New Mexico and reconnected during my sophomore year.

Having come from a working-class family, I was the first in my family to go to college. Neither of my parents had finished high school. My father, William, a mechanic, and my mother, Helen, a seamstress, drilled into me early, and often, the importance of a college education. Being a very adaptive, only child, I was studious and earned my parents praise for good grades and good works. While this devotion to achievement had served me well in school, it had also led me to become a risk-averse pleaser, serious, and rather boring. These issues became the fodder for my own therapy.

Being a free spirit, Rebecca had introduced me to a world I had not before known, including an appreciation for music, travel, alcohol, marijuana, and sex. We were truly opposites and that difference had intrigued me from the start. I always wanted to please and she was very much her own person. I often wondered what she had seen in me. I think it was that I put no demands on her and pretty much liked whatever we did together. We dated at the university and got married between my undergraduate and graduate school years, staying at the University of New Mexico for my doctorate in psychology, while she held down various jobs to support us.

Her voice pulled me out of my musings and back into the room.

"Can I pour you a glass of wine, or would you prefer a beer?" she asked as she moved toward the built-in bar.

She remembered my preference for beer. Having grown up in a working-class family, the finer and more expensive tastes for alcohol had eluded me until later in life. I had, however, graduated up to wine.

"I would love a glass of Cabernet if you have it," I said. I wanted to at least have the appearance of sophistication.

On cue, she poured me a glass of Cabernet from a bottle recently opened to allow it to breathe. It all felt a bit orchestrated and pre-meditated. She seemed to anticipate my next move. I continued to have a sense of unreality and suspicion about what Rebecca's real intentions might be.

She poured herself a glass of Chardonnay and, pointing to the leather couch and chairs in front of the fireplace said, "Shall we sit?"

4

I let her sit down first, not wanting to claim my seat until she had taken hers. She chose a comfortable looking Eames lounge chair covered in brown and white cowhide. I selected a comfortable leather side chair opposite her, not wanting to be tempted by sitting too closely. I put my glass of Cabernet on the glass table between us.

"Tell me," I said. "How can I help?"

"The police arrived at the gallery very shortly after I placed my nine-one-one call," she said. "Needless to say, I was a mess."

"The police quickly realized that Blake had been bludgeoned with a blunt instrument and had died on the spot. They found a sculptured obelisk-like piece in the same room on the floor near the side door covered with blood. In addition, a very expensive painting was missing, evidenced by the vacant space on the gallery wall. It had been where an Albert Bierstadt painting had been. Its estimated value was over a hundred thousand dollars. The gallery was a crime scene," she went on. "After a few questions, one of their female officers escorted me home so that I could change."

I wanted to touch her arm to console her, but our chairs were too far apart. So, putting on my most empathic face I responded in horror, "You must have been terrified. How did you get through it?"

"It was awful, Scott. I was, and still am, in shock and disbelief," she said as tears came to her eyes. "The female officer asked if there was someone I could call to come and spend the night. I could only think that I wanted to be by myself. She waited until I had cleaned up, changed, and had settled in before she left. I was grateful that she had been with me and grateful when she left around midnight."

"I can't begin to imagine what you were going through," I said weakly. "How did you possibly get to sleep?"

"I poured myself a stiff whiskey, took a sleeping pill, and went to bed. I slept until ten."

For once I was quiet, not knowing exactly what to say that wasn't lame or excessive. Finally, I asked, "It must have been the next day that you called me. What led you to call?"

"Shortly after waking up, a Detective Miguel Montez from the Santa Fe Police called me and asked if he could come over to get my statement from the night before," she continued. "Of course I agreed, although it was the last thing I wanted," she continued.

The name Miguel Montez rang a bell with me. As I thought more about it, I recalled that I had competed against him in track in high school. He had gone to a rival Catholic boys high school and was a cracker jack athlete in multiple sports. I remembered that I had liked him and that we would often talk between events. I also recalled how bright he seemed. I decided to keep my knowledge of Miguel to myself for the time being.

"He came over and, for two hours, I reviewed the events from the night before, one step at a time question after question. It was both excruciating and annoying, like I was being considered a suspect," she lamented. "He said that I would have to go down to the police station to take my fingerprints and a DNA swab to eliminate me as a suspect. I was both horrified and livid. I called our family attorney, Charles Kahn, to accompany me to the police interview."

"When Detective Montez left, I found myself sobbing and shaking. I was beside myself. Blake had just been brutally murdered and I had to be eliminated as a suspect. Really," she said with disbelief. "That was when I called you. You were the first person that came to mind who really understood me and, more importantly, whom I knew would not judge me. I am so sorry to have dragged you into this, but I have nowhere else to go."

As she explained her calling me, I had to seriously manage my own frustration. In essence, she had no one else to turn to or she would have. It seemed that even in Blake's death, I was the consolation prize. I really had to put on my big boy pants for this one. She also continued to heighten my wariness regarding her true intentions.

"Why don't we finish this over dinner?" she suggested.

I was hungry and ready for dinner.

5

"I thought we would keep it casual tonight, fill our plates in the kitchen, and sit around the fire pit on the back porch," she suggested.

"Sounds good to me," I said enthusiastically.

She chauffeured me into the kitchen area. Even though it was immediately off of the great room, I had not noticed it coming in. The kitchen kept the same upscale southwestern style as the great room. The cooking space was ample with a large gas range, windows on the cabinet doors, and an ample wine refrigerator. This was in addition to the huge double refrigerator. The kitchen had a terrazzo tile floor that was different from the wooden planks in the great room. I later determined that it was a heated floor. In front of the cooking area was a large, beautiful, dark wooden countertop like you might see in a very expensive farm style house.

The beautiful countertop held several slightly elevated serving dishes with candles underneath them to keep the food warm. I was astonished that with all or the turmoil of the past few days, that Rebecca had the time or the energy to put such a feast together, especially since cooking was never one of her talents.

"How did you find the time to prepare all of these dishes?" I asked in astonishment.

She laughingly said, "Oh, I didn't. We have had a full time cook and housekeeper, Rosita, since we got married. She cooked all of this, set the plates and utensils out, and even started the fire in the fire pit." to which she pointed outside the kitchen door to the portal.

For the moment, I could see why Rebecca had been attracted to Blake and this lavish lifestyle. Under different circumstances, I would have married Blake!

Rebecca clearly remembered my love of Santa Fe style Mexican food. In the serving trays were enchiladas, pozole, calabacitas, warm sopapillas, honey and seasoned green chile to top things off. I had not had these delicacies since I had moved away, and my mouth began to water.

Santa Fe style food is like no other in the country. The mixture of red and green chile with ingredients like cilantro, the use of native corn in the pozole, and the diced squash calabacitas with onion and garlic are just some of what sets this New Mexican food apart from any other. Add on the fry bread puffy sopapillas with honey and you are only a short step away from food heaven.

The wine, the food, her appearance—were they all orchestrated to manipulate me or was I just overreacting based on our history? I had learned in therapy what is often obvious to others, "All that glitters is not gold." I did want her intentions to be noble ones, whatever they were.

Forgetting, for the moment, why I was really there, I encouraged Rebecca to go first then I began filling my plate with the delicacies in front of me. When we completed our parade through the buffet line, we made our way out to the fire pit. I was anxious for what came next.

6

Once we had settled into our seats with our food and drinks on small trays by the fire pit, we began to talk again. I was particularly interested in why anyone would want to kill Blake.

"Tell me, Rebecca, why do you think anyone would want to kill Blake? Or do you think it was some random event by a local looking to rob the gallery?" I queried.

"I should probably start at the beginning, Scott," she said tentatively. "And this is the hard part. I have never forgiven myself for the way I treated you. You never deserved that. You were always kind to me and never controlling or mean. Honestly, I had never been given love so unconditionally as you gave it to me."

Well, I can't say that felt great, but I needed to hear more.

"When I met Blake, I know that he appealed to my wild side. You may be surprised to know that, since our divorce, I have gone to a therapist myself to try to figure myself out."

"I had no idea since we have not communicated in eleven years," I said somewhat defensively.

She continued, "I know I hurt you and I had to understand what I was experiencing so that I would not self-destruct or hurt anyone in the future."

"Good for you, Rebecca. I am sure that took a lot of courage. What did you learn?" I asked.

She continued, "I learned what had probably been obvious to you. My wild side, my independence, my self-serving nature had all been to establish myself as separate from my strict, unrelenting, and intolerant parents. I had seen my older sisters lose their own identities and acquiesce to my parent's demanding and unyielding nature. They both became very compliant and fearful of doing anything that would have irritated or brought on the wrath of my parents. Interesting enough, once they

24

both graduated from college, they moved as far away as they could from them. On the other hand, I developed a 'fuck you' attitude as my means of coping. I was determined not to allow them to over-power me. It was interesting how little resistance they actually put up once I started being my own person. Like so many bullies, they caved when I fought back."

I was surprised, and pleased, to hear her insights. "I remember your parents, Rebecca," I replied. "I always thought it strange that you did not want them included in our lives. We rarely saw them and, when we did, it was cursory."

"Yes," she replied. "I did not want to be around them anymore than we had to be."

"I'm confused, though," I said quizzically. "You mentioned that I never treated you like they did and, in fact, that you had never been treated as well as I treated you. So, why did you have the affair with Blake and subsequently leave me?"

As I asked the question, I realized how totally weird this conversation was. It only added to the eeriness of the entire situation.

"Scott, I determined after I asked you to come that I owed it to you to be direct and honest with you. You deserve that," she began.

"Please, continue," I said curiously.

"When Blake and I married, he was already well established being ten years older than me. He was wealthy, well-connected and had a lifestyle that, on the outside, looked exciting and appealed to my desire to be recognized in those circles. Life with you Scott had become predictable, you going to work as a therapist and me going to the store to work selling faux Santa Fe clothes to faux rich tourists. We had a routine, having a drink every night after work at La Fonda, buying groceries, hiking on Saturdays. I have since learned that my free spirit was drawn to excitement. Blake brought that. As awful as it sounds, there is an exhilaration in having an affair—the secrecy, the possibility of getting caught, the hidden rendezvous. While I knew it was wrong, I was vulnerable to Blake's charms and pulled into his influence. He represented something I would never have otherwise had—freedom from the mundaneness of my life."

I reacted defensively, "I am sorry the life we had was so dreary for you."

She quickly responded, "Scott, I know how crass and insensitive this seems, but I want you to know that I am not the same person now as I was then."

"Could have fooled me," I said sarcastically.

I was beginning to feel very uneasy, defensive, and wondered if now would be a good time to leave. I had already seen this movie before. Furthermore, I did not need another dose of humiliation. I had grown beyond that.

"Look Rebecca, I did not come here to be flayed by whatever shortcomings I had eleven years ago. If that is your intent, we should stop now and I can fly home tomorrow," I said with more than a little anger in my voice. For the first time, I felt powerful.

"Scott, I knew this would be a difficult conversation. I am begging you to let me get through all of this. If, at the end, you still want to leave, I will not stand in your way."

Then I knew I was in the driver's seat.

"Very well, I will wait to decide once you have finished," I said half-heartedly.

She continued, "It did not take long for me to begin to experience the unseen cost of life with Blake, but by that time I was already committed."

"Cost?" I said.

"I knew that, in Santa Fe, Blake was a powerful and well-known figure. He knew the governor, our senators, the local police. He was at every gala, fund raiser and social opportunity. There was a certain notoriety in being seen with Blake. I say notoriety because it soon became apparent that Blake's wealth and donations were really a way for him to buy influence. In spite of that, there was a thrill in rubbing shoulders with the powerful elite. Unfortunately, I bought into this lifestyle hook, line, and sinker. The excitement of being seen with these situational-celebrities, having photo-ops at grand events, and seeing my picture in the paper in the society section gave me a false sense that I was someone other than the daughter of a government worker." She took another sip of her wine and paused.

Intrigued, I said, "Please, continue."

She looked away and continued, "I am not sure if Blake ever really loved me or if I was just another of his conquests that became more permanent. When we were together, he was always kind and loving. We rarely fought and he kept most of his business dealings to himself. He satisfied my longing to be a free spirit through travel, social events, introductions to the rich and famous, and a fairly unlimited expense account. I never had to lift a finger. We had a cook, a gardener, and a chauffeur when I wanted one. To a casual observer, our lives were perfect.'

Rebecca took another sip of her wine and went on, "I know he liked me draped over his arm at the social events, as his eye candy. Being so much younger than him, he took pride in my appearance, and he made sure I always had a serious wardrobe budget to look the part of a rich man's wife. His entire life and the empire he built were all based on his need to be seen as the smartest, wealthiest, most charming, and cunning person in the room. And he usually was."

I did not want to get too far astray from the reason I came, so I interrupted, "So, Rebecca, what does this have to do with his murder and me being here?"

7

Taken aback by my persistent need for relevance, Rebecca answered. "I am not certain, Scott, but I know that over the years, Blake had created his share of enemies. I was too naïve to dig deeply into his business affairs, but there must be something there."

I knew I had to ask Rebecca the elephant-in-the-room question.

"Rebecca, I need to know something before we continue, and it is crucial as to whether or not I stay," I challenged.

"Scott, please let me stop you there," she insisted. "I loved Blake. I had absolutely nothing to do with his murder. It has been a total and extremely devastating shock. For all of our differences and interests, we had developed a rhythm to our relationship. He always treated me well and I did not ask too many questions. Our lives were full."

I studied her voice and body posture to see if they matched her words. She spoke in a quiet but resolute and sad tone. Her body was slightly slumped, and she seemed genuinely broken at that moment. I was satisfied that she was telling me her truth.

"Then, Rebecca, why am I here?" I persisted.

"There are two reasons, Scott. First, believe it or not, there is no one here that I trust as much as I trust you. In the circles in which we have traveled, the relationships tend to be shallow, superficial, and self-serving. Even though we were very different, I always trusted you to have my best interests in mind."

I resisted being flattered, but what she said was accurate. I did always have her best interest in mind.

"And the second reason," I countered.

"The second reason is that I always saw you as a problem-solver in your work as a psychologist. You would relate to me some of the conundrums your patients faced and describe the methodical, systematic way you would begin to unravel their problems to help them find solutions that would help them get unstuck," She explained.

As she said this, it was not lost on me how I was unable, at the time, to methodically and systematically unravel the problems of my own marriage—problems I did not even know were there. She was right, however, that in my relationships with my patients I had much greater objectivity and cleaner boundaries. I was told I was a good therapist with good clinical instincts.

"So what am I here for?" I impatiently asked.

"Scott, I need you to help figure out who may have wanted to hurt Blake," she pleaded.

"Look, Rebecca, I am not a detective or a private eye. I would be out of my depth on this. This is something for the law enforcement professionals to manage," I argued.

"I don't trust anyone, Scott. I don't know the motives the police may have; or Blake's business associates; or anyone else Blake may have been in touch with. I do know that I am a person of interest, and the police are wasting valuable time and resources looking at me when I had nothing to do with his death. I know you can help. I remember when we would talk about your cases how clever you were at always understanding your client's motivations and what drove them. I know you can be of help. I am willing to pay you for your help. Money is not an object. Please say you will help me," she said plaintively.

"Rebecca, this is a big ask and I need to sleep on it. I will give you my answer tomorrow. If I decide to stay on, we will need some kind of a plan so that we will both know what our expectations are. Agreed?"

"Agreed," she said quickly. "Here is a printed copy of Blake's obituary. If you do decide to stay, you may find it helpful in some way.

We spent the rest of the evening with Rebecca filling in some of the details of their lives, catching up and learning more about the person Rebecca had become and vice versa.

Feeling tired, at eleven o'clock, I texted the taxi driver and met him in front of the gate. Before I left, Rebecca reached out to give me a hug and we agreed to meet for lunch tomorrow at the Compound on Canyon Road.

I clearly had a lot of thinking to do. What was Rebecca's real reason for having me here? It all seemed too simple and staged. Was I being played like so many years ago? Was I out of my depth and should this be left to the law enforcement professionals? A good night's sleep could only help.

The driver left me off at the front door of La Fonda. I was really beat and looking to get a good night's sleep. I waved to the front desk clerk, took the elevator to my floor, and walked on to my room. As I entered my room and turned on the light, I saw the message light blinking on my hotel room phone.

BOZEMAN
ELEVEN YEARS AGO
8

Once I had gotten over the initial shock that not only was Rebecca having an affair in front of my nose, but she was divorcing me, I found the humiliation overwhelming. Being a psychologist and counseling other couples, I felt so exposed that I was being betrayed without even realizing it. The irony was not lost on me. The sayings "the cobbler's children have no shoes," or "physician heal thyself," took on new meaning. I decided that I needed to take bold steps in a different direction if I was ever going to heal. There was little reason for me to stay in Santa Fe except for the familiarity. My family ties died when my parents passed away.

As I reflected on where I might go, I recalled fondly the car trips we took when I was a kid. My parents were not wealthy, but even on a mechanic's earnings they always managed to squirrel away enough money to take a family vacation. My parents always thought of our vacations as providing me a view into the world outside of Santa Fe. All of our vacations were car trips to nearby states, and for most of them we camped. I recalled one trip that I particularly enjoyed to Montana. It was as far as we had ever gone as a family. As I reminisced, Montana seemed like as good a place as any to land and, hopefully, rebuild.

Within a month after the divorce was final, I had closed my private practice, referred my patients to other therapists, packed up my belongings and headed to Bozeman, Montana in my used Volvo. I had been able to salvage some money from the divorce and had enough to live on for about a year if I was frugal.

The long drive to Bozeman gave me ample time to think about what to do next. I had determined that continuing to berate myself for what had been obvious to everyone else had little merit. Nevertheless, her affair and the divorce, had shaken my confidence and I knew I was going to need some help to sort myself out and begin again. Fortunately, one of my Santa Fe psychologist colleagues knew someone in Bozeman, with whom she had gone to graduate school, and to whom she could refer me. I was grateful to have a contact in Bozeman and have my own therapist to begin the work of rebuilding.

I knew that on the life-events stress scale, I was at the top. A divorce, a new location where I knew no one, limited funds on which to live, and not having a job, all at once put me in a high-risk category. However, I was determined not to approach life as a victim but to begin the process of understanding myself better and moving forward.

Once I arrived in Bozeman, I put my anxiety to work to drive me to get my life organized. Within one week, I had located a small one-bedroom apartment, set up an appointment with the female psychologist to whom I had been referred, and began looking for work. Within two weeks, I had several good employment leads and some interviews scheduled. I had determined that trying to start a private practice was not a good idea either business wise nor, especially, personally. I needed the structure, and income, of a real job.

I was lucky, that as a result of recent changes in the psychology department, the local university needed a full-time Lecturer for some of their introductory psychology classes. A Lecturer is at the bottom of the academic pile and non-tenured. However, having a steady income and the structure of a job was what I needed. In addition, being an instructor gave me access to the university community in which I could attend faculty events as well as university functions. The position even carried with it health insurance and the opportunity to contribute to their retirement plan. Also, being divorced in a university setting is almost a modern-day norm. There is no stigma in having been through a failed marriage, so my humiliation was significantly lessened.

I remember my first session with Doctor Jane Marbary, the psychologist to whom I had been referred. After a few introductory pleasantries, I began talking, then dissolved very quickly into tears and sadness. I thought I had been handling my emotions better, but maybe I had just been avoiding them. It did not take long for us to get down to the work of therapy. I was ready and she was very good, gently guiding me down the path from sadness and self-blame to anger and, ultimately, on to acceptance. This happened over time and, eventually, came with a realization that the deteriorating relationship and subsequent divorce with Rebecca were in some ways an inevitable path on my journey to self-growth.

I saw Doctor Marbary weekly for three years. We had more ground to cover than even I, as a psychologist and therapist myself, had realized. Even though I was required to experience therapy as part of my doctoral program, the depth Doctor Marbary was exploring was new territory. Issues about my parents, and even *their* parents, surfaced as instrumental in making me such a pleaser. While I could see similar problems in my patients, I had become blind to the same problems in myself. It seemed that new revelations came to me regularly, especially that first year of therapy. As a result of being in therapy, I made the decision not to open a private practice.

Other aspects of my life in Bozeman began to blossom. I enjoyed teaching and the camaraderie with other faculty members. I was treated like a peer and not an underling, in spite of my Lecturer position. I had made my small apartment my home and was volunteering at the local food bank. The salary at the university, while not being significant, had been sufficient to meet my needs with even a little left over for savings and entertainment. I embraced the Bozeman lifestyle and began skiing again, hiked mountain trails, and even tried fly fishing. I intentionally held off on dating, being cautious and wanting to develop a better understanding of the role of intimacy in my life.

By the fourth year of university teaching, I had moved up from Lecturer to Assistant Professor, a position that had tenure possibilities. However, I still saw teaching as an interim step to whatever might be next, and not a career. I did not want to be on the "publish or perish" treadmill to becoming a full Professor. Also, the politics in universities puts national politics to shame, with ongoing posturing and subtly questioning the competence, productivity, or quality of colleagues. I had determined that for me it was not long-term.

During the beginning of my fourth year at the university, I received a call from a university colleague in the psychology department, Joni Rychlak, also a licensed psychologist. In addition to her responsibilities at the university, Joni had been the local consulting psychologist for a regional firm specializing in applying psychology to business. The university had fairly liberal policies regarding outside engagements of their staff, as long as it did not interfere with their teaching and research responsibilities. Joni was about to embark on a one-year sabbatical to conduct research on the effects of trauma on communities. Her work would take her out of Bozeman. She wondered if I might be interested in filling her shoes on an interim basis during the year she would be gone.

Joni knew that I had a background in psychological assessment, crisis intervention (previously with families), and evaluating family systems. She convinced me that my previous work with individuals and families would be effective in working with businesses and business executives. She had already received approval from the home office in Denver to have the discussion with me. Because I was continuing to explore my career options, I scheduled a time to talk with her and the regional director, Emma Maxwell. While I had little experience with business directly, I had conducted workshops in communication, systems theory, group development, group dynamics, and conflict management. The work sounded intriguing to me, and I was up for the challenge.

The conversation with Emma Maxwell and Joni centered around some of the work to be expected. The work included evaluating candidates for key positions in companies; leading workshops for executives and their teams; and consulting with executives on such issues as succession planning, leadership, and identifying their own fears and impediments to success. Emma assured me that business development would be handled by the home office along with billing and collections. I was advised that there could be some travel, but that currently there was an abundance of work in Bozeman and within a day's drive from Bozeman, including Billings, Helena, Butte. The home office would provide some initial training in business fundamentals, and individual and organizational assessment, and I would be able to improvise with clients once I was working with them. While I would be paid on the basis of the work I performed, the payment far exceeded what the university paid for a similar amount of work. It seemed that I had nothing to lose, and I was ready for an adventure.

After Joni helped me understand the administrative aspects of the work and had introduced me to her current clients before transferring them to me, I was off and running. As promised, during the university's Spring Break, the home office provided me training in the form of a week's face-to-face education in business, executive assessment, and organizational assessment. It was intense and exhilarating. I began to feel my world widening as I had found a place where I could put my previous training as a psychologist to work.

I took to the work very well and quickly developed more work with existing clients, while identifying new clients with whom to work. The clients ranged from municipalities to the fields of healthcare, manufacturing, banking, and more. Many of the businesses were small and medium sized, often privately held and with the founder still involved. The variety of work kept me on my toes, always learning some of the nuances of these companies, their businesses and those who ran them. At the same time, I began to see that the same issues surfaced time and again, regardless of industry or company. The problems I came up against were ultimately human. I found that even high-level executives were insecure. Their personalities included the same personalities I had seen in private practice, ranging from the narcissistic to the risk-averse pleaser. The difference was that I had less time to determine their personality and had to be quicker, and more direct, in my work to help them.

After about six months in consulting work, while continuing to teach a full load, I began to recognize that consulting to businesses and applying psychology to the workplace were my passion. The variety of work, the fascinating people, and the complexity of problems seemed to be a perfect fit for both my background and my interests. It was much more stimulating, and challenging, than my work at the university had been. For each business, I was trying to solve interesting and complex problems to help individuals, and businesses, succeed. I was developing new skills and aptitudes while increasing my workload. I began to wonder what would happen when Joni returned. I did not have to wait long to hear the answer.

One evening while I was wrapping up a day's work, having both taught and attended client meetings, the caller ID on my phone indicated a number I did not recognize. Usually, I do not pick up such calls and either let them go unanswered or go to voice mail. Curiosity got the best of me, and I answered.

"Hello," I said somewhat irritated expecting the call to be yet another spam call about buying a car warranty or some kind of insurance.

"Scott," a female voice inquired.

"Yes, this is he," I replied.

"Hi Scott, this is Joni. Joni Rychlak," she responded.

"Joni," I exclaimed, happy to hear her voice. "How are you? I have been thinking of you."

"I am doing well," she answered. "And you?"

Without hesitation, I went on to tell her how much I was enjoying the work and thanking her for inviting me to be involved.

"Well, Scott, that is why I wanted to call you. As you know, I have been spending my time conducting research on how communities are impacted by traumas. During the course of my research, the US Department of Homeland Security has become interested in how they can best respond to traumatic events, like floods, school shooting, and homegrown terrorism. Long story short, they have offered me a job in Washington as part of their research staff, and I have accepted."

Stunned, I was quiet as the words sunk in.

"Scott, are you still there?" Joni quizzed.

"Yes, I am here," I muttered. "I am just trying to take it all in."

"Well," Joni continued. "I have already spoken to Emma today to let her know. She told me of the great work you have been doing and while she would miss me, she indicated I had left the Bozeman business in good hands. In fact, I was a little miffed that she did not lament more at my departure," she joked. "I will let the university know tomorrow, but I wanted to let you know so that you would not be caught totally by surprise or hear this from anyone else."

I was speechless.

"Wow, Joni, this is unexpected, but I am thrilled for you. It sounds like your research work is really being appreciated. Not only will the university miss you, but I will miss you as well. You have been a great friend and colleague," I responded.

I was privately thinking that this really was an answer to prayer from the standpoint that I really loved the consulting work and was beginning to have pangs of disappointment that when Joni returned, I might have to step aside. But now!

We talked for another few minutes, wished each other the best, and promised to stay in touch. As the call ended, I could not hide my excitement.

The next day, I received a call from Emma. She asked if I had spoken to Joni and what my thoughts were. I did not hesitate to let her know of my love of the work and that, while I would miss Joni, I loved what I was doing.

"Scott," Emma continued. "You have been doing outstanding work there. We have polled some of your clients, and they are very pleased. In the short time you have been there, you have added additional work with existing clients and even begun work with some new ones. As a result, we are prepared to offer you a full-time position, if you are interested. We would actually pay for a small office in the center of town. In addition, we would encourage you to continue teaching on a smaller basis, perhaps as an adjunct or visiting professor. We can work those details out as we go along. What do you think?"

For the second time in twenty-four hours, I was speechless. The thought of moving into a position that I had already "tried out" and loved was thrilling. And to think that I would be making fifty percent more starting with the consulting firm than I was making teaching, and without all of the university politics. Well, I was more elated than I had been at any time since moving to Bozeman.

Once again I heard, "Scott, are you there?"

"Oh, sorry Emma. Yes I am here. I am just trying to take it all in. The answer is yes, I would be very interested in your proposition." I exclaimed with gusto.

"In that case, Scott, I will be coming up to Bozeman next week and we can talk about the details. We are excited to have you on board. You are a great addition to the consulting team," Emma replied.

"Great, I look forward to seeing you then," I exclaimed, maybe a bit too excited.

"See you then," Emma closed.

That conversation with Emma had been seven years ago. Since that time, I had developed a very robust consulting business in Bozeman that included two part-time associates and a receptionist. We were still with the larger consulting firm. I continued to teach periodically at the university, but my teaching assignments had shifted from the psychology department to being a regular guest lecturer in the business school talking about leadership.

Personally, life was good. I had created a fairly large personal and professional network of friends. I was thriving financially and dating occasionally. I was still a bit cautious about commitment, but my trust level was getting better. Overall, life was good.

Then, I saw the name on my caller ID—*Rebecca Martin*. My stomach dropped. After all these years, what could she possibly want?

SANTA FE

THE PRESENT CONTINUED

9

The blinking phone light in my hotel room created both a sense of puzzlement and apprehension. The only person that knew I was here was Rebecca and I had just left her house. I then quickly rationalized that it was probably just the desk clerk checking in to see if I had any needs. I picked up the phone receiver and dialed nine to get my messages.

I was listening to a woman's raspy voice saying, "Doctor Hunter, this is Anna Pacheco. You do not know me, but I am the General Manager, and minority owner, here at La Fonda. I know you are here to see Rebecca Martin. I was a business partner with Blake's and may be able to provide you some information that would be beneficial. For obvious reasons, I do not want to meet here at the hotel with you. Meet me in the morning at eight o'clock at the restaurant at the Inn of the Anasazi on Washington Street. It is in walking distance to La Fonda. They have already set aside a private booth for us. See you then."

My mind was spinning. First, that I would receive an unsolicited call from someone saying that "they had some information that would be beneficial." Beneficial for what?

Secondly, that someone other than Rebecca would know I was there to be with her.

Finally, I was curious that this information would not have come from Rebecca.

I felt an uneasiness coming over me. In my previous role as a marriage therapist, I was keenly aware of what psychologists call triangulation. Triangulation occurs when Person A is upset with Person B but rather than dealing directly with Person B about the issue, Person A loops in another individual, Person C on the condition that their conversation is confidential. I often saw this triangulation in families when a parent roped in a child to discuss the issue the parent had with the other parent, swearing the child to secrecy. This is ultimately manipulation involving hidden agenda and the foundation of dysfunctional families.

Would this meeting put me in a triangulated position? Or would the information I received really be of legitimate use to me.

Recalling that I was to meet Rebecca at the Compound at noon to give her a final verdict on whether or not I would stay, I rationalized that this additional information could possibly help me make that decision.

It was close to midnight, and I needed a good night's sleep. I got in my night clothes, set my phone alarm for seven o'clock, turned off the lights and tucked myself under the covers. But my mind kept racing. Why was I really here? What real value could I add? Had I not made as much progress in therapy as I thought and was I once again just trying to be a pleaser? What was Rebecca's real motive? Was I just a pawn in a much larger drama? And who was this Anna Pacheco and what was she up to? And on, and on...

Through my therapy I had learned that we are at our worst when we try to analyze ourselves. We cannot be objective. However, I had also learned the importance of paying attention to my feelings. Gut instincts are always really pattern recognition at a sub-conscious level. So, my apprehension was related to some previous pattern in my life, but what was it? With that thought in mind, I drifted off.

The phone alarm went off much sooner than I wanted it to. I had a fitful sleep, full of anxious dreams and unanswered questions. I could really have had another couple hours of snoozing. Nevertheless, I knew I had a big day and had to get up.

As I stumbled out of bed, I opened my drapes to see another glorious Santa Fe day. The high altitude and the clearness of air here makes the colors jump out. The brilliant sun and deep blue sky provide perfect backdrops for any scene. I noticed what I had not previously, that my room was a corner room facing the historic plaza. For centuries, the plaza has been a gathering spot for Santa Feans and tourists alike. It is the center of both social and cultural life. It is rimmed with stylish, and very expensive, boutique retail stores and local restaurants. It is one of these stores in which Rebecca had worked. It is a magical place, part native American and part Hispanic all with a European feel. No wonder it is called "The City Different." The La Fonda is on the southeast corner catty corner from the plaza. On the north side of the plaza is the palace of the Governors a single story, block long, brown adobe structure with a long portal. Now a museum, it was the first seat of government and the oldest continuously occupied public building in the United States. The architecture of most of Santa Fe, and particularly in the center of town, maintained that adobe-style look. Much of the year, you would find Indians from many of the local pueblos selling their jewelry under the porch in front of the Palace of the Governors.

I quickly showered and put on some fresh clothes. I still had a new pair of pressed jeans I wore with a button-down white shirt and a brown suede blazer that I had worn often in my Santa Fe days. I noted that if I decided to stay, I would have to get my clothes cleaned or, heaven forbid, buy some new ones. I left my room, headed down the hallway to the elevator, down the elevator and to the lobby. As the elevator door opened, I noticed, and waved to, the young lady who had checked me in the day before.

"Is everything to your liking," she asked.

I smiled and replied, "Couldn't be better. Thanks for everything. By the way, I don't believe I got your name yesterday."

"Oh, I am Christina," she said demurely.

"Nice to meet you Christina. I am off to breakfast," I said, as I left out the side entrance.

I went out the side door and walked toward the plaza. I had not gone far before I could see the Inn of the Anasazi just a block from the northeast end of the plaza. I was more than just a little curious about what Anna Pacheco had to tell me.

The Inn of the Anasazi is a beautiful three-story hotel built in the pueblo style. It is accented with dark wood features and terrazzo floors in the lobby. Inside the restaurant are kiva fireplaces tucked in the corners and lit with scent of piñon wood. The ambience is understated elegance. I walked in through the small lobby to the restaurant. I informed the maître d that I was looking for Anna Pacheco.

Without thinking about it, he said, "Certainly, Doctor Hunter, Ms. Pacheco has been expecting you."

With that introduction, he led me to the far end of the restaurant to an almost hidden alcove. There sitting by herself was a stately looking, dark black-haired woman dressed in a nicely pressed white blouse with a silver heishi necklace around her neck. She had on a lovely, expensive looking, wool checkered jacket with three-quarter sleeves covering her blouse. She had a rich, but unassuming and sophisticated look that suggested both success and confidence.

She reached out her hand, and said, "Doctor Hunter, I am Anna Pacheco. Thank you for joining me."

I took her hand and politely replied, "The pleasure is mine. Please call me Scott"

She continued, "Please have a seat."

I sat down and awkwardly and said, "It is nice to meet you but please tell me why you called."

She explained that Rebecca had called her to make the arrangements for me to stay at the La Fonda and that Rebecca was picking up the tab. She then suggested that we order and talk over breakfast. She had already taken the liberty to have menus at the table.

Once I reviewed the menu, she summoned the waiter.

Seeing the menu made me again realize what I had missed in Santa Fe. The food cannot be found anywhere else.

"I will have the huevos rancheros with red chile and coffee," I ordered.

The waiter had previously taken Anna's order of toast and two scrambled eggs with green chile.

"Isn't it unusual to frequent the restaurant of the competition?" I ventured.

Anna laughed and said, "Santa Fe is a small town. We have an agreement with owners and managers of other establishments that when we have a meeting that is of a private, and confidential, nature we can meet in each other's restaurants in private."

I smiled and again asked, "So, please tell me what we are meeting about."

Anna began, "I was a partner of Rebecca's late husband, Blake, in some business ventures. As you can imagine, those of us who knew him are all in shock."

"Yes, I am sure it is a shock to those that knew him and Rebecca," I responded. "But what is this information you have that you think may be beneficial? And why would it be beneficial since I am simply here to console Rebecca and then return home to Bozeman."

Anna continued, "I know from Rebecca that she thinks highly of you and your skills as an observer of people. I also know that you and Rebecca were once married and that she and Blake had an affair that ended your marriage. If you do choose to stay, the information I have may help you sort through other relationships Blake had and perhaps identify those who may have not thought kindly of Blake."

I said warily, "I am intrigued, please resume."

10

Anna began again, "My family has been here since the sixteen-hundreds. They migrated first from Spain to Mexico and later from Mexico to this area long before New Mexico was a state. Unlike many of the early settlers who were farmers and had small ranches, my family was made up of traders and merchants."

"What does this have to do with why I am here?" I said a bit more testily than I had meant to.

Without acknowledging my irritation, she continued. "Because my family was involved as merchants and traders, they began a number of very successful business ventures and became large landowners in the area. As a result, I have often been on the inside when new deals were struck or new ventures in Santa Fe begun. Over the years, I have a very large, and what has become, a very powerful network. The Pacheco name is well-known and well-respected in Santa Fe business circles."

At that point, I recalled that at one time my father had worked as a mechanic for a dealership, Pacheco's Chevrolet and GMC.

I asked, "Anna, did your family own Pacheco's Chevrolet and GMC?"

She smiled and said, "Why yes, it was owned by my uncle, Ruben Pacheco."

It came to me now that my father had worked there and had admired Mr. Pacheco, as he called him. I related that to Anna and said, "Small world."

"At any rate," Anna continued. "Blake saw the advantage of leveraging my contacts to begin creating some of his own entrepreneurial efforts. You see, Blake was a relatively unknown here at the time. We are talking twenty-five years ago. He had come to Santa Fe from somewhere on the East Coast. Although he was young, he quickly became a fixture at social events and had a charming, if not charismatic, persona. He arrived in Santa Fe with his second wife, Lauren, also from the east coast. Blake immersed himself in the Santa Fe culture and bought a house in Tesuque where he would throw large parties and fund raisers. He seemed to have some money, but his background always seemed a bit murky. Regardless, he was able to quickly establish himself as a person who wanted to invest in Santa Fe. That appealed to those in positions of influence in the city, the mayor, city council members, and the like."

"I have a slim recollection of Blake, but obviously I did not travel in those circles," I recalled. "I only came to know more about him when I became aware of the affair he was having with Rebecca. Why wouldn't more people have investigated his background rather than give him the figurative keys to the city?"

Anna responded, "Keep in mind, Scott, that Santa Feans have always had a love-hate relationship with outsiders. We tend to dislike the wealth they have, the patronizing way they carry themselves, their often loud and boisterous manner. On the other hand, we are dependent on them, and tourism is among our top economic drivers. We have become adept at overlooking those things about outsiders we loathe because they help us pay our mortgages. However, there is always a level of disdain just below the surface. So when Blake entered the scene, and wanted to invest in the community, the only question people had was whether he had the means to back up his stated interests."

Shaking my head, I sadly concluded, "In a sense, it is a higher-level example of the master-slave relationship where exploitation becomes a tolerated means to an end."

Anna responded, "That is a harsher characterization than I would have used, but it is not far off."

"Initially, Blake's intentions seemed noble enough. He loved the Santa Fe art scene and wanted to extend the reach of art to his east coast connections. After we had a chance to get to know each other, he approached me and he discussed his interest in starting a gallery that would cater to artistic tastes, including southwestern art, but going even beyond to a wider variety of art. He told me that while he personally loved the work of noted southwest artists like R.C. Gorman, Frank Howell, and John Nieto, he envisioned a gallery that would also include artist from other mediums."

Puzzled, I asked, "Aren't there already enough art galleries in Santa Fe? And aren't there any number of galleries that have other mediums than southwest art?"

Anna smiled and replied, "There are about three hundred galleries in Santa Fe with any number of types of art, so I also pressed Blake on why he was interested in starting yet another one. But he was persuasive and energetic. He believed that there was a market that he could tap into that was currently under-supplied with fine art. He also believed that he could persuade already well-established artists to hang their art in his gallery. He said that with his contacts, and the credibility the Pacheco name lent to the gallery, it stood to be a great success."

Shaking her head, she continued, "I usually let my head dictate my business decisions. But Blake was so charming, convincing, and confident, I let my emotions take over. I agreed to become a minority investor, and to lend my name to his gallery. That was my first mistake."

"Well Anna," I responded. "I know the feeling."

At that time our waiter arrived with our breakfast plates. With the incredibly fragrant huevos rancheros calling me, it gave me a chance to pause momentarily and take that first bite. But I was anxious to hear more.

11

After a few moments to arrange our plates and cups, Anna continued. "Blake found the house on East Palace Avenue was going to be for sale with the current residents retiring. The house was fifty years old and, until then, had always been a residence. Blake knew that the house would have to be rezoned to commercial, but the risk was worth it given that it was the last available property of its kind in the old historic area. It would be one of only a few galleries that would have its own parking behind the building and still be within walking distance to the plaza. I will give him credit for his vision."

I offered, "He sounds like a real salesman."

"Yes, he was," Anna replied. "He also had the drive and charisma to carry it off. He convinced the City Council to rezone and got other minority investors to see his vision. He managed the remodel and turned the house into a charming gallery. Early signs were that his vision was going to pay off."

"Are you suggesting that his vision went off the tracks?" I probed.

"Well, the gallery seemed to be progressing, but I began to hear new rumors of his well-known philandering." Anna responded. "His lifestyle seemed to be fast and loose, taking advantage of the relationships he had in high places, he would periodically host a "men's business retreat" in a private ranch resort in the mountains northeast of Taos. These "business retreats" would include men of influence in the city including the mayor, the head of the Chamber, a state representative, and even one time, the governor of the state. On the surface, these retreats seemed to be gatherings to discuss the future economic development of Santa Fe. However, while those who were invited were sworn to secrecy, stories leaked out about lurid details, out of state escorts being flown in, and the retreats being more of a way for these men to cut loose than really business related."

"This behavior takes philandering to another level," I said bewildered.

"Yes it does," Anna replied. "In retrospect, it seemed to have been a well-orchestrated, and successful, attempt by Blake to curry favor with decision makers. Through a series of retreats over several years, he began to know, figuratively, where all of the bodies were buried. In other words, his influence was, in part, based on a kind of subtle blackmail. In addition, he was always generous with his donations to activities related to law enforcement, fund raisers for the Chamber and local hospital foundation, and other very public charities. So, when he would go in front of the City Council with requests, like rezoning, he was rarely turned down. And when new economic development opportunities emerged, he always seemed to have the first option investing. It seemed that even powerful people were fearful of Blake."

"Wow," I exclaimed. "Did Rebecca have knowledge of these behaviors?"

"I don't think so. By the time Rebecca got to know Blake, he had already divorced Lauren and had been in Santa Fe for over ten years. By the time Blake and Rebecca began their affair, his power and influence were already well established. His "men's retreats" had long since served their purpose and were no longer necessary."

I jokingly said, "It is kind of like the mafia going mainstream after having made their money in nefarious ways."

"Exactly," Anna smiled and answered. "You can begin to imagine how, over time, Blake would have men who began to resent the way he held unseemly knowledge over their heads for their influence. He also used similar tactics with the artists he represented in his gallery in order to manage their percentage of profit to his advantage."

"Whew," I breathed heavily. "The list of people who may have wanted Blake to disappear must have been a long one."

"That's the interesting thing," Anna said puzzled. "In spite of Blake's questionable business practices, people were somehow able to overlook his manipulative behavior because they continued to believe his goodness outweighed his badness. Not only was he charming, but he seemed to have a generosity of spirit. It was not unusual for Blake to contribute to an associate's child's soccer team, or have a surprise anniversary for an associate and his wife, or throw a birthday party for the mother of another associate. I must say, his attention to detail to the kind of emotional events meaningful to his partners and friends was unusual, and very effective. He held a seventy-fifth birthday party for my mother at the La Fonda ballroom and invited people dear to my mother whom she had not seen in ages. That kind of attention buys a lot of forgiveness."

I began to wonder if Blake was just a brilliant and cunning businessman or a full-fledged narcissistic psychopath. Described by Anna, his life had all the makings of a made for TV movie!

After a moment to reflect, I replied, "My Anna, you have certainly covered a lot of ground in a short period of time. There are two very important things I need to know."

"All right," she responded. "What do you need to know?"

I continued, "First, to what extent is Rebecca aware of Blake's manipulative behaviors, his questionable business practices, and the degree to which he may have pissed off more than a few people? When Rebecca and I had dinner last night, she acknowledged none of what you have told me."

"Second, what can I really do here that cannot be done by local law enforcement professionals? I am a psychologist, not a detective. My understanding of detective work is limited to classes and workshops I have had in forensic psychology. Oh, and watching Dateline and Forty-Eight Hours on television. Not exactly a resume for solving a murder case."

Looking intently at me, Anna seriously countered, "Scott, with respect to your first question, the relationship that Rebecca and Blake had was one of mutual benefit rather than one of deep intimacy. Blake needed greater legitimacy than he had been able to establish. He needed to demonstrate the commitment that he had to the community was more than just exploitation. He got that legitimacy by marrying a local woman. True, Rebecca moved here in high school, but she had been here long enough to be considered one of us. In addition, like you, Rebecca had been school mates with some of the individuals who became prominent in Santa Fe—the police chief, the mayor, and individuals on the City Council. It was not necessary to use these relationships for influence, only to give Blake believability. On the other hand, it is not a surprise to you to know about Rebecca's need for excitement and how easily she can become bored with routine. The lifestyle Blake provided her met this need. I do not believe that Rebecca wanted to know, or that she did know, about Blake's business dealings."

It hurt to hear her lay out their relationship like this. Once again, I felt indicted for not having provided a life for Rebecca that was interesting enough to satisfy her. On the other hand, I also knew that, since the divorce, I had grown to become a healthier individual and wanted more in relationships than simply excitement.

"And the second question," I asked.

"Ah yes, the second question," she began tentatively. "The police are going to want to solve this case very quickly. No one wants a thorough investigation. Remember that I said that Blake knows where all of the bodies are buried. Well, there are several people in powerful positions who will not want their laundry aired publicly. Not only could it bring about embarrassment, but it is also possible that some of their actions could have been illegal. It is quite possible that the police could point fingers at Rebecca, and others who are innocent, just to wrap this up quickly. Remember, the spouse is almost always considered a prime suspect. In addition, the thought of hiring a private investigator is risky because that person could be bought off, or intimidated, by those same people who want to solve the case quickly. With you, Rebecca knows that you will have her best interest in mind."

I obviously had a lot to think about before I met Rebecca for lunch. I felt the walls closing in and that Anna was suggesting that I, or what I could find out, was standing between Rebecca and some significant legal issues.

"I do not even know where to start, Anna," I said plaintively.

"Let me provide you some suggestions," she offered.

THE GUADALUPE
SIX MONTHS AGO
12

The Montoya family had owned the Guadalupe restaurant for over
forty years. It has become a meeting place for all the locals. It was
Santa Fe's version of Cheers, where everyone knew your name. It was
located down Paseo de Peralta, not far from the Capital Building, known as
"the Roundhouse." State legislators used to drive the short distance to the
Guadalupe for after-session drinks to regale the day's victories and to drown
the day's defeats. It was a different time in local politics back then. There
wasn't the vitriol and meanness that seems to exist today. Being a relatively
small state in population, it was not unusual for these representatives to
have gone to school together, to know each other's families and, in some
cases, to be related. They could banter by day and break bread together in
the evening.

Maria Montoya's grandfather, Luis, had started the restaurant as a
way for their local friends and family to have a place to gather that they
trusted, and served local food with which they were familiar. When asked
about how he came to the idea, Luis would tell the story of having had an
apparition when praying to Our Lady of Guadalupe in the Cathedral. Luis,
a devout Catholic, prayed at the Cathedral daily. One day while praying,
he had a vision of a safe gathering place for family and friends to meet. He
always believed the vision was given to him by Our Lady of Guadalupe,
thus the name of the restaurant, the Guadalupe. Luis had a carving of Our
Lady of Guadalupe in the foyer of the restaurant as a memorial to that early
vision.

Luis used to observe that with the explosion of international interest
in Santa Fe, all the newer restaurants were simply creating an image of Santa

Fe that was for marketing rather than being true to the culture. Green chile ice cream. Really? He saw these restaurants and their fare, much like the emergence of Kokopelli and the howling coyote, as being representative of a fictional Santa Fe. Luis would shake his head and lament that they were all a product of some fancy New York marketing firm, unrelated to the roots of the people and the land.

Upon Luis death fifteen years earlier, Maria's father, Roberto, took over running the restaurant after himself having been a state representative. When asked why he left politics to become a restaurateur, he would always laugh and say that, "More political decisions were made at the Guadalupe bar than on the legislative floor." With his belly laugh, he would chortle, "I am more in politics now than when I was elected."

These policymakers had become family, literally. Two of the legislators were married to Maria's cousins. And they were on opposite sides of the political spectrum. The Montoya family had created an atmosphere that was more upscale than some of the family-owned diners, but more casual than some of Santa Fe's ritzy restaurants.

It had been ten years ago that she had first met Blake Martin, one of the wealthy elites in town and owner of Martin's Fine Art gallery. He had come into the restaurant with his new "bought and paid for" wife and several other notables in his entourage. The first time he had come to the restaurant was in the evening. The menu at that time was a bit more formal in the evenings, more like a New Mexican steak house with green chile recipes included with ribeye steaks and salmon. In the evening, they used white linen tablecloths to go with the candle lit tables. They also had specialty drinks with fruit infused cocktails.

Maria remembered that Blake and his group were seated at a large round table. Prior to being led to their table, Blake had quietly pulled her aside and indicated that the bill for the evening would be his, always wanting to be the big shot. He was a tall, handsome man with a winsome smile and exuded a certain attraction. He was faintly flirtatious. On the one hand, she had been charmed. But on the other hand, she recalled, her internal sensors cried out, "Caution! Caution!"

That evening was the first of Blake's many visits to the Guadalupe. He became a regular, particularly at happy hour when he would hob nob with the legislators and typically buy a round of drinks. To an objective observer, it was obvious that his intentions were not simply buying friends, but something more ambitious, buying influence. Because of his charisma and engaging personality, he became popular with the legislators. He was often the center of attention entertaining the group with stories of his work with his artists, authors, celebrities, and his new business ventures. It was a sight to behold to see Blake work a room. It became a badge of honor when Blake selected your table for his imbibing. You had become a part of the in crowd.

Maria recalled the uneasiness that Blake's growing popularity created with her father. Blake had been responsible for bringing in new business to the restaurant. The new patrons that Blake introduced to the restaurant were big spenders and frequent guests. These guests were often influential in their own right, introducing their friends to the establishment. In addition, they would periodically rent out the restaurant for an evening, and sometimes even a day, to hold meetings, parties, or fundraisers. While the restaurant was not under any financial pressure, the guests Blake brought in helped with the inevitable shoulder season, the slow times between when the legislators were out of session and the tourist season had not yet begun. However, Roberto had the uncomfortable feeling that Blake, and his associates, were beginning to take over the restaurant, pushing some of the loyal and longer-term guests to the background. Roberto had even had some of his regulars complain that the outsiders were loud, demanding, and disrespectful, something both Maria and Roberto had also noticed. Roberto was becoming fearful that Montoya's was becoming a victim of its own success.

13

It was after about three years after Blake first coming to the Guadalupe that he approached Roberto late one weekday evening when the bar was about to close. As he was finishing his last scotch and soda, Blake suggested to Roberto that they combine their interests and hang high-end art on the walls of the restaurant.

When Roberto responded with a hearty laugh, Blake rejoined, "No, amigo, I am serious."

"Amigo." Hmm. In the back of Roberto's mind, he noted Blake called him "amigo." While many local Anglos in Santa Fe were bilingual and could converse back and forth between Spanish and English, when an outsider did it, particularly in a business setting, it came across as ingenuine, manipulative and patronizing. It was an attempt to imply that they were more than just owner and patron, they were friends. Having worked in the legislature and around legislators for so many years, Roberto's bullshit sniffer was finely tuned. He instantly knew to proceed with caution.

Knowing that a pitch was coming, Roberto continued sardonically, "Okay, amigo, tell me what you are suggesting."

"I have noticed that the Guadalupe is a real gathering place for wealthy, and discerning, clients," Blake went on. "Roberto, with your ability to create such a welcoming ambience and fine dining experience, coupled with the fine art I keep at my gallery, I think we could kill two birds with one stone."

Roberto thought to himself, "I wonder if I am one of the birds!"

"Continue," Roberto feigned interest.

"I regularly have more art than I can put on display at the gallery. I show the art that I think will sell, or is in vogue with customers, and I store the works of artists that are, at the moment, less popular. Your restaurant is perfectly suited to hang many of the works I currently store. We could sell them to your guests and we could both make a little profit. It could also serve as a joint marketing venture. Visitors to the restaurant would be interested in what other works the gallery holds and visitors to the gallery would be directed to the Guadalupe for the finest dining experience in Santa Fe." Blake continued putting on his best negotiators strategy.

"Remember, I have brought a lot of new, and prominent guests your way," Blake said, trying to ingratiate himself to Roberto.

However, the effect was just the opposite. Inside, Roberto went from cautious to beginning to feel angry. Blake's comments triggered old and deep wounds about how later-day gringos had run roughshod over the local Mexican and Indian natives, taking their land, their resources, and sometimes their women all the while trying to make the locals feel indebted to them. Now Blake was implying that he had been, in some measure, responsible for the success of the Guadalupe. Montoya's. Where the hell had he been years before when the restaurant was really struggling, Roberto wondered. Nonetheless, Roberto knew he needed to keep his composure.

"So," Roberto responded quizzically. "I get your second-class art to hang in my first-class restaurant in the hopes that the influential guests that you have sent my way might buy the art for dessert. Is that right?"

Blake immediately recognized his misstep and how much he had underestimated Roberto's own cunning and business savvy.

"Not at all, Roberto," Blake quickly replied. "I know what a good businessman you are and how well you relate to people. Well, really, you are the reason you have so many regular and influential customers. In fact, I have learned a lot by watching you over the past couple of years about how to more effectively communicate and negotiate."

Knowing he had some ground to make up, Blake continued to backtrack and resumed, "I admire the business you have been able to build at the Guadalupe. My offer was intended to present an additional opportunity for you to get some passive income and for us to each broaden our marketing reach. As for the art, we could agree together what to display, and it would not be second rate. Keep in mind that the works I represent begin at no lower than three thousand and go up to twenty-five thousand. Our cut on the commissions would be between three hundred to twenty-five hundred per piece. Over the course of a year, we are talking about significant income for just displaying the art."

Roberto could see that he had Blake on the ropes, so he thought he would try a little rope-a-dope technique and string him along for a while.

"Well," Roberto began thoughtfully. "Blake, as I see it, there is more of a risk on my side than on yours. It would be almost like me running an art gallery rather than a restaurant. What if my regulars hated the art? What if my legislator guests felt like we had made the restaurant too upscale for them to have their after-hours banter and negotiations? What if the restaurant was flooded with tourists who wanted to look at the art and not become paying customers? I am just not sure this is a good idea."

Blake took the bait. "Look, Roberto, what if I guaranteed an upside and managed the downside risk? I really think this could be a win-win proposition."

Roberto was intrigued. Had Blake come more prepared than was first evident? Had the tables just turned?

"What do you mean, Blake?" Roberto replied.

"Well Roberto, here is how I see it. We are both businessmen. Business is all about making a profit and growing it over time. Right?"

That question showed Roberto just how little Blake really understood him and his motivation. He could see his father, Luis, turning over in his grave at the thought of making the restaurant yet another Santa Fe marketing tool, unrelated to the people and their heritage.

Without waiting for a reply from Roberto, Blake continued, "What if I became a minority investor in the restaurant and we write into the agreement that for the first five years of our contract, I guarantee that you will receive a profit no less than you have for your previous three years. We would have independent auditors come in to create a fair evaluation of the business. We would determine the percentage that I would own, and I would give you a check based on the auditor's determination. At the end of each year, we would look at the proceeds of the combined restaurant and art sales and determine any additional profits to be split."

"Whoa, whoa, whoa," Roberto exclaimed surprised. "You are moving way too fast. You have just gone from wanting to put art on the wall to becoming a minority owner. This is not a conversation I am prepared to have."

The conversation had taken Roberto somewhat, but not totally, by surprise. Over the years, he had been approached by others, friends and foes alike, to become partners in the business. These folks, mostly locals, had seen the success of the Guadalupe and wanted to become a part of a prosperous enterprise. Ideas pitched to Roberto had ranged from the practical to the whimsical. They included expanding the space; putting on a second floor; buying out a competitor to have another location; franchising the concept; bringing in a play area with slides and kiddie pools to appeal to families; and on, and on. Presenters were always of the opinion that bigger is better, a proposition with which Roberto strongly, but privately, disagreed.

In every case, when a new business idea was pitched about the restaurant, Roberto was clear about what had made the Guadalupe successful. It had always been his, and the family's, conclusion to stay the course. However, he had not previously been presented with the specific idea that Blake had presented. He had to admit that the idea of having fine art in the restaurant was intriguing and that, in spite of his protestations to Blake, he was curious. However, he was definite that he had no interest in having any outside investors in the business.

Roberto thought to himself, that it was a good thing that he had been a legislator and had heard ambitious, and sometimes preposterous, plans being presented. He had learned that most ambitious plans were really self-serving and not for the good of the people being served. He knew that to become overly emotional in the face of these proposals of self-interest was to expose your vulnerabilities and pass the advantage to your opponent. Also, he had no interest inviting "minority investors" to become a part of the business. The restaurant was a family legacy to be passed down to subsequent generations. He knew that his family would string him up if he relented. But now was not the time to engage further in the conversation. This was a time to think, not to act.

"Blake, let's back up a bit and just take one step at a time," Roberto insisted. "Let me give this some thought and let's meet here in the morning. I will ask Jodi to make us some brunch. Let's meet at ten o'clock."

Seeing that the conversation had come to an impasse, but not without having peaked Roberto's curiosity, Blake agreed and exited the restaurant, looking forward to tomorrow's exchange.

14.

Jodi Diaz had been a part of the Guadalupe restaurant "family" for over fifteen years. Like many of the Guadalupe employees, she had come to Roberto seeking employment and wanting to improve the situation for herself and her then young son, Juan. Roberto saw Jodi as wanting a hand and not a hand-out. He noticed something in her that he respected, a willingness to work hard and a certain resilience. Jodi's husband, and the father of Juan, had died tragically in a construction accident. They had no life insurance, and the small locally owned construction company carried no insurance for the benefit of their employees. Jodi was left with the responsibility of a young child, only a high school education, and no real work experience. Nevertheless, she did not see herself as a victim and only wanted an opportunity to survive in dignity.

Beginning with waiting tables, she had learned the trade and was now one of two head chefs. With Roberto's assistance, Jodi had managed to secure a Culinary Arts degree from the local community college. She was now a credentialed chef. Roberto was as proud of Jodi as if she had been one of his own. The feeling from Jodi was mutual. Jodi represented to Roberto the values he, and his family, had regarding using the restaurant-to help the community through providing opportunities to those less fortunate who would work hard and persevere. In fact, the number of current Santa Fe businessmen and women who had worked for the Guadalupe in their youth was legion. This was one of the reasons that the Montoya family was not interested in the 'bigger is better' approach to business as it could conflict with their unstated, and mostly behind the scenes, mission of local philanthropy.

Roberto had texted Jodi the night before asking her to have one of her sous-chefs prepare a brunch for Blake and him in the morning. Not being one to disappoint, Jodi was not going to delegate something for the jefe's important meeting.

After the meeting with Blake the night before, Roberto had polled family members and some staff, like Jodi, about Blake's idea about hanging art in the restaurant. He did not bring up Blake's idea to be an investor since Roberto knew that was a non-starter. The opinions were mixed but there was agreement that if the process could be managed, and neither the restaurant nor its guests would be negatively impacted, it was worth a try.

Blake arrived promptly at ten o'clock, briefcase in hand. Roberto was waiting. Roberto ushered Blake to a corner booth. They were the only ones in the restaurant because it typically did not open until eleven thirty for lunch.

No sooner had they set down when Jodi came with coffee and juice. She had prepared one of her favorite dishes, a green chile and cheese omelet with a side of fried potatoes, frijoles, guacamole, and two mini blue corn pancakes with maple syrup. A meal fit for a king, or at least a business brunch for the boss.

Satisfied that her presentation was complete, Jodi quietly made her way to the shadows of the room and into the kitchen, always with an ear to respond to Roberto's calling.

"Well," Blake began eagerly. "Where do we start?"

In typical Roberto fashion, Roberto smiled and replied, "I think I will start with the omelet. What about you."

Blake laughed and said, "Well, I guess I should have put pleasure before business."

With that, both men began eating their hearty breakfast and talking about other, non-business issues like local politics, the dearth of snowfall, and their anticipation of a robust tourist season. Once their plates were cleaned, and they had both commented on the exquisiteness of Jodi's culinary prowess, they got down to business.

"Blake," Roberto commenced. "I have given your proposition a great deal of thought. In addition, I have consulted with some key family members. We are, how shall I say this, cautious but willing to give your idea about using the restaurant to hang your art a try. We will want to go slowly on this and, as I said last night, take one step at a time."

Roberto was careful not to surface any thoughts about Blake being an investor. He knew from his legislator days that you wanted to start with a small positive and not bring up the bad news until it was necessary.

Blake got Roberto's drift and did not push the issue of investing.

"Great," Blake responded enthusiastically. "I was hoping you would consider my proposition. I am excited and I hear the caution in your voice. I agree, let's take one step at a time. I did prepare some preliminary documents to review in hopes that you would consent." Blake continued as he reached for his briefcase.

Internally, Roberto was rolling his eyes, seeing Blake's aggressiveness, and knowing that he would have to manage him carefully.

For the next hour, Blake and Roberto discussed some their thoughts regarding how they would select the art; where it could be placed; how sales would be transacted; how they would split the profits; how they would cross-refer their respective customers; what constituted the art being a distraction rather than a benefit; and finally, how Blake would follow up on his offer to financially insure that the restaurant's profitability would not be negatively impacted by the venture. Neither of them raised the additional idea of Blake investing in the restaurant.

"If we can get all of the details worked out," Blake concluded, "I would recommend that we begin the venture by having an evening presentation of the artwork of a Santa Fe artist. Our gallery would pay for the restaurant for the evening including all the set-up fees, invitations, hors d'oeuvres, drinks and wait staff. We would have an invitation-only guest list that you and I would jointly create. It would be a great way to showcase the art, the artist and of course the restaurant. What do you think?"

Roberto was please by Blake's idea and generosity. In addition, it would be a great way for some of his folks to earn a little extra money.

"I think it is a great idea and it would be a fun evening," Roberto responded.

As luncheon customers began coming into the restaurant, the men began wrapping-up their conversation.

"I will have my attorney draft a proposal and you can have your attorney review it," Blake offered.

Roberto agreed, escorted Blake to the door, shaking his hand, and said, "I look forward to getting and studying your proposal. I am sure we will talk again soon."

15

It had been three months since Roberto and Blake had signed the proposal, and the new venture between the Guadalupe and Martin's Fine Art gallery was working out relatively well. True to his word, Blake had kept his part of the bargain and collaborated with Roberto on the art to be placed, not referring interested clients to the restaurant who would not also be paying customers, and providing a financial spreadsheet documenting monthly sales, profits, and the percentages due to each party. The only initial glitch had been training the wait staff how to respond to prospective buyers and creating a separate payment process for those purchasing the art. Roberto was seeing some new customers, both local and tourists, and business was going very well.

The private launch of the new venture had also gone well. The invited guests were appreciative of the opportunity to have a private showing of the work of a local artist and to actually meet her. Several works of her art had been sold that night. In addition, businessmen and women saw the restaurant as an opportunity to host other events, like weddings, bar mitzvahs, birthdays, Quinceañeras, and work retreats. It had gone so well, that Roberto suggested they have another private showing, this time with a wider variety of art and artists, and a different invite group. Blake readily agreed.

The downside of the successful venture was that Blake began bringing up the minority investment idea again. Blake had been subtle, but relentless. Roberto could see that Blake's strategy was to subtly gaslight Roberto overtime, sowing seeds of doubt to make Roberto think that he could not be successful without Blake and that the success of the restaurant was due, in large measure, to Blake's involvement.

Roberto was seeing first-hand what he had observed at a distance, that Blake's negotiation strategy was to alternate between being charming and ingratiating to trying to create doubt. Blake was the good cop-bad cop all rolled into one. While Roberto marveled at Blake's resolve and craftiness, he was also just as certain that he did not want the arrangement to go further than it had already.

Blake continued to up the stakes. He went from being a minority investor to talking about how the location was perfect for a boutique hotel, much like the Inn of the Anasazi. It would be a place for dignitaries to stay and dine when coming to Santa Fe for business or government work. The hotel would be cited by national organizations as a five-star regional favorite. When that strategy did not work, Blake would appeal to Roberto's philanthropic interests imagining how together they could create a foundation with proceeds from the restaurant/hotel and elegant fundraisers to provide financial assistance to local charities. The more Roberto declined Blake's offers, the more extravagant the next offer became.

The ideas were endless, but Roberto was just as resolute in sticking to the scaled down plan. Roberto went from being amused at Blake's creations to being irritated at his perseverance. Blake continued to allow his ambitions to blind him to the loyalty Roberto had to his family legacy and his staff. Roberto only need look at the statue of Our Lady of Guadalupe in the foyer, the inspiration for his father to have originally created the restaurant, to regain his footing and purpose.

The second art exhibit and reception were taking place this evening and the chefs and waitstaff were scurrying to manage last minute details. The final works of art were being put in place and the party was about to begin. The list of invitees to this event was a bit different from the first. Guests for the initial art party were people of influence known to either Blake or Roberto or both. They consisted of former clients of Blake's gallery, the mayor, members of the city council, some legislators, and some of the regulars to the Guadalupe. Both Blake and Roberto wanted the event to be both a success as well as a measure of good will. It had been a clever, and effective, strategy.

They both decided that for the second art party, they would expand their reach to prospective, and wealthy, clients who were less known to either of them. They elected to send personal invitations to the occupants of Las Vistas, a private gated country club community consisting of out of state homeowners and business executives who had retired in Santa Fe, plus a sprinkling of locals.

Roberto had initially been skeptical because of how controversial Las

Vistas had been when it first opened twenty years previously. It was initially seen as yet another group of wealthy outsiders intent on exploiting the locals for water and available land. However, the Club at Las Vistas community had upheld its commitment to stewardship, with a focus on sustainable water, wildlife conservation, community grants and scholarships, and the creation of a charitable foundation supporting children and adults with physical and emotional disabilities. While not all Santa Feans were in love with the development, it had become more accepted and judged with less disdain as their good works became more widely known.

It was after Blake's pointing out the many benefits to Roberto, that Roberto finally relented. As a result, they had sent out personalized invitations to over four hundred Las Vistas residents. As of the day before the art exhibit showing, they had received 250 RSVPs to attend. It promised to be a full house and excitement was high.

16

The Guadalupe had been transformed into a high-scale event atmosphere. Roberto had hired a string quartet to play classical music in the background. The waitstaff were all dressed in Santa Fe elegant attire—black jeans, long-sleeve white shirts, black leather vests, and black bow ties. High cocktail tables with fine linen tablecloths and faintly piñon-scented candles graced the large room. Everything was set for a lovely, and hopefully prosperous, evening.

Blake and his wife, Rebecca, arrived at the restaurant at six thirty. Guests began arriving at seven. Roberto and Blake alternated on welcoming guests and walking them through the evening. While there were several new faces, Roberto also recognized some previous customers and enjoyed making the connection to Las Vistas.

In Santa Fe, formal events were always very eclectic, in both dress and attendees. Santa Fe was unique in its history of attracting a wide variety of visitors and residents. It was not unusual to see famous celebrities, national politicians, and sports figures alongside artists, writers, and locals. These formal, and semi-formal, occasions always gave attendees the opportunity to display their particular version of Santa Fe style. Women adorned in brightly colored hand-woven shawls, sleek long skirts with slits and Concho belts, turquoise squash blossom necklaces, silver rings and bracelets, and elegant leather jackets, often with Native American designs. Men outfitted in expensive bolo ties, leather jackets, pressed jeans, custom boots, and cowboy hats. The song "Rhinestone Cowboy" often came to mind when Roberto saw these latter-day westerners from California and New York. It was always fun and, at times, amusing to see how these partygoers would express themselves with their version of Santa Fe. Tonight was no exception.

Because many of the guests knew each other, the conversation was plentiful and loud, often drowning out the music of the string quartet. In addition, the familiarity lent itself to lowered inhibitions and higher quantities of alcohol. An unanticipated benefit of the free-flowing alcohol, and the familiarity of guests, was the increase in testosterone when it came to spending money on the art.

The idea that money cannot buy class became evident when two Las Vistas neighbors, both well plied with booze, began out-bidding each other on a work of art neither of them knew anything about. The competition appeared to be all in good fun, but underneath it all you could see two faux cowboys wanting to show their colleagues, and neighbors, who had the biggest balls. In the end, one bidder relented, and the work of art only went for about fifty percent above the initial asking price. Blake smiled and Roberto could only shake his head.

It was not the last display of mostly friendly bantering and it often led to additional over-paying for art about which the buyer had little knowledge. Nonetheless, it was a good introduction to the Guadalupe by many who had never previously been customers. Likewise, it was an opportune time for Blake to identify some potential purveyors of his fine art (and cash in on their wealth, naivete and egos).

It was about nine o'clock when there was the sound of a slight disturbance at the front door. Maria had been at the front door reception area that was slightly hidden from the main dining area, checking off names as guests arrived. Because all the guests were personally invited, and there was a sign outside of the Guadalupe, "Private event tonight," Roberto thought there would be none of his regular guests trying to come in. He was surprised to hear loud, and somewhat angry, tones at the entrance. Fortunately, the guests were themselves talking and having a good time, so the commotion was barely noticed.

"Where is that son of a bitch?" the uninvited arrival spoke with a Texas drawl, slurred by some level of inebriation.

Roberto rushed quickly, but deftly, to the front.

"May I be of assistance?" Roberto inquired.

"I want to see that stealing bastard Blake Martin," the stranger exclaimed loudly.

Roberto was quickly sizing up the situation. He was being confronted by a tall, overweight, boisterous man in blue jeans, newer looking cowboy boots, a wrinkled white shirt that was partially untucked, and a wide belt with a large silver and turquoise belt buckle. He was topped off by a cowboy hat that was slightly tilted on his head. This was all under a brown leathered coat that looked expensive. He appeared to be in his fifties with shaggy salt and pepper hair tumbling out from under his cowboy hat. The stranger had a strong odor of alcohol on his breath confirming Roberto's earlier assumption that he was inebriated. Roberto knew he had to act quickly to diffuse the situation and not attract further attention from the guests.

With so many years of managing a restaurant, Roberto had come across numerous situations that he had to subdue before they got out of control. He knew that the more you can agree with a cantankerous guest, and the less confrontational you are, the less likely the guest would become even more belligerent. Roberto was a master at diversion to quell situations before they got out of hand. Roberto knew that he always had to have a plan in the event that something like this happened. Now with a houseful of very wealthy and influential guests, he knew he had to act quickly.

"I would be glad to help," Roberto quickly responded, thinking quickly on his feet. "Come with me and let's see if we can find him."

Continuing to stay calm and matter of fact, Roberto held out his arm to usher the guest to a side hallway out of sight from the other guests that led to the restrooms as well as a small private conference room.

"Where the fuck are you leading me? Goddammit, I was to see Blake Martin. I am going to strangle the asshole. He has messed with the wrong person this time," The man bellowed.

"Right this way," Roberto encouraged the man to walk down the hallway with him. "By the way, I missed your name. I am Roberto Montoya, the manager here. What is your name?"

"I am Tyler King. Now where the hell is Blake?" he exclaimed.

Continuing to try to divert, and create rapport, Roberto queried, "Glad to meet you Tyler. I don't think I have seen you here at the Guadalupe before. Are you from here in Santa Fe?" Roberto asked knowing the answer was no.

"Hell no," Tyler rejoined. "I am from Houston. Haven't you ever heard of King Oil?" Tyler said incredulously. "Now where is that scheming bastard?"

Roberto continued, "Blake is going to join us in our executive suite so we can speak in private. Please, right this way." Roberto knew that calling the conference room the executive suite would appeal to Mr. King's ego and give him the respect he thought he deserved.

65

In the meantime, Maria, knowing the emergency drill quickly left her reception position to get two people. First, she pulled Julio Gonzales aside to enlist his support, if needed. Julio had just returned from active military duty in Fort Benning, Georgia, retiring after thirteen years of service. He had been a highly trained, and decorated, Special Operations Ranger involved in several covert missions overseas. Roberto was helping Julio with his reentry into civilian life by giving him a job that both knew was temporary until Julio could finish his education as an attorney. He had been able to complete two years of law school while in the military and was scheduled to attend the University of New Mexico School of Law in the fall to complete his JD degree. To say that Julio was physically fit was an understatement. He was buff, focused, and had a presence about him that, while being understated, was also very confident. Maria briefed him on the situation and asked Julio to go down the hall to stand outside the conference room, just in case.

Julio smiled and said, "It would be my pleasure."

Maria's second stop was to pull Blake aside and let him know that Tyler King was there to speak with him, inebriated and very angry. She noticed immediately that the color drained from Blake's cheeks as he gasped for air.

"Shit," he pronounced. "What the hell is he doing here?"

Maria counseled him, "Listen, Blake, Dad is a master at diffusing these situations, just follow his lead. Do not do anything to escalate the situation or make Mr. King any angrier than he already is. Agree with him and promise to meet his soon to discuss his concerns. The goal is to have this conversation be short and free of any further disturbance. Got it!"

"Yeah. Okay. I just don't know why he had to come here tonight," Blake said resigned as he headed for the conference room.

Julio was already stationed outside the conference room as Blake made his way down the hall toward him. Blake felt some relief knowing that there is safety in numbers and that Julio could handle the situation if it did escalate.

As Blake entered the room, he could see that, as Maria had suggested, Roberto was speaking to a much less agitated interloper.

The conference room was a richly decorated small room that Roberto had designed for those legislators who needed privacy to discuss impending bills or policy. It had a small mahogany table with six leather executive chairs and tongue and groove wainscoting. At the far end was a small bookshelf with a shelf for alcohol at the base. The room gave the aura of important people discussing important ideas.

Tyler King had settled into one of the comfortable chairs and Roberto had already poured him a glass of water. He was clearly less agitated than when he had come in.

"Hi Blake," Roberto said in an inviting and warm tone. "Mr. King and I were just getting to know each other."

"Good evening, Tyler," Blake said with the best congeniality he could muster under the circumstance.

"Look, Martin," Tyler said confrontationally not wanting to use Blake's first name, "You have completely fucked me over with that fake piece of shit you sold me trying to pawn it off as a Blumenschein original. I want my goddamn money back plus damages or, believe me, I will fucking bury you!"

Ernest L. Blumenschein was one of the original founding members of the Taos Society of Artists in 1915. The group consisted of very well-established artists who had gravitated to Taos to form what would become an art cooperative. Their works were shown in traveling shows across the United States. It was common now for their originals to sell at art auctions in the mid-six figure range.

Blake replied in the most apologetic manner he could gather, "Tyler, I am so sorry that you do not believe that what you bought meets up to your expectations. Please, bring it to the gallery and we can sort this out."

It was clear that Blake was squirming. This was new territory for him to be on the defensive. He had always been able to charm, or intimidate, his audience and now he was on the ropes. Roberto had not seen this side of Blake before.

"Meet my expectations, really," Tyler exclaimed disbelieving. "I paid you two hundred fifty grand for the painting, and you assured me it was an original. I had my own art estimator examine it and he said it was a fake, worth only a fraction of what I paid. Look you asshole, either you make this right or I will fucking bury you. I will bankrupt you in court and the only color you will be seeing will be an orange jump suit."

Even though his agitation had been reduced, the anger in his voice was evident.

"Please, Tyler," Blake pleaded. "Bring the painting down to the gallery on Monday and I will have my folks take a closer look at it. I truly want you to be satisfied with your purchase."

Appeased for the moment, Tyler responded, "All right, Blake. I will be there Monday. But you had better be prepared to make good on this or you will be in a world of hurt. Understood?"

"Understood," Blake said plaintively.

With the apparent conclusion to this part of the conversation, Roberto took over.

"Mr. King," Roberto said appearing to be deferential. "I would love to have you and your family come back to the Guadalupe and be our guests for dinner. I would enjoy getting to know about you and your time in Santa Fe. Just let me know a good time for you."

Beginning to sober up a bit, Tyler replied, "Thank you, Roberto. We would look forward to that."

With that conclusion, Roberto opened the door and led Tyler down the hall and to the front door. They passed Julio on the way and Roberto gave him a wink as they passed, his version of "all clear." Roberto noticed that Tyler did not reach out to Blake to shake hands and Blake followed them to the door to ensure that Tyler was leaving. The entire conversation only took about fifteen minutes. Again, Roberto's ability to manage difficult situations saved the day.

Once Tyler had exited and the door was once again closed, Roberto exclaimed to Blake, "This cannot happen again. You must deal with your clients at your gallery and not here. We can discuss later."

Without waiting for an answer, both Roberto and Blake reemerged and joined the festivities. It appeared that no one had even missed them.

Roberto knew that this incident would require more conversation with Blake, and knew they had to have it relatively soon.

17

It was after midnight when the last guests departed. It was clear that the evening had been a great success for both the guests and the event. To the guest, they were complimentary of the restaurant, the food, the service, and the wait staff. Twelve of the fifty art works had sold, one above asking price. In addition, there appeared to be serious interest in several the other art pieces. Blake assured interested parties that he would follow up with great below-market pricing. He was nothing if not a salesman! Blake was smiling ear to ear and Roberto could see what was coming next.

However, Roberto was concerned that the event had almost gone too far. Having wealthy inebriated guests, most of whom were not locals, gave him an uneasy feeling. As he passed the statue of Our Lady of Guadalupe, he was again reminded of his father's vision of the restaurant—a safe gathering place for friends and family "where everyone knows your name." Roberto was beginning to feel that the Guadalupe could become just like those restaurants that created a fabricated marketing image of Santa Fe and that his father had railed against. In addition, the disruption, and near catastrophe, of an angry and intoxicated intruder had almost ruined the evening. Any previous concerns that Roberto had about expanding the business relationship with Blake had only been confirmed tonight.

A Blake escorted the last guest to the door, smilingly he came over to Roberto saying "Hey, amigo, how about a night cap?"

There was that "amigo" again with Blake trying to overcome any tension between them with goodwill. Bracing himself for what he knew was coming, Roberto responded, "It has been a long day and I am beat, maybe another time." He was tired and did not want to have the discussion now.

Blake rejoined, "Oh, come on Roberto, just one to celebrate the evening."

Roberto relented, hoping to keep the conversation superficial, "Okay, just one."

Roberto poured both of them a brandy and they sat at one of the now-cleared tables.

Blake lifted his brandy glass to Roberto with, "To a great night and a great partnership."

Without replying, Roberto clinked glasses with him.

"Look, Roberto," Blake continued. "I am really sorry for the issue with Tyler King. It is really just a misunderstanding that I know I can sort out next week. Believe me, he is by far the exception of my art clients. Actually, I have never had an unhappy customer in the past."

Roberto doubted that this was the case, but kept that thought to himself.

"Roberto," Blake began. "This partnership has exceeded all my expectations. It has expanded both of our customer bases and introduced us to those who recognize the finer things in life and are willing to pay for it."

Roberto was silent, knowing what was coming next.

Blake continued, "Neither of us knew when we began this process that we would discover something so successful and special. What I have seen has deepened my conviction that if we were to become more fully business partners we could create something really extraordinary. With your incredible background in hospitality and my contacts, we could build something truly unique. The location here is truly outstanding and by just putting a couple of floors above the restaurant for luxury rooms we could create an unparalleled world-class boutique hotel. Can you not see the vision?"

Roberto had been putting off this discussion, shadow boxing and distracting. He had not wanted to bring the hammer down on the idea of Blake becoming an investor, hoping upon hope that Blake would be satisfied with the agreement that they had already reached. He also had enjoyed some of the new attention the Guadalupe had received. In addition to the art showing, the local newspaper and radio stations had hyped the new look inside the restaurant. There had been a certain satisfaction to having received the recognition. However, he was unwavering in his father's vision for the Guadalupe-that it stays in the family and always be of service to the local community. It was time to be straight with Blake.

"Blake," Roberto began tentatively. "I agree, it has been a good partnership and it has exceeded my expectations as well. I was not sure having art in the restaurant was a good idea. You knew of my concerns when we began. I must say that the benefits have far outweighed the liabilities. Business has been up, particularly during times that have customarily been slower. I have been able to hire a few more staff and that is always a joy."

"Great," Blake countered smiling. "It looks like we are thinking the same way."

"Well," Roberto continued. "Not exactly."

Puzzled, Blake said, "What do you mean?"

Roberto began to explain, "When my father Luis started the Guadalupe over forty years ago, he envisioned a gathering place where the locals could come with their friends and families and always feel welcome. When I was in the legislature, my group of friends expanded and they became part of our extended family, coming here to continue enjoy each other's company, to banter and to continue their political discussions. Even before our partnership, I worried that we were becoming so popular that the locals were beginning to feel a bit less welcome."

"Not to worry, my friend, the local people will always be invited," Blake disputed.

"Hear me out," Roberto interrupted. "The Guadalupe is more to me than just a successful enterprise. It is a sacred trust, in some way a ministry, in the way we hire young residents, give them opportunities, and send them on their way. It is a legacy I cannot ignore."

Not to be denied, Blake said, "Roberto, I will make sure we continue to honor your father's original vision for the Guadalupe. We are only adding to it. In fact, we can even set up a foundation to support the youth of Santa Fe. I am sure your father would approve of that."

Exasperated, Roberto knew the time had come.

"Blake, I value what we have done, and I appreciate our business relationship (being careful not to say 'friendship'). I would like to continue what we have begun with art in the restaurant. However, I will never pass on any part of the ownership of the Guadalupe to anyone else. It is a sacred pact I have with my father, my family, and the locals whom my father so wanted to be served."

Looking more angry than dejected, Blake loudly put down his brandy glass and refuted, "Goddammit Roberto, not only are you the most stubborn man I have even met, but you are also looking a gift horse in the mouth!! Don't forget that most of your success these last few years has been because of my influence and the people whom I have introduced to you and to the Guadalupe. You used to have slow seasons, now you are busy all the time. It has been me that has kept you going during those times, not your cheap ass friends and family."

With that, Roberto got up and said, "This conversation is over. Go home and get some sleep and we can talk in a more civil manner at a later date."

Blake abruptly got up, and as he stormed out the front door he looked back over his shoulder and said, "Roberto, you will regret this!"

18

"Nine-one-one. What is your emergency?" the efficient 911 operator
asked.

A shaky, and rapidly speaking, voice on the other end of the line
cried out, "A fire. There is a fire in the building just down the street. Quick,
please send help!"

The operator took down the caller's information, confirmed that he
was not in any danger, and dispatched a call to the nearest fire department.

In short order, fire trucks surrounded the building. What was quickly
determined to be a four-alarm fire brought fire trucks, equipment, and
firefighters from three of the surrounding area's fire departments. The black
smoke and blaze could be seen for miles. The heat from the fire could
be felt over two blocks away from the burning building. The scene was
a beehive of activity with firefighters hooking up hoses, pulling hoses to
strategic spray areas, and getting ladders ready while waiting for additional
instructions.

Fortunately, the fire took place in the middle of the night, so no one
was hurt. The first 911 call came in at 2:28 AM. The call came from a late
shift employee stocking shelves at a local pharmacy. As he left the pharmacy
to go home, he noticed the fire down the street and immediately called 911.
The first fire truck arrived at about two forty-five. Because the building's
infrastructure was mostly wood, the fire grew aggressively. By the time the
first truck arrived, the entire building was up in flames. Crackling noises
came from the building as big timbers holding up the roof collapsed and
small explosions from highly combustible materials periodically erupted.

The Incident Commander, that individual in charge of the firefighting
team, had quickly sized up the scope and scale of the incident. His job
was to quickly make a risk assessment and to determine the appropriate
mode of operation to be employed. His risk assessment quickly determined

that either there were no lives to be saved or, if people were still in the building, there was little potential to save their lives, or the building itself. Given his risk assessment, he determined that a defensive mode was most appropriate. At this point, the goal of managing this incident was to protect any additional exposed areas and to extinguish the fire from an exterior position. His first rule was always, "no one gets hurt." Given the aggressiveness of the fire, he wanted to ensure that none of his team would be injured. Once he had made this determination, he gave the team orders to focus on protecting the land and buildings adjacent to the fire rather than try to save the building itself.

It was very unusual in Santa Fe to have a major fire. While there had been the occasional major building catch fire over the years, most fires were small, residential houses related to gas leakages, fireplaces with flues not properly cleaned creating chimney fires, or brush fires that had gotten out of hand. The few numbers of past restaurant fires had all happened in the kitchens and had all been quickly contained since the Ore House fire on the plaza over thirty years ago. Santa Fe had strict building codes, including that buildings in the historic part of the city could not exceed five stories and newer buildings had to adhere to Green building codes. However, the Incident Commander mused, this building was older and may have been grandfathered in.

The Incident Commander wondered to himself, "Why in hell would there be a fire in the middle of the night in a building where there were apparently no employees, there had been no previous fire code violations of which he was aware, and in such a prominent area? The forensics on this should be interesting. And why, of all places, the Guadalupe?"

SANTA FE

CONCLUSION

19

Breakfast with Anna had given me a lot to think about. Walking back to the plaza from the Inn of the Anasazi, I reflected on our breakfast conversation, and I realized that the list of folks who may have wanted Blake dead was long and filled with powerful people. These included the police, local politicians, business associates and partners, and current or former clients. And those were only the ones that were obvious. What may be the surprise here is that Blake's life had not been taken before now. His charming personality had buoyed up his misdeeds and covered up his many attempts to coerce and exploit for his own benefit. In some respects, I had to admire Blake's chutzpa. As a psychologist, I know that there is a fine line between being a narcissist and a psychopath. In fact, many of the largest companies in the US are run by very smart, high-functioning psychopaths. Their deviance is tolerated because of the benefits stakeholders receive as a result of the psychopath's ability to persuade, manipulate, and deceive, all the while, creating plausible deniability. Blake had all of these characteristics, and more. His success had been, in no small measure, a result of his exploitation of others.

I kept wondering to myself, "How could Rebecca not have known about his business dealings and the underbelly to his personality? Did she really not know, or did she choose to ignore it? Or were the benefits she received from his dealings sufficient for her not to probe? Was she just another stakeholder oblivious to his deception and only focusing on her own greed?"

I had a lot to think about before my lunch with Rebecca. I was still conflicted about whether or not to stay and provide assistance, but I was leaning on staying. Blake's homicide was, as Winston Churchill had commented about the Russians, "A riddle, wrapped in a mystery, inside an enigma." There were so many variables and so many interesting paths to follow to unravel the truth. It was reminiscent of some of my work with organizations trying to decipher those characteristics of their management which were facilitative and those that created obstacles. I was up for a good puzzle. The fact that my ex-wife was involved did complicate things, more than a little.

After a short rest in my room, I had decided to walk from La Fonda to the Compound restaurant on Canyon Road. The Santa Fe city center is very walkable, and very pleasant. The streets are lined with high-end clothing and jewelry stores; restaurants and cafes with al fresco dining; and boutique hotels. The tree-lined Santa Fe River is two blocks from the plaza and is a pleasant walkway to the entrance of Canyon Road. The morning temperature was slightly cool, the sky a deep blue, and the air fresh and crisp, reflecting Santa Fe's high altitude. In addition to the fascinating culture, it is the depth of colors, the deep blue of the sky and the shadows created by the bright sun that attracts the many artists to Santa Fe.

I arrived at the Compound a few minutes early. Rather than rush inside, I decided to reacquaint myself with the galleries on Canyon Road. Much had changed since my last visit before I left eleven years ago, but much had stayed the same. Canyon Road was still a single lane with art galleries on either side of the street. The art in these galleries is much more eclectic than would be expected in a southwest gallery. While many of the galleries had changed hands in the intervening years, the ambience remained the same. Galleries continued to be housed in old adobe homes, many designated as historical sites. This was not like the art districts in New York, Chicago, or Los Angeles. The strict building codes required the galleries to conform to the tradition in which they had been constructed. As a result, Canyon Road had much the same look and feel as it did a century ago.

After briefly wandering into, and out of, a couple of galleries, I made my way down to the Compound restaurant to meet Rebecca. Like many of the Canyon Road art galleries, the Compound had originally been the centerpiece of a group of houses in what was then known as the McComb Compound. It had been transformed into a restaurant in the 1950s. It was given a mid-century modern flair in the 1960s and continues that look today. The restaurant maintains its adobe exterior. Inside, the walls have a light tan texture, the white ceilings are lined with supporting wooden beams called vigas, and the tables all have white tablecloths and candles. The mood is one of elegant coziness with award-winning food to match.

I asked to be seated on the outside patio with a table that was more private. Rebecca arrived shortly thereafter. Dressed in form fitting jeans with a brightly colored woven shawl over a white blouse, and her hair pulled back, she looked beautiful. I had to keep myself in check and remind myself again that this was the woman who eleven years ago had betrayed me. That thought kept me focused on the business at hand.

I stood as she approached, still being cautious. She quickly gave me a hug and said, "I was worried after our time together last night that you wouldn't show up."

"I told you I would," I said mildly defensively. "I know we have a lot to talk about."

Unless Anna had called her, which I doubted since I had just recently left our conversation, Rebecca did not know about the new information I had from Anna.

While the waiter was pouring our water, and not wanting to dive into business too quickly, I suggested we order lunch. Rebecca agreed.

Still being full from my large breakfast, I decided to go lighter for lunch. I ordered a Tuscan Lettuce salad topped with salmon. Rebecca ordered the house made pappardelle pasta bolognaise. She also ordered a glass of Chardonnay. I decided to stick with water.

Once our ordering was out of the way, Rebecca began, "Well, what have you been thinking?"

I briefed her on the unexpected voice mail and subsequent breakfast with Anna Pacheco. I told her some, but not all, of the avenues Anna thought I might pursue. I still was not sure whether or not Rebecca had conspired with Anna to have her meet with me or, if it was like Anna had said, she just wanted to fill me in about Blake in the event that I did stayed.

Rebecca seemed surprised that Anna had called me, but also pleased.

"Scott, I had no idea that Anna was going to call you, especially since she had not met you. Anna has been a friend of the family and a business partner with Blake on some ventures. She would have an opinion of Blake that would be different from mine," Rebecca continued.

Still not being certain about any hidden motivations in meeting with Anna, I decided that now was the time to put all my cards on the table.

"Rebecca, I have had a lot to digest in a short amount of time. I still find the fact that you called me in the first place to be weird and a bit unsettling. However, when Anna let me know of the relationships that Blake had in Santa Fe, including with the police, politicians, and others, I can see the difficulty in getting an unbiased, and clear eyed, view of what happened to Blake and how justice will be served."

"Please, continue," Rebecca urged.

"Obviously, if you were not my ex-wife, and if I had not grown up here, I would not be interested at all. There are some questions I still need to have answered to give me greater clarity. You must be transparent and truthful or there is no need to continue the discussion," I responded somewhat harshly.

"Okay." Rebecca said plaintively. "I promise to be truthful and transparent."

With that assurance, I began questioning her.

20

I knew that by questioning Rebecca more, I was falling victim to a basic psychological principle, that of cognitive dissonance. This principle suggests that we all seek psychological consistency in what we believe, and that we actively seek out information to support our beliefs. When we are faced with inconsistencies, it creates stress. To reduce this stress, we either seek new information that helps us accept the inconsistency (called rationalization) or we walk away altogether. By having picked up Rebecca's phone call in Bozeman, I had already elected not to walk away. Therefore, I had to find reasons to reduce the incredible inconsistencies, and stress, in order to stay. In other words, I was hooked. In part, my rationalization had been that, like solving problems in the companies in which I worked, this puzzle fit my skill set better than I first realized. Now, just like working with business executives, I still needed to ask tough questions to get below the surface.

"Rebecca," I began. "I have a difficult time believing that you were totally unaware of Blake's business dealings and some of the questionable relationships he had developed. You are by no means stupid, so, let's begin there."

Rebecca took the last long sip of her Chardonnay and lifted her glass to the waiter indicating she wanted a refill.

"You are right, Scott," Rebecca began, somewhat shakily. "I have not been totally candid with you."

Taking a sip of her new glass of wine, she resumed. "It was not long after Blake and I were married that it dawned on me that, in many respects, our marriage was to benefit his standing in the community, and his business dealings, more than any attraction he had to me. In fact, it was only shortly after we were married, that we had sex less and less frequently, and always when he had too much to drink. However, in public, his fawning over me suggested to others that our marriage was more than perfect. I began to realize that I was simply his eye candy."

As Rebecca began to reveal more about their marriage, while it was hard to hear, Blake's behavior began to fit those behaviors of a narcissist. Narcissists, like psychopaths, are unable to experience empathy, reveal vulnerability, or ever admit to shortcomings. Because of this, relationships with narcissists are typically short-lived and exploitative. When the relationships are longer lasting, it is always because the relationship provides the narcissist a means to an end, not because there is any depth of feeling for the other person.

Rebecca lamented, "My attempts to address the lack of intimacy in our marriage were always met with derision and denial. He would say that he was fine, it must be my problem. After a while, I realized that the relationship was not going to get better. I did not want another divorce and I realized what a mistake I had made in the first place by having had the affair and divorcing you. I had to develop another strategy. I began to think about how, under the circumstances, I could get what I wanted understanding the marriage was going to be privately a sham."

I wanted to be empathic and say something like, "That must have been difficult." or, "I cannot imagine the pain you felt." But I knew I had to be careful and try to say somewhat emotionally detached myself.

"So how did you get what you wanted?" I quizzed.

Without hesitation, Rebecca said, "Having grown up in a middle-class home, we never had money for extravagances. I knew that Blake had money, so I determined to spend it on myself, in part to get even. I began to realize that Blake was not going to challenge any of my purchases. He still needed me to accompany him to public events, and he wanted me to look the part of a wealthy businessman's wife. So I hired a personal style consultant and we began buying clothes, jewelry, and even the BMW I picked you up in. I would let Blake know, but as long as I did not push him for more in the relationship and accompanied him to his public events, he did not protest."

"Did the strategy work for you?" I queried.

"It did to some extent," she replied. "It was fun to have nice things. In addition, I had a few girlfriends I would have lunch with. Blake wanted to entertain, and it was fun to meet interesting people, some of influence.

But after a while, I adjusted to a life that, on the surface was exciting, but was in fact, very prosaic. Our relationship became one of two people sharing the same house but not the same life."

"Surely you must have become aware of some of Blake's business dealings," I challenged.

"Well," she began tentatively. "I heard rumors, but Blake was always secretive with me always saying that things were fine. He mostly provided me a monthly calendar of events for which he expected me to make myself available. And I did so obediently."

"What about the rumors?" I pushed.

Taking another sip of her wine, Rebecca continued, "My girlfriends, like Anna, would occasionally drop hints that Blake had offended someone, or that some business partner was pissed at him. But they would never give me more details. I began to get the sense that Blake was not well liked, but he was able to maintain a believable façade when we were together in public."

I was again trying to take in everything Rebecca was telling me and align it with what I had known about her. When we had been married, she had been spunky and adventuresome. Using her defiance to separate from her parents did not sync with the more passive and conforming woman with whom I was now speaking. Something felt odd and out of place, but I could not put my finger on it. Had Rebecca really tried to make the best of a bad situation, or was there something else?

"Rebecca," I probed further. "It is a real stretch to go from pissing off business associates to being killed. Can you think of any reason any particular person would want to kill Blake? And why?"

"I am being totally truthful with you Scott when I say that I can think of no one who would actually want to kill Blake. Every time I would accompany Blake to an event, or even dinners we would host, those whom I met were always kind and gracious. I never saw anything that caused me to be suspicious. Of course, people are always on their best behavior in the company of others," Rebecca responded.

I thought to myself, "Well, not everyone was kind and gracious or Blake would not have received a deadly blow to the back of the head with a heavy sculpture."

"Rebecca, is there anything else at all that I should know to help me make my decision?" I said, knowing that I had already made up my mind.

"Well, there is one thing, but I do not see how it would be related. In fact, I debated with myself as to whether or not I should even mention it," Rebecca said tentatively.

"Anything could help, Rebecca, please tell me," I urged.

Thoughtfully she began, "Well, in the past few months before his death, and for the first time, Blake was beginning to question some of my purchases. Like I said before, I pretty much had *carte blanche* for years, spending whatever I wanted. He started to ask me things like, 'Do you really need that?' or 'Why did get that?' It was very unusual behavior and I just decided he had been in a bad mood and tried to forget it."

"Were you aware of any financial issues that Blake was facing?" I probed.

She continued, "No, not really. He seemed to become somewhat moodier after the recent fire at the Guadalupe restaurant."

My ears perked up. Anna Pacheco had mentioned that one person to whom I should speak was Roberto Montoya, the owner of the restaurant that had recently been burned to the ground in a fire of undetermined origin. I decided to get more information from Rebecca without tipping my hand about what Anna had mentioned.

I encouraged her, "Tell me more."

She took another sip of her Chardonnay before answering. "The Guadalupe was a restaurant that Blake visited regularly, usually for business lunches and meetings. I only went there when there was some kind of social event or fundraiser. The restaurant is a Sant Fe staple and very popular among the locals, including politicians and businessmen. Blake became friends with the owner, Roberto Montoya and they decided that it would be mutually beneficial if they could join forces, so to speak."

"Join forces?" I asked.

"According to Blake, the restaurant was struggling and he wanted to help Roberto out. Because Roberto, and his family, were well connected in Santa Fe, Blake saw their partnership as a win-win," she explained.

"Partnership?" I asked curious as to how Blake had presented the relationship to Rebecca.

"Why yes," she continued. "Blake thought that if he could display some of his art in the Guadalupe, it could broaden the restaurant's clientele and bring in some higher paying customers. Blake would refer customers that came into the gallery over to the Guadalupe and Roberto would refer his customers who showed an interest in the art over to the gallery. Blake

82

told me that he hoped it would help Roberto salvage the restaurant since there were so many other fine restaurants in town competing for the same customers."

"How interesting," I said as I thought to myself that this is not exactly how Anna had portrayed the relationship.

"Yes," Rebecca continued. "Blake even paid for a couple of evening art events at the restaurant inviting some of his wealthy acquaintances to introduce them to the Guadalupe, and of course, the art, in hopes that they would become new customers for Roberto. He always asked me to attend, but I always left early."

"And how was this partnership going," I asked trying to keep my skepticism in check.

"Blake told me that the partnership was going so well that he and Roberto had big plans. They were going to expand the restaurant two more stories to build a small luxury boutique hotel on top of the restaurant. Blake seemed excited," she observed. "I was flattered that Blake told me as he rarely talked to me about business."

"Then what happened?" I pressed.

"After the second art party, Blake came home very late. I had already gone to bed and did not hear him come in. But the next morning, I could tell something was wrong."

"What did you notice?" I wondered.

"Well, Blake usually got up early and went downtown for coffee before opening the gallery. That day, he was at home in his office studying some financial books he kept. I greeted him cheerfully, asking how he thought the art party had gone. He was in a very foul mood and said, 'Get the hell out of here, can't you see I'm busy.' Needless to say, I huffed off myself and left the house," she clarified.

"I thought you said his mood changed after the fire," I observed.

"It did. But I first noticed the change that morning after the art party. The actual fire was only a couple of days after the party. His mood continued to be ugly. I also heard that one of his gallery customers was upset with him. I chalked up his foul mood to stress and hoped it would change, so I just stayed out of his way."

"When was the fire?" I asked.

"It took place about four weeks ago. The fire department could not find a cause for the fire and identified the cause as undetermined," she exclaimed. "After the fire, Blake was hard for me to be with, always grousing and storming around the house. I just left him alone."

After another sip from her glass, Rebecca said, "That is a long answer to your question about any concerns Blake had about financial issues. As I talk about it, I guess with the restaurant venture falling apart, he may have had more concerns than I realized. It is actually good to talk about all of this. I really haven't had anyone else to talk to."

When I heard her last comment, I knew to be cautious. My instincts as a psychologist were to dive in by being empathic and going into a therapist mode or try to rescue her. I was not in the habit of ignoring others feelings, but in this case I knew that the boundaries needed to be firm and not permeable.

After a long silence, I continued.

"Rebecca," I said in response to all of her thoughts. "I will stay here for two weeks and see what I can come up with. I know you do not trust that an impartial review of Blake's death can be completed given his ties to influential people. For that matter, I am not even sure that I can be impartial. I also know that the list of those who did not like Blake was a long one. I will offer what help I can. But only two weeks."

Rebecca put down her glass and with tears started streaming from her eyes said, "Oh Scott, thank you so much. I was afraid that you would leave without offering your help. I know I do not deserve any of your attention, but I am so very grateful. Please name your price. I will pay you whatever your fee is. Of course, I will also pay for whatever charges you incur. Thank you, thank you, thank you."

With that she held her face in her hands and wept.

When she lifted her head, I could not help but notice the absence of tears relative to her weeping. Was I seeing things, or was I being played? Without reaching out to comfort her, I replied, "Rebecca, I do not want to be paid for this. I am doing it to see if I can be of assistance. I may come up with nothing, who knows? We will just have to see. You picking up the tab for La Fonda is sufficient."

I knew from my work with business executives, that at the point you decided to take a fee for your services, expectations were created and the nature of the relationship changed. From a psychological perspective, when money defines a relationship, roles shift, and a boss/subordinate dynamic ensues. I wanted my work with Rebecca to be as clean as it could be. By not accepting a fee, I continued to be in charge of the interaction and could walk away at any moment. If she paid me, she would define the parameters of my time and work, with whom I could speak, and down what paths I might venture. I was not going to let that happen.

Again, she looked up and said, "Thank you Scott. I cannot tell you how much I appreciate this."

We finished up the lunch with a few more pleasantries and then departed, Rebecca driving her red BMW with the top down and me walking. I thought to myself, this must in some way be a metaphor, but I could not exactly explain how.

Now the work began. Where should I start? I knew that if I was going to be successful finding out anything, I had to renew my acquaintance with Miguel Montez. Otherwise, if he found it I was snooping, I would be silenced or seen as an obstruction. In addition, I needed to get his support to have the conversations I knew I needed to have. As I began walking back toward the plaza, my cell phone buzzed in my pocket.

21

I noticed the 406-area code on my phone. That was the code for all of Montana, probably something related to my work.

"This is Doctor Hunter," I answered.

"Hi Scott, it's Dorothy," replied my administrative assistant in Bozeman.

"Hey, Dot," I replied. "What's up?"

"Are you having fun on your little rendezvous?" She bantered.

When I opened the Bozeman office, Dorothy Weston was my first hire. That was seven years ago. She took care of all of the back-office work, including scheduling, office management, bugging clients about payments, and any other details about which I needed to be aware. She was about sixty, very smart, reliable, dependable, and with a wicked sense of humor. She had become someone whom I trusted, and she knew about some of the details of my trip to Santa Fe. In addition, she had a great bullshit-detector and would not let me deceive her, or myself.

"Couldn't be better," I joked back. "But you did not call me to check up on my mental health. What is going on."

As much as I liked Dorothy, I did not have the time, nor inclination, to spend much time with chitchat.

"You have had a couple of calls from clients wanting to know your availability for some consultation. Jeffrey Collins, the CEO of St. Augustus Medical Center called, and Rich Hinsen called from Hinsen manufacturing. How do you want me to handle them?" Dorothy asked.

Since I had just made up my mind to stay in Santa Fe for two weeks, I had not yet let Dorothy know my schedule.

"Thanks for the update," I said gratefully. "I have decided to stay in Santa Fe for two weeks. I will likely be back late two weeks from today. Can you put them off until then?"

"Sounds serious," she replied with a chuckle. "Sure, I will simply let them know that you are unavailable. If they have some serious needs, I will escalate them to the top and take care of them myself."

I always appreciated Dorothy's ability to handle difficult situations in a calm and confident manner. I had developed a high level of respect for her judgment and the competent way in which she handled clients. In addition, I had relied on her as an initial screener for any women in whom I might be interested personally. With her lifelong history in Bozeman, and her ability to quickly size up people, she would often give me a thumbs up, or down, on dating prospects. So far, her judgment had been spot-on. The women on whom she had given a thumbs down, and that I had pursued anyway, had always ended poorly, even with my level of cautiousness. In short, she kept me out of relationship hell.

"Thanks Dot," I said, wanting to get off of the phone. "I will let you know if anything down here changes the schedule. Have a great two weeks, or as good as you can have without me."

"I'll try, but it will be hard," she joked. "Take care."

We hung up and I left the conversation knowing that I could forget about my work in Bozeman until I returned. Now time to renew an old acquaintance.

22

I called the main number of the Santa Fe Police Department. A serious and to the point operator answered, "Santa Fe Police Department. How can I direct your call?"

"Yes," I responded. "May I speak with Detective Miguel Montez?"

"Can I let him know your name and what this is in reference to?" she queried.

"I am Scott Hunter, an old friend in town for a few days and I would like to reconnect," I said tentatively.

I thought to myself that the operator probably handled multiple calls per day and mine was on the lower level of importance to her.

Nonetheless, she cooperated and replied, "I will see if he is available."

As I waited, I knew that Miguel would be suspicious of my calling him at this time. While we had not spoken in years, I was fairly sure he knew that I had been married to Rebecca. I hoped he would take my call. I remembered Miguel from our high school competition, and I knew that he was smart. I recalled that he had been the valedictorian of his high school class and his photo had been in the paper for having received a scholarship to study criminal justice at Sam Houston State University in Huntsville, Texas. Sam Houston State University has one of the oldest, and most prestigious, criminal justice programs in the nation, with unique relationships with INTERPOL, the FBI, and police departments across the nation. It was quite an honor to be accepted, much less to be given a full ride scholarship. Beyond that, we had not kept up and I did not know how he would respond to me.

I could hear the phone connect on the other end.

"Scott Hunter! Well, I'll be damned! Are you still holding a grudge for me kicking your ass in the regionals when we were seniors? Or are you wanting a rematch?" Miguel said with a deep laugh.

Relieved that he remembered me, and sounded glad to hear from me, I countered, "Well Miguel, it was the price I had to pay to date your sister. I knew that if I would have beaten you, you would never have let me come near her."

Miguel's sister, Joanna, had attended many of Miguel's track meets. She had caught my eye during my senior year and I struck up a conversation with her. Joanna went to the Catholic high school for girls, so I only saw her at the track meets. We had only a couple of casual dates. I was too shy to pursue it any further and the dates were at the end of the track season, so I did not see her after that.

We both chuckled, then Miguel observed, "I guess you have heard about the brutal murder of your ex-wife's hubby, Blake Martin? I don't need to consider you a suspect do I?" he bantered.

"No, no, I am not a suspect. I would like to buy you a cup of coffee if you have the time. I would love to catch up and let you know why I am in town," I said hoping that he would agree.

Miguel quickly replied, "I would like that, Scott. Seriously, though, because of your relationship with Rebecca, we need to clear you as a suspect. We are always required to eliminate people who may have had a motive to murder the victim, even if that motive is an old or weak one. We always begin with family members, spouses, and, in your case, the former spouse of the victim's wife. It is just a formality, but a necessary one. Why don't you come down to the station to make your official statement? I will request a rapid review of it and then we can get that coffee."

I knew that having to make a statement was a possibility when I called Miguel and I was anxious to comply and get it behind me. When Blake was murdered, I was facilitating a strategy meeting for the CEO and Board of a Bozeman hospital. The retreat began on the Friday afternoon that Blake was murdered and went well into the evening. We continued until noon the following day. I knew the date, time, location, and individuals involved and knew they would all vouch for my time with them.

"Sounds good," I replied. "I can be there is a few minutes."

I was at the station in about twenty minutes. I went to the reception area, gave my name, and told the officer in charge that Miguel Montez was expecting me. He paged Miguel. It would be the first time Miguel and I had seen each other since high school. Miguel was still easy to recognize as he came down the hall, smiling, and reached out his hand to me.

"Good to see you, Scott. Thanks for coming in," he greeted me.

"Great to see you, Miguel. You look just the same as I remembered," I said, not exaggerating much.

"You are looking pretty good yourself," Miguel replied. "Let me take you to an interview room and we can take your statement. I have asked for a rapid review which means that once you give me details on where you were the night of Blake Martin's homicide, we can get the information verified quickly and be on our way. I will have one of our officers take your statement."

He led me to an interview room, introduced me to the officer he referenced, and I gave my statement. Once I had given the information on the details of my whereabouts the night of Blake's murder, the officer asked me to wait in the interview room, assuring me he would return as soon as he could get the information verified. Because I had my contact list in my cell phone, I was able to provide the officer with the phone numbers of the hospital CEO, the Chairman of the hospital Board, most of the Board members, and my administrative assistant, Dorothy.

Surprisingly, the officer was able to return in about thirty minutes with a thumbs up. He indicated that he had made a couple of calls and that the statement I had provided had been verified. I was free to go.

Miguel met me saying, "Sorry to have put you through that, Scott. It is just a necessary procedure. Now let's go get that cup of coffee. There is a locally owned coffee shop on Rodeo Road called Java Joe's. It is quiet and out of the way of the tourists. How about meeting there at around four o'clock? I can go home from there after we visit."

I quickly agreed. The coffee shop was well known to me. It had been there for some time and had been a favorite of my parents when they were alive. It was already approaching mid-afternoon, so I requested an Uber and headed to Java Joe's.

23

J ava Joe's was just as I had remembered it, an understated coffee shop within a strip mall in the southeast part of the city. Walking in felt familiar. I almost expected to see my folks drinking coffee in the corner laughing with their friends. Of course, this time it was different. Nevertheless, it still felt like a safe and welcoming place.

The coffee shop was very quiet this time of the afternoon. I walked up to Carmen, the barista, at the counter, and ordered a flat white with two Splenda, my go to coffee. I also told her that I was expecting a visitor, Miguel Montez and gave her three five-dollar bills to cover both of our coffees and a tip. She mentioned that Miguel was a regular and thanked me for the payment.

I picked a spot in the corner to sit that would be a bit more private. Within ten minutes, Miguel arrived. Seeing me in the corner, he approached me with a big smile and a firm handshake. He looked trim and fit with dark hair, olive skin, a tall, muscular frame, and twinkling eyes to go with his bright smile.

"Scott, it is so good to see you after all these years. It has been over twenty years since we last met. And as for my sister, Joanna, she is married with children, so the answer is still no," he said with a deep laugh.

"Miguel, the last I saw of you was the photo in the *Santa Fe New Mexican* with an article about your scholarship to Sam Houston State University. I expected you to be the Chief by now," I smiled as I said it.

"Well," he rejoined. "There has been a lot of water under the bridge since then. Let me get my coffee and we will catch up."

As Miguel walked to the counter, Carmen put a cup of coffee on the counter with, "Your regular, Miguel. And it is already paid for."

Before taking the cup, Miguel reached across the counter and gave Carmen a friendly hug with a, "Muchas gracias, mi amiga."

As Miguel sat down, I invited him to fill in the twenty plus years since we had seen each other.

Miguel's journey had been an interesting one. He had gone on to secure both his Bachelor's and Master's degrees in criminal justice. He had worked in a series of FBI field offices in Texas and in the southeast. He had risen from being an Agent to the rank of a managing a Field Office in Atlanta. He said that a fair amount of his work had been the investigation and oversight of domestic terrorist groups. The next career step for him would have been a political appointment with more seniority but less job security.

Miguel concluded by saying that "I was becoming a high paid manager and paper pusher and further away from where the real action was taking place. When we would coordinate our efforts with local police departments, I always felt a pull to be back in a position where I could actually see the difference I was making. In addition, my parents were getting older and most of my family was here. I married a local girl, so the pull to Santa Fe overcame the pull to fame and fortune. When a detective position opened up here, I applied and got it. That was six years ago."

I replied with admiration, "What a great journey you have had. With your credentials and experience, I am still surprised that you are not the Chief of Police."

"That is another story, my friend. Tell me about your life," he countered.

I gave Miguel my back story including getting my doctorate, opening a local private practice, and getting married to Rebecca. I told him about being blindsided by Rebecca's affair and leaving town in humiliation. I also told him about the rebuilding process in Bozeman, including some immodest examples of my work with high-powered CEOs. I then told him about the recent, and fateful, call I had received from Rebecca and her subsequent request for my help to find Blake's killer. I mentioned how uncomfortable I had been with her request, but that I had taken the opportunity to return to Santa Fe. I also told him that I had met with Anna Pacheco, but I did not elaborate.

Miguel responded, "Scott, I had heard you were now Doctor Hunter. Congratulations. I had also heard about the break-up of your marriage and Blake Martin's role in it. I only heard about this when I returned to Santa Fe. I did not know where you had gone after that, but I always wondered. I had always felt like you were a kindred spirit even though our contact was confined to the track field. Joanna also thought you were a good guy. Sorry for what you have been through."

I continued, almost apologetically, "Miguel, as I told Rebecca, doing investigative work is not my specialty. I am a psychologist. True, I have become adept at understanding, and helping, powerful people in the business world, but criminal work is altogether different."

After several silent moments, Miguel said quietly and seriously, "Scott, obviously I cannot tell you any information about an ongoing investigation other than the official updates you would see in the news. Maybe now is a good time to tell you why I am not the Chief of Police."

Surprised, and curious, about Miguel's response, I said, "I would love to hear your story."

He began, "Well Scott, the short story is that coming back to Santa Fe with my criminal justice and FBI experience, I came to the position with fresh eyes. Early on in my work here, I could tell that, in the Police department, there was a suspicion of me and a certain skepticism. While I worked to reacquaint myself with former friends, it seemed that there was a feeling that I was going to pull rank, or be somehow dismissive, with those who had stayed here and worked their way up. It is the unanticipated downside of "local boy makes good" story. People began distancing themselves from me. Or at least that is what I thought."

Miguel continued, "I became very sensitive about what I said and how I acted. I did not want the confidence I had in myself, or in my work, to be misinterpreted as arrogance or demeaning. I continued to perform my work at a high level and stayed away from any activities that would appear to be anything but transparent. However, the distancing continued. So, I began becoming suspicious myself and wondered if my fellow officers were trying to hide something from me. My work with the FBI taught me to honor my instincts. If I felt something was not right, there was probably some kind of problem to uncover."

I smiled to myself as I thought about the times I have encouraged clients to trust their instincts, knowing that they were some form of unconscious pattern recognition. I thought Miguel was probably on to something.

"I began asking questions and the response was immediate. The Chief called me into his office and asked if I was trying to cause problems within the ranks. This only confirmed that I was on to something and that whatever the problem, it was pervasive. I knew that if I was going to find out of any problems within the department, I would have to do it on a more clandestine basis. Fortunately, my training provided me the skills and tools to do just that, look below the surface without revealing my intentions," he said seriously.

"Wow," I exclaimed. "This all sounds a bit dangerous and spooky. So, what did you do?"

Miguel went on to tell me about the methods he used including tracking internal phone calls and emails, looking at schedules, and even looking at the activity at the motor pool.

"The Bureau," he continued, "focused on both themes and triangulation as investigative tools. Themes are when the same event, or similar events, happen on multiple, seemingly unrelated, occasions. Triangulation occurs when two or more individuals are interacting with a third party or scheduled for the same event, particularly when the event is suspect. I was trained to look for corroboration and the validity and credibility of my sources of information. I had to do all of this while abiding by existing laws and without creating more scrutiny. Needless to say, the investigative work was slow, and I had to proceed cautiously. However, every time I found any activity that was suspect, it invariably led me to more irregularities. It was like unwinding a ball of string where multiple pieces are tied together to create a whole. At the same time, I needed to make certain that the responsibilities which I was assigned to oversee continued to be managed in a professional, and timely, manner."

"Miguel," I continued, "this all sounds like something I would read in a spy novel. It also sounds really stressful. What did your investigating uncover?"

"Obviously, Scott, I cannot tell you anything that has not already been made public. However, once I had a portfolio of evidence of police wrongdoing, I presented it to the Chief. I knew that the information I had was reliable, and that I had uncovered multiple issues related to subtle, but irrefutable, corruption and influence. The Chief was both astounded and profoundly shaken. This evidence led to the Chief resigning along with a few other high-level officers. They did so without me having to go to the press or to the City Council. I knew that many of these individuals were basically good people who had been manipulated by a very crafty individual. Most of them were lifelong Santa Feans with families. I saw no reason to darken their names when they had already resigned. None of the violations, in my opinion, reached the threshold of being a punishable offense. In addition, I did not want the personal publicity."

Miguel continued, "After all of the hoopla and speculation about the police department resignations had subsided, I was asked if I would consider being a candidate for the Chief of Police position. Of course, I declined. I knew that, if the evidence that I had collected became public, there would appear to be a conflict of interest and could further damage the reputations of several individuals. Also, I knew the reality that declining to be interviewed for the position would likely close the door to my advancing to the Chief's position in the future. Actually, I was okay with that. As I found out with the Bureau, the higher up you go, the more political the work becomes. I had left the Bureau because I want to make a difference at the local level, and I can do that best in the position I currently occupy as a lead Detective."

As Miguel unpacked his story, my mind was spinning. I began to wonder if what Anna Pacheco had told me about Blake's courting people in high places, included the Chief of Police and some of his colleagues and cronies. I also wondered if Blake could have included others like City Council members or even members of the state legislature. Could Blake's relationships with these officials been responsible for the downfall of the Chief of Police? Maybe I was coming to conclusions prematurely. Given the circumstances, I had to know a bit more.

"Miguel," I began both admiringly and cautiously, "I cannot imagine the amount of courage this must have taken. I appreciate the way you went about managing your findings. You clearly could have used it for your own self-aggrandizement or ambitions, but you didn't."

"Scott," Miguel interrupted, "Santa Fe is a small town with deep roots. It is common to see individuals with whom you work at social events, church, or even at the grocery store. When people are going through hard times, it is important to allow them to maintain their dignity. The culture here is characterized by the ties we all have to family. Sangre, as we call it, or blood ties. In my judgment, their resigning was sufficient enough payment for their transgressions. Who am I to judge?"

I may not have totally agreed with Miguel's conclusion, but I very much respected the sincerity and decency of his convictions.

Changing the subject slightly, I said, "I have been made aware of Blake's 'retreats,'" I said with finger quotation marks, "and the way he courted people of influence at these faux business meetings with drugs and women. I am also aware that he had been able to use his sway over city officials to get his way. Yet, I have a question. Was it Blake Martin's undue influence, or blackmail, that was at the root of their downfall?"

25

Miguel was quiet for several seconds, seeming to be thinking about his response. Miguel thought to himself that, after only being in Santa Fe a short time, Scott had already surfaced some information that could be helpful in the investigation. As crazy as the thought was to Miguel, he wondered if Scott could be of any help to him in the investigation.

We had already been at Java Joe's for over an hour. I was fearful that Miguel was going to decide to use my question to make his exit.

"Scott," Miguel began slowly and reflectively, "with regard to your question, I obviously cannot answer you. So far, everything I have told you is relatively harmless and not covered by any kind of confidentiality conflicts. While I like you and I think I trust you, I have to treat you like any other public figure. I cannot answer your question about that part of the investigation. In addition, there are two other confounding issues. First, you were married to Rebecca and, as you know, she is a person of interest in Blake's murder until we determine that we can exclude her as a suspect. Secondly, she has asked you to help her find Blake's killer. As you said yourself, you are a psychologist, not an investigator, nor do you have any affiliation with the local police department. However, I am surprised that, after having been in town only a very short time, you have found out that Blake was involved in questionable practices that he used to manipulate people in power. I must say, I am impressed."

I was pleased that he found the information about Blake's underhanded behavior insightful, but I knew everything he was saying was correct and that I was reaching when I asked him about Blake. Yet the fact that he would not deny that it was Blake who was the at the root of the downfall of members of the police left the door open for interpretation. If it was not Blake, I believe he would have said so. Coupled with the information I had received from Anna Pacheco, I had to believe it had been Blake at the root of the undue influence or even blackmail. I also suspected that he was going to conclude our conversation on that note, so I was surprised when he continued.

Miguel continued, "It has occurred to me that for the very reasons I just cited, you may be able to help. You may be more of an investigator than you thought."

Astounded and perplexed, I said, "Really. What do you mean?"

Miguel added, "Within the department, we are short-handed. We all have more to do than we have time or resources. In addition, Blake's murder is a very high-profile case. In such high-profile cases, with high levels of scrutiny from both the media and the public mean our every move is watched. I get several calls daily wanting to know the status of the case. Just managing the press is a full-time job. In addition, there is very little time for sleuthing. When one of our investigators tries to have conversations with people who might be associated with the case, they are regularly followed by the press because "the public wants to know." Sadly, we see the press has moved from reporting the news to making the news. In order to keep the murder in front of the public until it is solved, the press is preying on the public's fear that this is not an isolated event."

Miguel continued, "By having an outsider with whom the press and the public are less well acquainted, we could possibly get some information that would otherwise take more time, or we would not have gotten it at all. Even though you are from here, you have been gone for some time and would not bring about the same level of suspicion as either a local or some big shot New York investigator. In addition, your work being a psychologist to high-powered individuals lends itself to the kind of probing problem-solving we need. It is a risk using you, Scott, and your work would be totally off the record. Also, it would be all one-way. I cannot divulge information to you that is confidential, but I would be asking you for anything you find that may be of assistance. Also, you can never divulge to anyone, especially Rebecca, that you are doing anything on my, or the department's, behalf. In addition, we can't speak about Rebecca, or her involvement, until she has been cleared as a suspect. You would be more like an undercover police informant who is not benefitting, personally or financially, from any information you may provide. I can only point you in a couple of directions to explore."

Once again, my mind was swirling. This offer was totally unexpected. I did have to give it some thought.

"Look Scott, I have to get going. Why don't you think about it overnight and give me a call in the morning?" Miguel said.

Again, my mind was swirling. He gave me his cell phone number and I promised to give him a call the next day.

With that, Miguel got up, waived to Carmen, gave me a vigorous handshake, and proceeded to leave the coffee shop. Almost as an afterthought, Miguel turned back to me as he left and said, "Make sure to look at the early edition of *The New Mexican* tomorrow."

I texted for an Uber, got up shakily, and went outside to wait for my ride. I had a lot to think about.

26

I arrived back at La Fonda at about six o'clock. I realized that I had only arrived in Santa Fe two days ago. I could not believe how much had already happened. I felt a combined sense of exhilaration, anxiety, and fatigue. I was afraid that if I stopped, I would fall over in a deep sleep. I knew that I needed time to reflect on Miguel's offer as well as have a drama free dinner.

Instead of venturing out of the hotel, I decided to order room service. The room I was in on the Concierge level was a suite with a living room and small dining table and chairs. It was perfect for dining alone. I telephoned the order and then went down the hall to the Concierge Lounge to pick up a couple bottles of beer. As I picked up the beers, I chuckled to myself as I thought of the saying, "You can take the man out of the country, but you can't take the country out of the man." I grew up drinking beer with my dad and, for me, wine was for more public occasions. When I really wanted to think, there was nothing like a cold beer for a companion.

I was afraid to lay down as I waited for room service, fearful that I would crash. I popped open the first beer as I began rehashing the events of the past forty-eight hours. As a psychologist, you are trained to always try to separate sound from noise. From all of the data points you have been bombarded with, which are the ones that stand out as being relevant and thematic. From the opinions and information you have been given, what information is really important to understanding the person or situation and what information is simply static that can throw you into unproductive searches.

Knowing that my time was limited, I began running through what I knew.

First, I knew that Blake Martin had been brutally murdered in his own gallery by one of his own pieces or art, a heavy sculptured obelisk statuette.

Second, Blake had been married to my ex, Rebecca for over nine years, a marriage that increasingly seemed one more of convenience than deep and abiding love.

Third, Rebecca had called me to assist her in finding Blake's murderer.

Fourth, Anna Pacheco had sought me out and provided more information about Blake, his personality, and a couple of leads for me to consider.

Fifth, I learned about one of Blake's business relationships that had gone south with Roberto Montoya and the fire at the Guadalupe.

Fifth, Miguel Montez had confirmed, by his silence, that Blake was likely the cause of several top individuals leaving the Police Department due to Blake's uncovering influence pedaling.

I also thought about questions I needed to have answered to provide me some direction in my search for Blake's murderer.

I still was uncertain as to why Rebecca called me in the first place. While her suspicions of the police department seemed to be, in some measure, confirmed by Miguel, why me? Additional questions surfaced.

Rebecca had indicated that Blake was beginning to object to her freewheeling spending. Was this really an indication of any financial woes Blake was experiencing? Or was Rebecca exaggerating? And, if so, why?

How could I identify, and then whittle down, the list of those who might have wanted Blake dead? And why? From what Anna Pacheco had said, the list could have been long. It might even include some of those police officers whose demise could have been blamed on Blake.

Who could I really trust in this process? Miguel had sworn me to silence if I were to do any stealth work for him. This included not revealing information to Rebecca, since she continued to be a suspect. I believed I could trust Miguel. I was not so sure of Rebecca.

At that moment, a knock on the door signaled that room service had arrived. I opened the door to the waiter who placed the tray on the small dining table. I signed the bill and showed him out.

I was hungrier than I realized. I had ordered the chile-spiced, oven-baked rainbow trout with rice and fresh vegetable. The food was hot and looked amazing. As I ventured into my meal, I continued to review the various aspects of the case, what I knew and what I needed to know.

By the end of the meal, and my second beer, I had come to the conclusion that if I was going to make any progress toward finding Blake's murderer, I would have to accept Miguel's offer, and his terms. I was also anxious to follow-up on Miguel's suggestion that I look at tomorrow mornings edition of *The New Mexican*. While I was thinking about it, I rang the front desk requesting a copy be sent up to the room upon delivery in the morning.

At that point, fatigue and the beers began to have their effect. I brushed my teeth, dawned my night clothes and tumbled into bed. I decided not to set my mobile phone alarm and was asleep within minutes.

27

I woke up with a start. I had overslept, at least for me. It was almost seven o'clock. In Bozeman, I am used to waking up at about five-thirty, working out and eating breakfast before going to work. It took me a moment to reorient myself. Ah, yes, I was in Santa Fe doing some investigative work on behalf of my ex-wife. Okay, it was all clear now. I had to laugh. I also remembered that the early edition of *The New Mexican* should be at my door. I quickly got out of bed and opened my door to find the newspaper in a sack attached to the door handle. I pulled the paper out, sat down and opened it up. There on the front page was the story to which Miguel had eluded:

Police have determined that murder of local art dealer is an isolated event

By William Simmons

In a press conference earlier this morning, Police Chief John Trujillo indicated that the recent murder of art dealer, Blake Martin, was both an isolated incident and a targeted event. The Chief said that the department wanted the public to rest assured that this was not a random event, nor did the department believe that the public was in any danger. The Chief went on to say that they department had received numerous tips and was developing a list of Persons of Interest. However, he did not elaborate on either.

The murder of Martin has rocked the Santa Fe arts community. It is the first homicide of any gallery owner in recent memory. Speculation around the murder has centered on rumors regarding possible drug trafficking to even include human trafficking. However, none of these rumors has been confirmed. The Chief would not elaborate on a possible motive citing that it was an ongoing investigation. Since Martin's arrival in Santa Fe, he has been known as both an entrepreneur and a philanthropist. Martin, and his wife Rebecca, have hosted several charitable fundraising events for various causes including the police and fire departments and Arts for Kids. He was also known for his support of various legislators on both sides of the aisle.

The article went on to describe much of what had been previously reported, including the numerous other investments in which Blake had been involved.

I quickly turned on the television to the local station. There across the bottom of the screen below the reporter was a streaming banner BREAKING NEWS. The reporter was in the process of detailing what I had just read in the paper. She had no more information than what I had already read. In essence, this was the Chief's attempt to give the press, and the public, some reassurance without really providing any new information. It was his attempt to proactively, manage what was coming out of the department.

At just that moment, my mobile phone rang. On caller ID was Rebecca. How timely, I thought.

"Good morning, Rebecca," I answered, knowing it was her.

"Oh Scott, have you seen the news. Isn't it just awful?" she wailed.

Perplexed by her response, I was slow to react. When I finally did, I said, "Yes, I just read in the paper that the Chief of Police indicated that Blake's murder was both targeted and an isolated event to reassure the public that a madman was not on the loose."

Quickly she responded, "Yes, but did you see that he didn't say he was excluding anyone as a person of interest, and that means me. I always knew the bastard was out to get me. How humiliating. I can't even go out of the house without people whispering that I had something to do with Blake's murder. I was going to try to get out today, but the fucking Chief just ruined that."

I quickly recognized that this was not about the news, but it was about Rebecca. I also knew that I needed to be careful about the words I chose. I did not want to further enflame her by challenging her assumption, nor did I want to suggest to her that she might still be a person of interest.

"Rebecca, I am sure that the police have to keep their findings close to their chest and that they will exclude you as soon as they can," I said, hoping she wouldn't take things further.

"I hope you are right, Scott. Actually, I was hoping I could spend some time with you today to better understand your strategy, but I can't come out and photographers have stationed themselves just outside my gate. I can see them on our security cameras. So, I do not think you should come here."

Relieved, I responded, "Well, Rebecca, I have several leads I want to follow so I was going to begin making contacts right after breakfast."

"Okay Scott, I will let you get on with your day. Thank you for the reassurance. Please let me know if you discover anything of interest," she requested.

"Will do," I replied as I readied to push the End Call button my phone.

"Oh Scott," I heard Rebecca say quickly. "Wait. One more thing."

I quickly discontinued trying to end the call and said, "Yes. What else?"

"Well, after our conversation yesterday about any other people I thought would want to hurt Blake, I thought of one more possibility. It is probably nothing, but I am trying to let you know everything I can think of," she said quickly.

"Sure, what is it?" I inquired.

Rebecca continued, "Scott and I were at an art showing at the Guadalupe before the fire. It was an invitation only affair to introduce new, and wealthy, potential clients to both the Guadalupe and the artwork that was being presented there from the gallery."

"Go on," I encouraged.

"Well," she resumed, "there was some kind of disturbance at the front door of the restaurant and Scott was rushed out of the main room to deal with it. When he returned, he was visibly upset, at least to me. When we talked later, he mentioned that some tipsy buyer of one of the gallery paintings was apparently dissatisfied with his purchase and had shown up at the event to straighten the matter out. Blake assured me it was nothing to fret over and that he would handle it later. Like I said, Scott, it is probably nothing, but I wanted to let you know."

"Thanks, Rebecca. I will look into it. In the meantime, the best you can do is to stay low and don't worry too much. Talk to you when I have something," I concluded and hung up.

The phone call, though brief, had a lot to it, I thought. It again confirmed Rebecca's own sense of entitlement. She was more concerned with how she would be seen than that the Chief had indicated that Blake's murder was an isolated event. In addition, she was upset that because the Chief had not specifically excluded, nor included, anyone, it must mean that she was being singled out for the murder. This inconvenienced her because she was not able to go about her daily life like she was used to. I had seen Rebecca's narcissism when we had been married but wondered if she had she become even more entitled living the high life with Blake.

The time was approaching eight thirty and I had not showered or eaten breakfast, and I had a call to make to Miguel. I quickly showered, slipped on my jeans, my leather sneakers, and a long-sleeve Polo shirt and was ready to begin the day.

To Rebecca's point, I had been thinking about starting by using Anna Pacheco's name to meet with Roberto Montoya. I had even thought about asking Anna to make the introduction. Because of the fire at the Guadalupe, it made meeting with Roberto even more of a priority. Now that Rebecca had indicated that a disgruntled customer of the gallery had shown up uninvited to the invitation-only art show, I could use this as an excuse to meet with Roberto. However, I did not want to get ahead of myself, so I decided to call Miguel prior to making any moves.

28

Idialed the mobile number Miguel had given me. It rang a couple of times and when I was about to discontinue the call, I heard, "This is Miguel Montez."

"Miguel," I said almost tentatively, since he had not answered quickly, "This is Scott Hunter calling you back."

"Scott. Good to hear from you. Sorry for not answering sooner, I was just getting out of a briefing with the Chief about the Martin murder. Well, what's up?" he asked.

"I have been thinking about our conversation yesterday. By the way, it was great to catch up," I said, somewhat deferentially.

Miguel replied, "I thought so as well. Have you made any decision regarding my offer?"

"I will say that you certainly know how to stir things up," I continued. "I went back to my room and thought through what I already knew and realized that I cannot make any progress on identifying possible suspects without some direction. So, yes, I would like to discuss your offer in more detail."

"Have you had breakfast yet?" he asked.

"No," I responded. "I was just about to go get some. What are you thinking?"

"I had to leave home early this morning, so I haven't eaten either. There is a small restaurant on Palace Avenue just behind the Cathedral called the Palacio Café. It is quiet, out of the way, and has a good breakfast selection. Let's meet there is, say, fifteen minutes," he requested.

"See you there," I said as I hung up.

I gathered my small briefcase, pad, and pen, put on a light jacket, and headed out. The Palacio Café was only about a seven-minute walk from the La Fonda.

I reached the restaurant just as Miguel arrived. We shook hands and he directed me to a table in the corner. He had called ahead and asked that we be seated apart from anyone else. This morning, that was not a problem as there were only two other tables occupied.

We sat down followed shortly by the waitress with our menus and coffee. The restaurant was small and dark but inviting. It had a mom-and-pop feel to it, with local art on the walls and the daily specials written on a black board above the counter. I had been eating at a rather rapid pace, so I decided to stick to oatmeal and berries. Miguel ordered a breakfast burrito.

Once we got the ordering out of the way, Miguel began by asking, "Did you see *The New Mexican* this morning?"

I filled Miguel in on both reading the story in the paper and the call from Rebecca in distress.

Smiling, Miguel said, "Did you expect that response from Rebecca?"

"No," I responded. "I thought it was odd and I had to reassure her that it was not all about her."

Ignoring my reply and wanting to move on, he continued, "So, Scott, I am assuming you are ready to go undercover?" As he said go undercover, he smiled and put finger quotes around the words.

I smiled and said, "Yes. I am ready."

Miguel responded with some enthusiasm. "Great. I had a chance last night to look at your website, and I am impressed with the work you have done. I do believe your skills will be a good fit for what I have in mind. In particular, your ability to interview people and draw conclusions about them on that basis. I must reiterate, however, that while I can point you in a direction, you absolutely must keep our relationship, and what you find, confidential. You will share information only with me. I will not be asking you to look into anything related to Rebecca, and you must keep any information that you find out away from her, obviously. In the event that you are suspected of working with the police, I will deny it. Are you good with all of that?"

I had spent a lot of time thinking about going stealth. I knew it was the only way I could be of any help. So, I responded, "Yes, Miguel. I understand."

"Good," he said. "Let me fill you in."

Miguel then went on to review the investigation. The Martin homicide was very high profile. He repeated what he had said the day before about managing the press and the department's inability to pursue any leads without the press being involved. In addition, the department was short-handed. Because most murders in Santa Fe had either been because of some kind of domestic dispute, or gang and drug related, it was unusual to have to involve high profile people in an investigation. In fact, many of those on the police force were somewhat intimidated interviewing wealthy, influential people. He went on to say that because I interviewed high profile people for a living, he believed I would be a good resource. Having sworn me to confidentiality, he went on to give me some of the details not known to the public.

As I suspected, Miguel reported that the Chief's press conference served to both calm the community and to begin to flush out some suspects. This is a police technique to suggest that they have more information than they actually have, and to generate some leads and tips. By turning up the heat on targeted folks, we often see them begin to make mistakes, tell other people, or go into hiding.

I thought to myself that Rebecca's call earlier, just after the press release, was evidence of this. Because she had not been cleared by the police as a person of interest, her anxiety had been raised, thus her call to me. However, I contradicted myself, there is no way she would seriously be a suspect. She had witnesses at Geronimo restaurant at the very time Blake had been killed. I also reflected on some of my executive clients in business how, under stress, they would display behaviors that were different from their typical style. Behaviors such as becoming too bold or mischievous, acting as if the rules did not apply to them. Some would become more withdrawn and independent, moving away from others. In any case, pressure, and the resulting anxiety, could cause anyone to act differently, and dysfunctionally. Interesting parallels I thought.

Miguel went on to say that this murder was likely premeditated because the security system had been disarmed. Because galleries in Santa Fe can have millions of dollars of art, they all have high end security systems including cameras, alarms, and calls directly to the security company and the police. In the case of Blake's murder, while it was late in the day, there had been no CCTV tapes or other indications as to who may have entered the gallery. Because the security system had been disarmed, it could have been an employee, or a former, disgruntled, employee who knew the master code to the system. In any case, the system appeared to have been disarmed for several days prior to the murder. The police were in the process of working with the security company to determine how the system could have been disarmed without their knowledge.

Miguel continued by saying that there were no fingerprints left behind. The obelisk sculpture had fragments of latex, indicating that the murderer had been wearing latex gloves to hide any fingerprints. Blake had been killed by a single blow to the head. Because of the forcefulness of the hit, and that it was on the head, the police believed that the killer was likely a man, and one of above average height. They believed that Blake had his back to the killer and either did not hear the killer's entrance, knew the killer, or saw the killer as a customer. With both the forcefulness of the blow and the disarmed security system, this seems to be personal. Also, the back door to the gallery that accessed the parking lot was, by Rebecca's report, open when she arrived. The only vehicles in the parking lot were Rebecca's BMW and Blake's Range Rover HSE. They found some other tire tracks that were still being studied.

"Scott," Miguel, went on, "I have to reiterate that none of this is public knowledge. You must keep this to yourself. Do I have your commitment on that?"

"Of course," I reacted, a bit defensively. While I knew that it was Miguel's job to make sure I would not share this information, I had already committed to him that I would keep it confidential.

Our breakfast orders came and the waitress gave us a warm-up on our coffees. It was a good time to take a deep breath and soak in what I had heard.

I restarted the conversation, having gotten over my initial defensiveness. "Miguel, I am flattered that you would take me into your confidence, and believe me, I will honor it."

"Great, Scott. I do have a couple of leads I would like you to follow up."

I was eager to hear what the next steps would be.

29

Miguel began, "There are a couple of areas we want to pursue. First, we are looking into any current or former employees who worked at the gallery. We believe that it is best that we look at them ourselves. If the press discovered we were looking at former employees, it would not come as a surprise to them. Along the same lines, obviously, we are going to interview Rebecca in order to eliminate her as a suspect. Again, this will be of no news to the press. The press is hungry for something more salacious than former employees or the spouse. In a similar manner, we will be looking at Blake's finances, including insurance, Wills, and the books for the gallery for any transactions that seem to be unusual. So, our way of managing the press is to investigate the obvious."

"However," he continued, "there are a couple of leads I would like for you to follow. We have been made aware that there have been some gallery customers who have been dissatisfied with their purchases. These purchases have been in both the five and six figure dollar categories. It is not unheard of for a dissatisfied customer to want to take revenge on a gallery owner, although clearly murder is an extreme. We have had gallery owners who were suspected of fraud reported to the state Attorney General's office. We have had at least one very unhappy customer at another high-end gallery file multiple lawsuits suggesting that the art he paid for and the art he received were very different paintings. We have also had negative ads taken out in ArtNews magazines and even once a full page add in the Wall Street Journal. However, there has not been to date any physical assaults between gallery owners and unhappy customers. Interestingly, we have heard that one of these customers showed up uninvited to an invitation-only event at the Guadalupe restaurant to confront Blake. We would like you to take a closer look at him."

The look on my face must have been one of mild surprise, because Miguel asked, "Do you know something about this?"

I then told Miguel more about my meeting with Anna Pacheco and how she had made a couple of suggestions for me to consider to begin my inquiries. She suggested that I speak with Roberto Montoya regarding the fire at the Guadalupe as well as a fracas at a premier event that Blake had experienced with an uninvited attendee and customer. I also said that Anna had suggested that Blake had made more than one business partner unhappy. I recollected to Miguel that Rebecca had also mentioned the same disturbance. However, I told him that neither Anna nor Rebecca seemed to know the identity of the angry interloper. Finally, I told Miguel about Rebecca's observation that Blake had been visibly upset at some failed business dealing with Roberto Montoya.

As a psychologist, I look for themes, and clearly one was emerging—the disturbance at the Guadalupe had now been mentioned three times in three different conversations.

Miguel frowned. "Well, so much for keeping persons of interest to ourselves. I am always surprised by what a small-town Santa Fe is, particularly with those longer-term locals, like Anna, who have deep roots. Given what you just told me, we also need to ensure that we keep Anna on the Do Not Tell list," he said, again using finger quotes around Do Not Tell. "We will need to proceed cautiously, Scott."

Miguel sighed and said, "We need the name of the disgruntled gallery customer to whom Rebecca referred. I believe Roberto Montoya will know his identity. I want you to set up a time to talk with Roberto. Tell him that Anna Pacheco suggested he would be a good contact for you as you think about settling in Santa Fe. I know that is not your goal, but with Anna's influence and Roberto's good will, I am sure he will be willing to meet with you. As you speak with him, you can get him to open up both about the fire at the Guadalupe, which is still under investigation, and his relationship with Blake. I would expect you to guide him in such a way that he will reveal the disgruntled individual to you without raising too much attention.

"That's a tall order," I said. It required me to do a kind of maneuvering that I am not used to. In my work with business executives, I have found that executives are often more fragile than their lofty positions or large salaries would suggest. In fact, over the years, I have learned the importance of finesse and nuance when delivering personal critiques to their management style. My biggest mistakes as a consultant have been when I have believed that the unvarnished truth would be the most impactful way to help executives change their behavior, only to find out that, to paraphrase Jack Nicholson in *A Few Good Men*, "They can't handle the truth." I have been kicked out of more than one executive's offices for being too direct. As a result, I have learned that to be most effective, I needed to be patient, listen, and present critiques in such a way as to not raise the defenses of the executive. So, I knew that, when talking with Roberto, I would need to listen, boost his confidence, and disarm his defenses down, as I plied him for information.

Miguel shot back, "If it was easy, Scott, I would do it myself. This situation calls for your expertise. Are you ready to get started?"

"Sure," I replied, "but how do you suggest that I get this initial interview time?"

Handing me a sheet of paper from a small note pad he kept in his pocket, Miguel said, "Here is Roberto's mobile number. I know he had a small business office for the restaurant, and other matters in which he is involved, just a few blocks east of the Plaza, across the street from the Hilton hotel on Sandoval street. Since the restaurant fire, I believe he will be there. Give him a call and tell him that Anna Pacheco recommended that you talk with him. They are old friends, and he will be happy to make your acquaintance."

"Once Roberto and I have talked, how do you want me to get information back to you?" I asked.

"After today," Miguel replied, "we will mostly have to communicate on the mobile phone number I gave you. It is a private phone. Do not call me at the station. For the foreseeable future, we should not meet in public places like we are today. If I want to call you, I have your number. Ready to get started?"

"I am ready," I said eagerly.

With that conclusion to our discussion, Miguel rose, held out his hand to mine to shake, and picked up the check. I mildly protested, but he prevailed and encouraged me to call Roberto. I left out the front door to go back to my room and clean up before making the call. I wanted to sort out my thoughts before actually calling Roberto.

30

It was ten fifteen when I left the Palacio Café. The short walk back to the hotel was refreshing. The bright sun and the crisp air were invigorating. Being in the center of Santa Fe, I realized just how much I had missed the home of my youth. I loved the blending of the Native American, Hispanic, and Anglo cultures. I also had missed the food, the architecture, the art, and the people. Maybe a return someday would still be achievable. My adrenaline was pumping like crazy, now into high gear. I was both excited and scared. This was new territory for me, but I was up to the task. I cleaned up and dialed the phone number for Roberto.

After two rings, a woman answered with a spritely voice, "Montoya enterprises, this is Marcy. How can I help you?"

"Good morning, Marcy," I replied cheerfully. "I am calling for Roberto Montoya. Is he in?"

"Of course," she answered. "Who may I say is calling?"

"My name is Scott Hunter. I was referred to Roberto by Anna Pacheco," I said as confidently as I could hoping to get an appointment.

"I will get Mr. Montoya," Marcy said dutifully.

After a few seconds, a warm voice on the other end came on the line, "This is Roberto."

"Good morning, Mr. Montoya. I am Scott Hunter and I was referred to you by Anna Pacheco. I have been away from Santa Fe for some time and am considering returning. Anna thought that you would be someone who would be a good source of information as to the business landscape in Santa Fe. I know this may be unusual, but would you be willing to allow me to buy you lunch in the next few days?"

Roberto laughed and said, "Scott, any friend of Anna's is a friend of mine. Actually, I have lunch plans, but if you have some time this afternoon around two o'clock, I am available here at my office."

"That would be terrific. Where are you located?" I asked, knowing the address from Miguel, but not wanting him to think I was too aggressive in wanting to see him.

"Yes," he replied. "I am in the office building across from the Hilton on the corner of Sandoval and Water. I am on the second floor, office two-fourteen. See you at two o'clock."

Gratefully, I replied, "Thank you so much. I will see you at two."

We both hung up and I sat back in my chair, pleased that I was able to get a confirmed appointment.

As I did when meeting with business clients, I began to review what questions I had for Roberto; how I would develop some kind of bond with Roberto; and most importantly, how I would get around to talking about the Guadalupe restaurant to get the name of Blake's disgruntled customer. I always found it helpful to walk, and talk to myself, to review upcoming meetings. I thought that this would serve two purposes. I could reacquaint myself with downtown again and I could visualize the meeting with Roberto. I reached for my jacket and left the hotel walking west toward the plaza.

I decided to check-out the park near the old Federal Court House. The Federal Court House is where I had registered for the draft back in the day. The park surrounding the Court House was tree lined with benches to sit and a sidewalk stretching around the park that was about a half mile walking distance. Even during tourist season, this was just far enough away from the plaza that it was rarely busy. It was the perfect place to clear my head of distractions and begin thinking about my upcoming meeting with Roberto.

I crossed the plaza and began walking down Lincoln Avenue. The park was about a four-block trek along a street lined with boutique men's and women's clothing stores, galleries, and coffee shops. It was fun to see what had been renovated, and what hadn't. As I approached the corner of Lincoln and Marcy, something familiar caught my eye on the far side of the street. I had to do a double take to make sure that what I thought I saw was real.

"Well, I'll be damned," I thought to myself, as there across the street coming out of the Tea House, a specialty coffee and tea shop, was Rebecca, arm in arm with a snappily dressed man. I momentarily hid in the shadows wanting to size up the situation without being noticed. It was eerie seeing Rebecca out when just a couple of hours earlier she had been complaining

116

that she was basically being held hostage in her house by the press.

The man looked to be in his late forties or early fifties. He was medium build with a full head of dark hair. He had on beige slacks, a navy blazer, a light blue shirt, and a tie. It is unusual in Santa Fe to see people dressed up like he was. Even professionals usually do not wear ties, and when they do they usually wear bolo ties showing off southwestern art and turquoise on the clasps. The only professionals who dressed up were bankers and attorneys. I wondered if this was the attorney that Rebecca mentioned whom she had called when she was about to be interrogated by the police.

I could tell by the way they were interacting that they were not strangers. I had to decide quickly whether or not I wanted to come out of the shadows to meet them or stay back and observe. I decided to wait and watch. I wanted to manage the conversations I had with Rebecca. I did not want to be in a position where she would begin asking too many questions about what I was finding, nor did I want to take the chance that she might become suspicious. I decided that I would manage my communications with her by calling her when I had something to report. As I continued to watch them walk down the street, they turned away from me and walked toward what I could see was Rebecca's red BMW parked on the street. The man opened the car door for her, they hugged, and he continued down the street and out of sight. Rebecca drove away.

I was a little more than perplexed that Rebecca was out of her house and not appearing to be in great distress, and also, that I happened to see her with someone else. I had to remind myself that this wasn't, as baseball player and philosopher Yogi Berra used to say, "déjà vu all over again." There was probably a good explanation for their meeting. If he was her attorney, they would have had good reason to be together. I wondered why they would have chosen to be in a public place for a private conversation. I decided to go into the Tea House to nose around and see if there was anything I could pick up from the internal staff conversations.

The Tea House was a combination retail specialty tea shop as well as a place to meet for tea and scones. It had not existed when I had lived here before. In fact, it had been a small office supply store. I walked in trying to look like a prospective customer, not an undercover whatever I was, and began browsing the vast tea selection.

"Tea lover, are you?" I heard being asked from a pleasant female voice behind me.

117

"Well, I am kind of an amateur, really," I said sheepishly.

I thought I would take a chance and see if my hunch was right. "Actually, I am waiting on a friend. I am running a little late, so I hope he is still coming."

"But of course, take your time looking. I am sure your friend will be here shortly," the lovely lady offered.

"Maybe you know him," I said quizzically. "His name is Charles Kahn."

"Oh, my," she exclaimed. "You just missed him. He had been here not ten minutes ago with another person, a woman."

Having had my hunch confirmed, I decided to leave saying, "Well, darn. That is what I get for being late. Thank you so much. I will be back another time when I can receive a proper education about your fine teas."

She smiled, saying, "Any time. I would be pleased to provide you with an introduction and a tasting to discover just what kind of tea palate you have."

With that, I opened the door and stood outside for a moment wondering about my next move.

I decided that other than seeing Rebecca with Charles, I really did not have anything new to consider. I went ahead and continued my walk to the park to continue to think about my upcoming meeting with Roberto. Unfortunately, I found that the image of seeing Rebecca with Charles Kahn disturbing and it continued to interfere with my thought process. I kept explaining to myself that there must have been a good reason for them to have met. Being a family friend in addition to her attorney made sense. What kept bugging me, though, was the discrepancy between what she had told me about being house bound and finding her out of the house, and seemingly in good spirits. Ultimately, I decided that if I was going to be clear headed with Roberto, I would have to put this observation on the back burner for now. Also, I could hear Miguel's voice in my head as a warning to stay clear of any questioning of Rebecca.

I made my way to the Federal Court House park and began walking around the park on the sidewalk in the cool shade of the large oak trees rehearsing in my mind the meeting to come with Roberto.

The next time I checked my watch, it was one-thirty. I was stunned that I had been so lost in thought that I had missed lunch. I rarely miss a meal, and never voluntarily. Well, I would make up for it tonight, I laughed to myself. Knowing I had a twenty-minute walk in front of me to Roberto's office, I began the trek looking forward to our meeting.

31

I arrived at Roberto's office about ten minutes early and opened the door to be greeted by Marcy, whom I had spoken with earlier.

"You must be Scott," she said sunnily.

"Yes. And you must be Marcy," I replied trying to match her disposition.

"Roberto is just finishing up on a call. Can I get you anything? Coffee? Water?" Marcy offered.

"Water would be nice," I responded.

"Sparkling or still?" she continued.

"Sparkling, if you have it," I exclaimed surprised at my choices.

"Ice or without?" she asked efficiently.

I smiled at her service, remembering that the engine of Roberto's enterprise had been the restaurant. He had even trained Marcy to be service oriented.

"With ice would be perfect," I said.

"I will bring it in to you with Roberto," she said smiling and looking over her shoulder to see Roberto coming out to greet me.

"Scott," Roberto said warmly, reaching out his hand to shake mine. "Come in. Has Marcy taken care of you?"

Roberto had a presence about him that had elements of both confidence and graciousness. He was tall, had a full head of salt and pepper hair, and was dressed in slacks and an upscale polo shirt. He appeared to be a man who was comfortable with himself and comfortable in the company of others.

"Hi Roberto. It is a pleasure to meet you. And yes, Marcy is getting me some water now," I answered, waiting for my next instructions.

Roberto pointed to a small, dark wooden conference table flanked by four black leather chairs. His office had a rich, professional feel to it with wood floors and Native American rugs, an executive L-shaped desk in front of custom-made bookcases, the conference table, and a wall-mounted presentation board with dark brown mahogany doors. The plastered walls had wainscoting on the bottom third. A combination of framed awards and plaques and Southwestern art graced the other walls. He also had a large window looking west out over the street. I was impressed. It was an office similar to some of my executive clients.

"Take a seat, please," Roberto offered.

I knew from working with executives that there is always a particular seat at a conference table that they prefer to use. It is typically associated with positional power, both conscious and unconscious. To those who work regularly with the executive, the "boss's chair" is sacrosanct, and everyone knows that even if they are the first to the meeting, they are not to sit in that chair. As a visitor, it is more difficult to know. However, it is usually a safe bet that the seat closest to the executive's desk is the executive's default chair. Suspecting that, I took the chair furthest from the desk. I knew that "you only have one chance to make a first impression," beginning with the handshake and extending to where you sit. I had learned this from more than one misstep. This also pointed to another truth, and that is that the executive's office is not one of equality.

Looking more closely at Roberto I could see what appeared to be fatigue on his face. He was more slumped in his chair than I expected and slightly less energetic. I wanted to keep that in mind as we talked, not wanting to outwear my unsolicited visit.

As I sat down, Marcy placed my iced sparkling water on a leather glass coaster with an engraving of a restaurant with "Guadalupe" running along the top of the coaster.

I nodded my appreciation to Marcy and Roberto began, "Well, Scott, how do you know Anna and how can I help you?"

I had expected this opening question and was prepared for the answer. I knew that with both Anna and Roberto having long family histories in Santa Fe, they would no doubt be running into each other and that my visit with Roberto would come up. I knew I had to be careful in my responses. If I were too direct too soon, the meeting would be a short one. On the other hand, to delay the truth too long would only incur suspicion and skepticism.

I replied, "I have just recently met Anna. I am originally from Santa Fe and have been gone for several years. I have come to Santa Fe on some personal business am considering returning. Anna suggested that you would be someone who would have a good sense of the Santa Fe business world."

While I knew I was skirting the truth, and it felt uncomfortable, I also knew that there was enough truth in what I said that it would not get me into any trouble with Roberto.

"Hmm," Roberto responded and asked, "Hunter, Hunter. Are you related to William Hunter?"

Both surprised and not surprised, because Santa Fe is a small town, I replied, "Yes, he was my father. Did you know him?"

Roberto livened up a bit and said, "Yes, I did. He would often work on our cars whenever they needed repairs. He was someone I could always trust to fix my automobile problems and not try to sell me anything I did not need. I always thought he was a fine, honest, man. I did not know your mother. I was sad when I heard, several years ago, that he had passed."

"Small world," I mused.

"Small indeed," he responded and continued, "So tell me a bit about yourself. I am assuming you graduated from high school and left Santa Fe. Is that right?"

I took the time to review with Roberto my history about college, getting my doctorate, practicing in Santa Fe, getting divorced and leaving Santa Fe. I knew that it would come up about Rebecca, and I was trying to fit my being here in Santa Fe into a larger picture that included my return.

Listening attentively, Roberto replied and said, "All of our family went to the Catholic boys and girls schools, so I was unaware of you, except that I knew your father. I am a bit confused, however, about what I can do to help you. If you are a psychologist, why would you need to know about the business world? And why have you decided to return?"

I went on to explain my shift from private practice to using psychological principles in management, and some of the work I had done with companies. But I knew that this was the moment of truth and either the conversation would be terminated or the fact that he knew my family would have created enough goodwill that he would allow me to continue conversing.

I took a deep breath and continued, "The personal reason I have come back now is that the divorce I referenced was to Rebecca Miller, who later became Rebecca Martin, wife of Blake Martin. I came back to essentially support her, at her request, to get through this time."

I immediately saw Roberto's complexion blanche as he again slumped down in his chair.

Knowing that I only had a small window, I persisted, "But I do want to return to Santa Fe. My roots are here and it is time for me to face my past. I am very interested in understanding the business landscape, and I believe that Anna directed me appropriately."

The fact was that even my brief time in Santa Fe, after eleven years, had given me some sense of coming home. While Bozeman had given me a place, and time, to heal and redirect my career, it never felt like home to me. Maybe that was why I had never really had a serious relationship, knowing subconsciously that I was not long for Bozeman. I would have to sort this out at another time, but my words to Roberto did not seem totally disingenuous.

After a long pause, Roberto observed confused, "So you came back to support your ex-wife whose husband was recently brutally murdered? And, in the process, you have decided you may want to return? I'm sorry, but this sounds a bit absurd."

I was having to think on my feet now, knowing that what he said was right, and that I had to somehow manage my response to acknowledge his reservations and to be able to move past them.

"Yes, Roberto," I began tentatively, "I have had the same exact thoughts, and it does sound absurd. To be honest, I have never quite felt at home in Bozeman, and have had a restlessness. When I received Rebecca's request for support, my first inclination was to immediately decline. Our divorce had been contentious, and I left town feeling betrayed. As strange, and morbid as it may sound, Blake's death meant that I could revisit my reasons for leaving and reconsider a return. So, ultimately I said yes with the idea in the back of my mind that I could use the time to determine if returning to Santa Fe felt right."

Roberto shook his head saying, "Well, Scott, it's your life and I hope you find what you are looking for. I need to tell you, though, that I do not want to be associated with either Blake or Rebecca. You may know that Blake and I had some business dealings together, and they were not going well. Also, four weeks ago, my restaurant, the Guadalupe, burned to the ground in a fire for which the fire department still has not released the cause. We are still sorting through the aftermath of the fire, including insurance, potential liability, even possible Chapter 11 in the event the fire department does not rule in our favor. The fire occurred shortly after a very contentious argument that Blake and I had about him becoming a fuller partner with me. I refused and he became very angry. I am not saying he had anything to do with the fire, but it seemed very suspicious given the timing."

I became more solemn and said, "Roberto, I am truly sorry for the fire and whatever happened between you and Blake. I cannot imagine how awful the fire must have been for you, your family, and your employees. Of course, I also have no lost love for Blake given the affair he and Rebecca had. Other than offering some short-term support, I want to be clear that I have no intention of a future with Rebecca. However, I am interested in understanding the business climate here to see if there are any possibilities of work, as a possible bridge to me returning."

At that point, Roberto said with a sigh, "Scott, I would like to help you, but I am up to my eyeballs in trying to manage all of the financial and legal issues associated with the fire. However, my daughter, Maria, could be of real help. In fact, she is more tuned in to the Santa Fe business scene than I am. She is usually here, but today she is out trying to see what is salvageable from the fire. I will ask her to meet with you to further discuss your interests, if that is okay with you."

Seeing the impact all of this had on Roberto, I of course accepted his proposal with, "That is most generous of you, and I would love to talk with her."

At that, Roberto bellowed, "Marcy, can you join us for a minute?"

Upon Marcy's return, Roberto continued, "Would you please set up a meeting with Scott and Maria in the next day or so?"

Marcy demurely replied, "It would be my pleasure. Mr. Hunter, if you could just let me know your schedule and contact information, I would be happy to schedule a meeting with Maria."

I could see that this conversation was over. I thanked Roberto profusely, gave Marcy my schedule and mobile number, and departed.

The conversation with Roberto was disturbing to me. It gnawed on me that I was in the middle of Rebecca and Miguel. Knowing that I had a clear allegiance to Miguel, I could not inform Rebecca about my "undercover" sleuthing. While I did not take a fee from Rebecca, she was paying for my expenses. I had anticipated having to make some difficult decisions, but I was unprepared for how my affiliation with, and support of, Rebecca was going to present such a problem.

Under other circumstances, I would have just walked away from this altogether. However, both the meeting with Miguel and the opportunity to become reacquainted with Santa Fe, led me to stay for the remainder of the two weeks. It would also give me some measure of satisfaction if I could assist in finding Blake's murderer and clearing Rebecca. At the same time, I knew that I would have to further distance myself from her.

I had a decision to make, and the sooner I made it the better it would be for everyone.

32

I left Roberto's office to walk back to the hotel. I had been there longer than I realized, and the time was approaching four o'clock. As I was walking back toward the plaza, my mobile phone rang. I could see by the caller ID "Montoya Enterprises" that it was likely Marcy calling.

On the second ring I answered, "This is Scott Hunter."

"Yes, Mr. Hunter, or I should say Doctor Hunter, this is Marcy," she said with a lightness in her voice.

"Hi Marcy," I replied. "You are certainly efficient."

"Thank you," she said gratefully. "I called Maria and she is available to meet with you here in her office in the morning at nine o'clock if you are available then."

"Nine works great, Marcy. Thank you! See you then," I said.

Cheerfully she responded, "My pleasure. I will have coffee and scones available. See you tomorrow at nine o'clock."

We both hung up. I was again impressed with the level of service I was receiving.

I had to have a conversation with Rebecca, and I was debating whether to have it in person or over the phone. I knew the best way was face-to-face, but I was not looking forward to it. When consulting to executives about having to have difficult conversations, I always encourage them to be clear about their expectations, be direct, and have the conversations as soon as they could. I needed to heed my own advice.

I called Rebecca's number hoping to be able to see her in person before dinner time.

On the third ring, Rebecca answered, obviously seeing my caller ID, "Well hi, Scott. I did not expect you to call. What's up?"

"Hi Rebecca," I said trying to sound casual. "Do you have a few minutes before dinner to have a short conversation, in person?"

She paused momentarily then replied, "Sure. We could meet now. I am just wrapping up work with my attorney. Come on over."

"Great. I will be there in about fifteen minutes," I said.

We both hung up.

The central part of Santa Fe is very walkable, and you can walk from any two points in the center of town in less than thirty minutes. But today was warm and I did not want to be either sweaty or out of breath when I arrived, so I used my Uber app to secure transportation.

My car pulled up and it was the same Uber driver I had the day before who had driven me to Java Joe's. I gave him the address and he knew the route. I was there in just over ten minutes.

As before, I pushed the button on the microphone, and we were buzzed through the gate. The driver left me off at the door and, as I was getting out, Rebecca showed up at the door with her attorney, Charles Kahn, who was just leaving. I had been correct in my earlier assumption; he was the individual I had seen Rebecca with coming out of the Tea House.

"Hi Scott. Welcome. I don't think you have met Charles," Rebecca began. "Scott, this is Charles Kahn, my attorney. Charles, this is Scott Hunter. We had just wrapped up when you called and Charles was just leaving."

Charles and I both extended our hands to shake. He had on the same clothes as before, but without the tie or sport coat. He was nicer looking than I had noticed before. He looked, and acted like an attorney, confident and professional, assertive but not aggressive.

Charles said, "It is a pleasure to meet you, Scott. I know Rebecca is glad you are here to support her."

"Nice to meet you, Charles. Rebecca told me how helpful you have been in working with the police," I said, a bit stiffly.

I found it interesting that Rebecca did not identify me as her ex-husband. I wondered if that was to skip over an awkward moment or that Charles already knew.

"Well," Charles finished. "I must be off. Sorry to just meet you and run, maybe we will have a chance to catch up at another time."

"Another time," I replied as the door closed and Charles walked to his parked car.

Again, I noticed something familiar about how they interacted. It did seem to be a bit more than just client and attorney. Maybe I was just super-sensitive and making up things. Or was something really going on.

Was this instinct at play? Or paranoia? Or, heaven forbid, jealousy?

"What a nice surprise," Becky said with a bit more cheeriness that I wanted to hear in her voice knowing that I was going to change our arrangement. "Please, have a seat. Can I get you anything? Water? Tea? A glass of wine?"

"No thank you," I responded and began. "Nice to meet Charles. I am sure he is a real help with all of the legal issues surrounding Blake's death."

I was trying to see where Rebecca might take this and see if there was anything more to it than just a professional relationship.

"Oh, my god," Rebecca exclaimed. "I couldn't have made it through this without Charles help, both professionally and personally. He has been such a good support."

I wanted to push, just a bit. "Charles has been a long-term attorney for you and Blake?"

"Yes, about five years," she said a bit brusquely. "Now tell me, what's up?"

Closing the door to the Charles conversation, I decided to forge ahead.

"Rebecca, I have been rethinking our lunch yesterday and what I mentioned to you then."

She frowned, saying, "What do you mean."

I continued, "For some time now, I have known that Bozeman would not be my home long-term. While it is beautiful and vibrant and the people are wonderful, it has never felt like the place where I wanted to end up. In the short time I have been here, coming back to Santa Fe has surprisingly felt more like home. When I left, as we discussed, I was bitter and negative. I identified the city with my own sense of disenchantment. I am not saying that I have decided to come back, but I do want to use some of the time I am here to explore the possibility. I am still interested in being of assistance to you, but I do not want you to pay my expenses since this has become partially a time to reacquaint myself with the city. I would not feel comfortable having you pay for my expenses knowing that I will be using some of the time to do investigating unrelated to identifying clues related to Blake's murderer. So, I will work with Anna Pacheco to redirect all of the expenses directly to me."

I paused to let it sink in. It felt good to begin to disentangle this web. I was feeling uncomfortable with the pretexts and having to spin stories. This would free me up considerably.

"Oh, Scott." Rebecca replied. "I thought you were going to tell me that you were going to go back to Bozeman immediately. I appreciate your honesty. While I would have preferred for you to spend all of your time helping me identify possible murderers, I do understand your conflict. I am still perfectly happy to continue to pay your expenses knowing that some of your time will be on my behalf."

I had anticipated this answer and was firm in my decision.

"Thank you, but I will have a clearer conscience if I pay for them myself. I am working to follow up on some leads, and when I have something concrete, I will let you know."

I knew that Miguel had been firm in telling me not to release any information to Rebecca, but if I did not at least indicate an interest in trying to help, I feared she would become angry. I felt certain that Miguel would eliminate her as a person of interest and when he did, I believed that I could give her some information, as long as it would not jeopardize the police investigation.

I did not want to get into a lengthy discussion with Rebecca, so I got up to leave.

Rebecca responded saying, "I was just about to have Rosita put something on for dinner, can you stay?"

I was also prepared for this invitation. "Thank you for the offer, but since I have been gone from my work for a few days, I have some emails I need to attend to."

That was actually true, I always had emails I could attend to.

"Well," she said almost dejectedly, "keep me informed."

"I will," I said as I opened the door and made my exit.

It was then I realized that I had not ordered another Uber. However, it was cooling off and I decided the walk back to the hotel would be a good time to sort through what I had learned. I also realized that I was hungry and began thinking about where I wanted to eat dinner. As I walked back, I thought it would be a good idea to call Miguel to give him an update.

33

I pulled out my mobile phone and dialed the number Miguel had given me. This time, Miguel answered on the second ring.

"Hey, Scott," he began. "I did not expect to hear from you so soon, but I am glad you called. What's up?"

I brought Miguel up to date on having seen Rebecca and Charles Kahn coming out of the Tea House together and how confusing it was following her desperate call after seeing the morning's article in *The New Mexican*. The fact that she said that reporters were basically preventing her from even leaving her house and then to see her there was very odd.

I went on to report that I had gone to Rebecca's house to change the arrangement we had of her paying for my expenses. I told him of meeting Charles Kahn who was just leaving her house as I got there. I repeated what I had told Rebecca, that because I was now looking to possibly return to Santa Fe, I could not in good conscience have her pay for my expenses feeling I would be duplicitous in taking her payments when part of the time I would be exploring options other than looking for any clues to Blake's murder.

Finally, I told him of my meeting with Roberto and how Roberto had recommended that I speak with Maria instead of him, and that I had a meeting with her in the morning. I also told Miguel that I thought Roberto suspected Blake of being instrumental in the Guadalupe fire. I mentioned that I thought Roberto looked tired and, maybe, a bit beaten down.

When I concluded, Miguel who had been listening attentively, said, "My, Scott, you have really hit the ground running. It has clearly been a good start. Your meeting with Maria should be an interesting one! Nice work."

It felt good to have Miguel's validation and was an encouragement to continue to get more information.

Miguel continued, "Scott, we have had an interesting day as well. Martin's gallery is still a crime scene and will not reopen any time soon. We will be having a second interview with Rebecca and her attorney in the next couple of days. In looking more closely at the crime scene, one of our forensic people identified bicycle tire treads in the parking lot. The forensic folks found this interesting because there are no bicycle racks in the parking lot, the lot is for the gallery only, and all of the other tracks have been from automobiles. We have already matched tire prints in the lot to Rebecca's BMW and Blake's Range Rover HSE. However, we may be lucky. As a result of an appeal on all of the local television stations, some folks, mostly tourists, have stepped forward with what they thought was possible evidence. One of the tourists had been walking down East Marcy Street a block north of the gallery. They were taking an iPhone video of the area at the time to record their stay in Santa Fe. The tourist was kind enough to allow us to download the video and forensics is just beginning to look at it now. The bicycle tracks may not lead to anything, but you never know. Look, you have had a full day, go get some rest and prepare for your meeting with Maria. Keep in mind that we are trying to identify the individual with whom Blake had the scuffle at the Guadalupe during the art showing just before the fire."

That reminded me of something Roberto had said, so I quickly asked before Miguel hung up, "By the way, Roberto mentioned that the fire department has not yet rendered an opinion as to the cause of the fire. He is worried that if the fire is seen as arson, his insurance will not cover the loss. Anything you can tell me about that?"

"Well," Miguel replied. "I know that the fire department has been sorting through a number of clues within the remains of the restaurant. They have been trying to determine where the origin of the fire was and whether it could have been related to a gas leak or something more sinister. Because the fire at the Guadalupe, like Blake's murder, is so high profile, I know the Chief is moving slow on this in order to be thorough. Because the Guadalupe is almost a Santa Fe institution for legislators and locals, the Chief wants to make certain that they are thorough in the examination of clues, and cautious in how they report their findings. Having said that, I think they will have something in a day or two to report. Stay tuned. In the meantime, go get some rest."

With that information, we both hung up.

I was almost back to the hotel. I remembered that I needed to let Anna know that all of the hotel and restaurant charges were to be paid by me and not Rebecca. As I entered the lobby of the hotel, I could immediately smell piñon incense. Nothing is more reminiscent to me of Santa Fe than that smell. Growing up, we had burned piñon wood in our fireplace. It always gave off such a sweet aroma. During the holidays, you would find Canyon Road street corners punctuated by small stacks of burning piñon wood, called luminarias, as groups walked up and down the street caroling and drinking hot chocolate. I was immediately taken back to those times when we would walk up and down Canyon Road greeting friends and neighbors as we celebrated the season.

It took me a moment to remember where I was when my reverie was interrupted by a, "Welcome back, Doctor Hunter."

It was Christina, the young lady who had been at the desk when I left this morning.

"Thank you, Christina. My, you put in long days," I marveled.

"The management here is great. I am able to work four days a week, but ten-hour days. It works out great for my family. Is there anything I may assist you with?" she inquired.

"Yes, Christina, there is one thing. I need to get in touch with Anna Pacheco. Do you know how I might do that?"

"Absolutely, Doctor Hunter. Give me a minute and I will call her and connect her to your room," Christina answered eagerly.

I thanked Christina and headed up to my room. I intended to freshen up a bit and then go back downstairs to La Plazuela restaurant for some dinner. As I walked into my room, the phone was ringing.

I picked up and said, "This is Scott Hunter."

"Scott," Anna answered. "Christina told me you wanted to talk with me. How can I help you? I hope your stay is going well and that you are comfortable."

"Hi Anna," I responded. "Thanks for calling. I hope you are doing well. I certainly enjoyed breakfast yesterday and getting to know you a bit."

"I enjoyed it too. What can I do for you?" She quickly replied getting down to business.

I went on, "The short of it is that I have talked with Rebecca, and I want all of the charges incurred here at La Fonda to be charged to me, not Rebecca. My time here has taken a bit of a turn and in addition to following some leads on Rebecca's behalf, I am also considering returning to Santa Fe. As a result, part of my time will here be exploring the possibilities of coming back to live. I did not want Rebecca to foot the bill for me exploring what possibilities for work, and living, are here. So, even though she protested, I want to pay my own expenses. I will have a cleaner conscience when I am looking for opportunities that are independent of any investigation work I do for her."

"Well." Anna jumped in, "I am delighted that you are going to stay and help Rebecca out, as well as to explore the possibility of relocating to our fair city. Consider me as a resource should you decide to come back. I am pretty well connected. As for the expenses you incur, how long do you intend to stay?"

"Thank you for being willing to serve as a resource," I continued. "I am staying for two weeks. At the end of that time, I think I will have a reasonably good idea about whether or not to come back."

"In that case," Anna interjected, "we have a weekly rate that I can extend to you that will help with the room charges. Since we are at the beginning of our shoulder season, the room rates have just dropped, and with the weekly rate, it will be manageable. I am pleased to be of any further assistance. By the way, have you made any progress on identifying possible suspects in Blake's murder? I saw the story in *The New Mexican* of the Chief of Police's interview. Reading between the lines, it does not look like they have much."

I knew from my discussion with Miguel that I had to be very careful about revealing too much to Anna, so I indicated that I was just beginning to follow the leads she had given me. Not wanting to prolong the conversation, I thanked her again and we said our goodbyes.

Now I was starved. I had a light breakfast and I had skipped lunch, so dinner at La Plazuela was sounding pretty good. I freshened up, put on a clean shirt, and headed down to the restaurant.

34

As the La Plazuela maître d greeted me, a wave of nostalgia overcame me as I remembered the last meal my father and I had here together. It was a short time before his death and a bittersweet memory. In his memory, I asked to be seated at the same table where we had dined before. In the eleven years since I had last seen the restaurant, few things had changed, and it still had its New Mexican charm.

The restaurant, situated in the middle of the hotel, had once been an open-air courtyard. Years ago, skylights had been added over the open-air ceiling to allow dining regardless of weather. In addition, the interior walls of the restaurant consisted of beautiful painted glass panes that complemented the hand-carved furniture, artisan lighting, flagstone floor, and water fountain in the middle of the room. The restaurant had maintained its Old-World charm while adding only slight upgrades.

The menu had changed to stay current, adding contemporary influences to the New Mexican cuisine. As I viewed the menu, I realized how hungry I was. I started with a Margarita and a side of guacamole. I decided to order the Filet y Enchiladas, a combination of a char-grilled steak marinated with a blanket of green chiles, accompanied by a cheese enchilada smothered in red chile sauce.

As the waiter brought the guacamole to the table, I heard a ping on my phone. Looking down, I saw a text from Anna, "Scott, I have something important thing I would like to discuss with you. Would you be willing to have a drink in an hour at the bar at La Posada?"

Socializing after dinner had not been on my agenda. I had really planned to go back to the room, reflect on the day, prepare for my meeting tomorrow with Maria, and hit the sack. I also wondered what was so important it could not be discussed over the phone. However, I realized that I was in Anna's debt for the break on the room rate, and that I needed all of the information I could get, so I replied in the affirmative. I hated to rush my dinner, but La Posada was only about a ten-minute walk.

Dinner had been delicious and had really hit the spot. At this point, green chiles on just about anything would have done the trick. Because I was about to see Anna, I limited myself to just one Margarita. The waiter brought the check, I signed it, and I was off.

Santa Fe sits at almost seven thousand feet elevation. The nights are cool, and I was surprised when I stepped outside the door just how quickly the temperature had dropped once the sun went down. It made for a brisk walk. La Posada is just a few blocks from La Fonda, just east of the Cathedral Basilica. I arrived quickly, and slightly winded.

Similar to La Fonda, La Posada has been a Santa Fe landmark as a hotel since the 1930s. It had previously been a brick mansion built in the 1880s. The hotel sat on six acres just blocks from the Santa Fe Plaza. Over the years, the hotel had undergone several incarnations and had hosted numerous literature and cinema dignitaries and other well-known personalities. The bar was in the main building in a dimly lit, but cozy corner with couches and small table booths.

As I entered the bar, one of the bar staff came to me and said, "You must be Doctor Hunter."

Surprised, I joked, "Why, I did not know I was so well known."

The waiter smiled, saying, "You fit Ms. Pacheco's description. Let me take you to her table."

I saw Anna in a corner booth. Her hair was smartly pulled back into a bun, much like you would see on a flamenco dancer. Tonight, she was wearing a red blouse with silver buttons adorned with a silver and turquoise Zia necklace. She smiled and, as before, held out her hand saying, "Scott, I am so glad you could come on a moment's notice. Please have a seat."

I sat and the waiter took my order of another Margarita, the one I had expected to have at La Plazuela.

"Well, Anna," I began, "we are again meeting in a non-La Fonda venue. This must be important. I am curious about your text, and why now?"

Anna, already with a gin and tonic in hand, replied, "Scott, I told you a lot at breakfast yesterday, but I was not sure you would be staying. You had not yet committed to Rebecca whether or not you would be staying, and I wanted to see how serious you were before I told you more. Now that I know you are committed to helping identify Blake's murderer, I thought you needed to know one more detail."

As Anna began talking, Miguel's words of caution were in my mind. I knew I had to be very careful to listen and not offer Anna anything in return that would compromise my work with Miguel.

"Okay," I responded, "that's fair. Please continue."

Anna went on, "I mentioned to you that one of Blake's charms was to identify what others needed and to provide it, creating an obligation vacuum.

"Obligation vacuum?" I queried.

"Yes," she continued. "It is when you have done someone a favor and, either explicitly, or implicitly, they owe you one in return. Kind of a quid pro quo, often uninvited and unwanted like the seventy-fifth birthday party he orchestrated for my mother. I knew nothing about what he was doing except for us to meet him at La Fonda. I thought it may have been for dinner. But both the scope and scale of the event went far beyond the pale, so to speak. The moment I walked into the room and saw a catered ballroom, full of friends of my mother's that she had not seen in ages, I knew I owed him. I did not know what, when or on what scale, but I knew I was in his debt. That is an obligation vacuum."

"Now I understand," I said. "And this is in keeping with his sophisticated manner of manipulating others ultimately for his own interests. Please go on."

She resumed, "Blake lived by the rule, "no risk, no reward," but he took it to another level. His appetite for recognition, power, and wealth drove him to take greater and greater risks. He wanted to dominate business partners, not just collaborate. He was not interested in being simply an investor, he always wanted to be in control, even though he was the minority investor!"

I interrupted, "I pretty much figured that out after our initial conversation. But what is different that you have not told me?"

"One word," she quipped. "Cocaine."

"Cocaine?" I answered, a bit surprised. "You mean Blake was involved with cocaine?"

Anna was quick to answer, "I do not think he was a user, but rumors have been rampant that he was a provider. I do not know his source, and I am not one hundred percent certain that it is completely true, but I have heard enough anecdotal stories that suggest that one way he would get wealthy and prominent people in hand was to introduce them to cocaine and then be able to use this to blackmail them. He was ruthless.

His objective was not to make money on the drug sale. In fact, he usually gave it away free. He was more interested in using the fact that they had used cocaine for his benefit. Remember, these are very well-respected, and highly influential, people. They are trusted and serves as model citizens in the community. The knowledge of them using cocaine, even though it was supplied by Blake, became the ultimate obligation vacuum—"I know something damning about you and you have something I want."

"Wow," I exclaimed. "This really opens up the possibilities as to motives other people may have had to want him dead."

"That is why I wanted you to know, Scott," Anna interrupted. "Over the years Blake had developed many followers, and many enemies. The possibility that he had provided cocaine to people of influence only increases the number of those whom Blake may have angered. That would include those whom he may have been blackmailing for favors, like city officials and legislators; business partners that he wanted to dominate; and, possibly, even family members of those whom he could intimidate. Add this to the list of people who did not like Blake for business reasons and you have a fairly long list."

"This is reminiscent of what we have heard about Jeffrey Epstein, luring in people of influence to have sex and drugs with underage girls. Very sinister and eerie," I replied sadly.

"I wanted you to know about Blake's reputation as a someone who had used drugs as yet another way to buy influence. I also wanted you to know of the trap Rebecca may have felt herself to be in. However, I have never spoken with her specifically about this," Anna responded.

When Anna mentioned Rebecca, it made me think of seeing Rebecca with Charles Kahn. I decided to take a risk and further my inquiry.

"Anna," I began, "when I saw Rebecca earlier today her personal attorney, Charles Kahn, was just leaving her house. What can you tell me about him?"

After a long pause, Anna replied, "Charles is a well-known attorney in Santa Fe. Because Santa Fe is a small town, it is not unusual for attorneys to provide a wide range of legal services. Charles is no exception. He has had a relationship with Blake and Rebecca for several years. He has helped draw up business contracts, as well as purchase agreements. He even helped them a few years ago rewrite their pre-nuptial agreement."

"Re-write their pre-nup?" I asked a bit confounded.

"Yes, their pre-nup," Anna went on, "I do not know the specifics on whether Rebecca pressed, or Blake wanted to be magnanimous, but the final document was provided for Rebecca, in the event of Blake dying first or if they divorce. Again, I do not know the specifics and Rebecca only mentioned it in passing, but I know Charles helped them with the final document."

"Anna," I interrupted, "can you tell me more about Charles Kahn and the relationship he had with Blake and Rebecca?"

After a pause, Anna continued. "Kahn has been in Santa Fe about ten years, give or take. When he came here from California, he joined a small law firm. Within a couple of years, he went out on his own. He was more of a generalist lawyer, undertaking any work that came his way. His previous law firm had some serious heartburn when he left because he took several clients with him. While that may be common in big city California, it is a no-no here in Santa Fe. In his own practice, he also became the defense attorney for some shady characters. He always seemed to find legal loopholes, or questionable connections, to get them out of trouble. In general, he was not highly respected in the legal community."

Anna took a sip from her glass and continued, "He arrived in Santa Fe already divorced. He was known as a lady's man but never got serious with any of his companions. He was socially active in town, frequenting fundraisers, and other big social events. He was seen as always being in a 'sales mode,' trying to get new clients. He was particularly adept at identifying older unmarried, divorced, or widowed women and convincing them to turn over their legal matters to him. He began working with Blake on legal contracts for Blake's business ventures. That legal work expanded into helping Blake and Rebecca with wills and, most recently, the pre-nup. It was common to see Kahn and the Martins together at social events. In some respects, Blake and Kahn were both seen as always being "on the prowl" for new ways to profit from the vulnerabilities of others."

My head was spinning and I had more questions I wanted to ask Anna, but decided that having had two stiff Margaritas and heeding Miguel's counsel, I would end it there.

"Well, Anna," I said wanting to close down the conversation. "This is all very helpful information. It also broadens the scope of what I will look for. Keep in mind, though, that I have told Rebecca I would be here only two weeks. I will work hard to see what I can find. Also, I really appreciate your earlier offer on the reduced rates at the La Fonda. It will help immensely."

"My pleasure," Anna added.

"I am really bushed," I said lamely. "And I have a lot to think about before tomorrow, so I am going to call it a night. Thank you so much for the additional information."

"I totally understand and thank you for meeting me here on such short notice," Anna concluded.

I waived to the waiter for our check and, in spite of Anna's protest, I picked up the tab and bid her a good night.

In walking back to La Fonda, the chilly wind in my face helped revitalize me. This investigation was beginning to feel like a bowl of spaghetti, pull on one strand and it is connected to four more. Where would it end? I hoped to get some rest before trying to figure out the meaning of all of this information.

35

I walked back into the hotel, gave a nod to the desk clerk who was new to me, and headed up to my room. As I opened the door, the blinking message light on the room phone indicating a voice message caught my eye.

"Well, shit," I thought to myself not wanting to have any more interactions tonight.

I dialed nine to get the message, "Hey Scott, this is Miguel. Sorry to bother you so late. I thought about calling your mobile phone but thought I might catch you in the room. Give me a call whenever you get in. I have some more information for you. Bye."

I was already on information overload and really did not want to have another conversation tonight. But, being an only child, I had always been taught to put work before pleasure. So, I dialed Miguel's mobile phone from mine.

On the first ring, I heard, "Hey Scott. I saw your name on caller ID. Sorry to bother you so late, but I have some news for you that may be helpful in your talk with Maria tomorrow."

By now, I was again fully present and knew that Miguel needed my attention.

"Hi Miguel. No problem. I just got in from having a drink with Anna Pacheco," I said. Actually, it occurred to me that it was good to let Miguel know about my time with her now so that I would not forget and surprise him at a later time.

"Anna Pacheco," he said surprised. "I hope you did not reveal anything to her about our work together."

"Of course not," I replied, almost irritated. "She texted me about something that she wanted to let me know that she had not previously told me. I just let her talk. Believe me."

139

I then went on to tell him of my previous conversation with her about hotel charges being sent to me rather than to Rebecca and her unexpected text to me. I further explained to him about her revelation about Blake and his potential dealing cocaine to lure and manipulate.

"So," Miguel replied, "she thought that Blake might be enticing his associates to use cocaine and use the knowledge of their using cocaine to further extract favors. Very interesting. Well, I have some interesting news for you. Just after we talked earlier, the Chief called for a special meeting of the murder taskforce and forensics. The forensics came back with information from Blake's autopsy and the crime scene. In addition, at the Chief's request, the Arson Investigators briefed us on their conclusions from the fire at the Guadalupe restaurant."

"Wow," I exclaimed. "Quite a day. I am anxious to hear what they were."

Miguel replied, "Two interesting findings have emerged regarding the homicide. First, they were able to find a shoe print left on the back stoop of the gallery. Because there had been some rain the afternoon prior to Blake's murder washing away previous prints, they believe the shoe print was someone who may have entered the gallery after the rain. The interesting thing was that the shoe print was a tennis shoe print, size nine. Their speculation is that it may have come from whomever was riding the bicycle. It may be a long shot, but a nine-size shoe would suggest either a large child, or a shorter than average adult."

Miguel had mentioned the bicycle tracks before, but I had discounted it as either a random kid goofing around in the parking lot or a delivery. Now, I was not so sure.

Noting my pause to think, Miguel went on, "Do you remember me telling you about the video we received from the mobile phone of the tourist on East Marcy that we were going to review?"

"Yes," I said with greater interest.

It was dusk, and the video was not of high quality. While the video wasn't of the best quality, it had images of our bicyclist. The bicycle was black with those oversized low-rider handlebars. The rider of the bicycle was a male who appeared way too large for the bicycle, dressed in baggy pants and a black hoodie, and appearing to be at least in his twenties, riding toward the gallery about fifteen minutes prior to what we believe was the time of the assault, and returning about seven minutes after our estimated assault time. In addition, it was clear that the bicyclist had a small backpack and, get this, was wearing tennis shoes. It is at least circumstantial evidence."

I wondered if this sighting was somehow related to Anna's earlier information that Blake had been dealing drugs. What did not make sense was that this person obviously did not appear to be someone described by Anna as either influential or important given Blake's very high-level colleagues and clientele.

Thinking that was all of the news about the gallery, I replied, "This really does put a different spin on things, doesn't it?"

"Wait," Miguel said eagerly, "there is more. The results of Blake's blood test came back, and Blake had a lethal amount of cocaine in his system. The cocaine had been mixed with a significant amount of fentanyl. He did not die from the blow to the head. He had a heart attack."

"What?" I said unbelieving. "A heart attack? This is beginning to sound really crazy and convoluted. Are you thinking this could have been some kind of drug related death and not related to any of the previous POIs?"

I was secretly proud of myself, using police lingo POI for person of interest. I was showing off to Miguel just a bit.

"We now believe that drugs are in play, but we are not ruling out anything," Miguel replied ignoring my cleverness.

"Okay, but what does this have to do with my meeting with Maria in the morning?" I asked, puzzled.

"Well," Miguel said excitedly, "There was one more shocker that came out in the forensics meeting. The Arson Investigators have just completed the final evaluation of the Guadalupe restaurant fire and determined that it was, indeed, arson. That is why I wanted to call you tonight prior to your meeting with Maria. It will appear in tomorrow's morning edition of *The New Mexican*. The Arson Investigator was going to call Roberto Montoya as a courtesy tonight to let him know what was coming. Maria will doubtlessly know as well. However, the Chief has decided not to release the additional information about the shoe print, cell phone video or cocaine yet. He does not want to give away too much information and have any suspects go underground. So he has not given that information to the press yet."

After a pause to let me soak in this new information, Miguel continued, "Now as you talk with Maria, in addition to trying to identify the unhappy customer who confronted Blake at the Guadalupe party, you can begin to see her reaction to the Arson Investigator's report."

I responded, a bit bewildered, "Miguel, the fire was a few weeks ago. Why is the Arson Investigation just now over?"

Miguel answered in a solemn tone, "The investigators wanted to be certain of their conclusions. The Guadalupe restaurant is a Santa Fe landmark, tied to the political and social activities of the city, and even the state. You may know that the Guadalupe has for decades been the hangout for legislators and influencers. It is a place where heavy negotiations have taken place and important deals have been struck. According to the senior Arson Investigator, most restaurant fires occur in, or near, either the kitchen or some kind of leaking gas line. Kitchen fires will create a hot spot, indicating where the fire has begun. However, this fire appears to have been started with an accelerant in the main dining room, not the kitchen. The investigators checked, and double checked, their data because the legal and insurance implications of an arson are far different from just an accidental fire. That is why it has taken longer than usual for them to reveal their findings."

Things were happening fast. I had an immediate rush of anxiety and apprehension. The notion of getting in over my head revisited me, but I was in too deep now. I took a deep breath, exhaled, and spoke, "All of these new revelations certainly opened other avenues that were not even visible before. I need to spend some time preparing for my meeting tomorrow with Maria."

Miguel interrupted, "Look, Scott, do not over prepare. Remember, the main reason you are seeing Maria is ostensibly because of your interest in networking as you consider returning to Santa Fe. It is important to be yourself. If you over prepare, you may come across as either stilted and stiff or as having another agenda. Just use your interviewing skills as a psychologist to draw information from her during the course of your conversation."

Miguel's counsel was the same advice my clinical professor in my doctoral program had given graduate students prior to seeing our patients. She would encourage us to be prepared but, in order to build any rapport, we had to listen, be empathic, and demonstrate a concern for our patient's plight. She counseled, wisely, that if we appeared scripted, we would be perceived as too formal and more like mechanics than like caring counselors. The advice was as good then as it is now.

"Thanks for all of the updates, Miguel," I said wearily. "You are right.

I think what I need is a hot shower and a good night's sleep. I will let you know how the meeting with Maria goes."

We said our good nights and I proceeded to bed, not quite making it to the shower. I set my phone alarm for six o'clock, knowing I had a big day ahead of me.

36

The sound of my phone alarm jolted me out of a deep sleep. It was six o'clock, and I knew I needed to get up and get going for my nine o'clock with Maria. By the time I had showered, shaved, and dressed, it was closing on seven o'clock. I decided again to forego a large breakfast and went to the Concierge Floor lounge. As I entered, there was only one other guest present and one of the wait staff. The room is set up somewhat like the living room of a house with couches, love seats and some small tables with chairs. This morning there was a buffet with various fruits, scones, scrambled eggs, a variety of cereals, juice, and coffee. I filled my plate with some eggs and one scone to go with my orange juice and coffee.

The television was by the couches and turned on to the local news. For the second morning in a row, there was a BREAKING NEWS banner across the bottom of the television screen. The reporter was giving the public the information I had received from Miguel the night before about the Arson Investigator's findings of the Guadalupe restaurant fire. The reporter did not have any more to add to the story than I already knew. Based on how Roberto had looked the day before, I was certain the news was hitting him hard. It would be interesting to see how Maria would react. I finished my breakfast and went back to the room to freshen-up, picked-up my notepad and pen and left.

I had a little time to kill before I was expected at Maria's, so I decided to take a walk along the Santa Fe River. The morning air was crisp as I exited the hotel and strolled down the two blocks to the riverwalk. The Santa Fe River is seasonal at best and is more of a stream than a river. It is a small tributary of the Rio Grande with a dam in Santa Fe canyon northeast of the city where the river flow is regulated. Like many cities in the southwest, Santa Fe is dependent on the annual snowpack in the mountains. If there is a healthy snowpack, the Rio Grande flow is sufficient and there will be ample water for residential needs. The Santa Fe River supplies about forty percent of the city's water supply. Residents have learned how to conserve water, and the city is one of the best in the country in terms of water conservation. Nonetheless, there have been times when water restrictions have been in place. Today, being near the end of the seasonal flow, the stream was just barely flowing. The river walk itself was lined with large elm, cottonwood and oak trees providing cool shade in the summer months. In addition, there were benches and grassy areas for relaxing. I decided to sit for a few moments to collect my thoughts.

Many of the facts being uncovered had the Guadalupe restaurant in the center. First, Rebecca mentioned that there had been some kind of problem between Blake and a supposed disgruntled client of the gallery that took place at the Guadalupe. She had also mentioned Blake's foul mood after that evening.

Next, the Guadalupe was burned to the ground just after the Roberto and Blake had some kind of business deal gone bad. Roberto had confirmed this by his dislike of any association with Blake and the possibility that Blake may be involved in the fire.

The final piece of information was that the Arson Investigator's report that the fire at the Guadalupe had indeed been arson, turned the case in a clearer direction.

I knew that my upcoming meeting with Maria had added importance, and the potential for some volatility, now that Maria and Roberto both had been able to think about the Arson Investigator's report overnight. I also had to wonder if the association between Blake and cocaine had anything to do with the falling out between Blake and Roberto. I hoped to find out the individual with whom Blake had an altercation; the degree to which Blake and Roberto were involved from a business standpoint; and Maria's perspective on the Arson Investigator's report.

Having collected my thoughts, I left the park bench and continued my walk to the office building where I would meet Maria. I arrived at the office just before nine o'clock and Marcy greeted me, less eagerly than before with, "Hi Doctor Hunter. Right on time. Maria is just finishing up a meeting and will be with you momentarily. Please have a seat. May I get you some coffee or water?"

"Good morning Marcy. Thank you for setting this up. I am fine for now, thank you," I responded.

I sat down in a rich dark brown leather chair in the waiting room. I did not have to wait long. The door to Maria's office opened, and preceding Maria out of her office was a tall, muscular, clean-cut man in his mid-thirties. He was wearing a tight fitting, but fashionable, polo shirt, black jeans, and tennis shoes. As Maria exited, she held her hand out to me and said, "You must be Scott Hunter."

I simultaneously reached out my hand to shake hers and said, "Yes, and you must be Maria."

She smiled and replied, "I am. And Scott, this is my friend Julio Gonzales. Julio has been working with us as he awaits his entry into law school in just a couple of weeks. He recently retired from the military and is on to bigger and better things."

Smiling and slightly uncomfortable with Maria's introduction, Julio also reached out his hand saying, "Nice to meet you, Scott. I know you are meeting with Maria, so I will be on my way."

We shook hands and Julio walked out of the office.

At that point, Maria invited me in and, like Marcy, asked if I would like water or coffee. I declined and she began, "I may be a bit distracted this morning. If you saw the morning news, you probably know that the fire investigation of the Guadalupe has just determined that arson was the cause. We are trying to sort through the report and all of the implications."

I quickly responded, "Yes, Maria, I heard and am so sorry for what you and your father must be going through. If you would like to reschedule, I completely understand. I know you must have a lot on your mind."

Maria graciously replied, "No, Scott, this time is fine as long as you know that I may get interrupted. We have already scheduled some meetings this afternoon with our attorneys and insurance agents to review our options. My father mentioned that you were a Santa Fe native and had been living away from here for some time. He also mentioned that he had known, and respected, your father. That in itself is an endorsement. Please, tell me how I can be of assistance."

For the first time I had a chance to fully take-in Maria. She had a confidence about her that indicated a comfort with herself and with her audience. She had jet black shoulder-length hair, big brown eyes, an unblemished olive complexion, and a facial symmetry that was striking. She wore a white blouse, a silver Zia necklace inlaid with turquoise, and a smart looking black velvet jacket with silver buttons. She was gorgeous and I was awe struck.

I caught myself after my short enchantment, and said, "Thank you for your time and I perfectly understand if you have to leave. Again, my condolences for the loss of the Guadalupe."

"Thank you," she said a bit impatiently indicating that she was ready for me to get to the point.

"I left Santa Fe several years ago for personal reasons. I have reestablished my life, and career, and I am exploring returning. Santa Fe has changed since I left, and I am out of touch with any of my previous contacts. Anna Pacheco suggested that your father would be a good resource and your father recommended you," I paused to let this all sink in.

"My father mentioned that you had been referred to us by Anna. She is a long-time friend and a very successful businesswoman. Dad also mentioned that you had some affiliation with Rebecca Martin," Anna added.

I knew this was a defining moment in the meeting. Under explain and I would be treated with skepticism. Over explain and I could be seen as trying to curry favor. I had to be honest, direct, to the point, and relatively short.

"I left Santa Fe because of my divorce to Rebecca. She subsequently married Blake Martin after having had an affair when we were married. I left humiliated and resettled in Bozeman, Montana, not thinking I would ever return. However, she called me last week out of the blue, telling me about Blake's murder and asking me if I would be willing to talk with her about supporting her through the investigation. It was a strange request given the circumstances, and I had to think long and hard before accepting her offer. Since I have been here, I have experienced a personal reconnection with Santa Fe that I thought was lost. I have also re-established clear boundaries with Rebecca so that I will support her to some degree, but I am considering moving back," I said, having rehearsed this part of my introduction since having met with Roberto. I steeled myself for Maria's response.

"Scott, it is important that you know that I have no love lost for either Rebecca or Blake. I believe that Blake may have had a hand in the fire at the Guadalupe and it has really been devastating to our family. I have seen my father age before my eyes. His life, his heritage, and his place in this community have largely been defined by the Guadalupe. While we in no way celebrate Blake's demise, I saw him as a person who would take advantage of anyone to advance his own position of power and wealth. Just before the fire, he tried to manipulate my father into letting him become a part owner of the Guadalupe. When dad declined, Blake stormed out of the meeting with a veiled threat. That was the last time we saw, or heard, from Blake. Two weeks later the Guadalupe burned down. Now we know, it was the act of an arsonist. To say I am suspicious is an understatement."

A long silence fell over the meeting. I needed to continue the conversation while empathizing with Maria. I wondered to myself what to say next.

37

As Maria thought again about the arson and about Blake's murder, her dark eyes, typically warm and inviting, were now steely cold. In spite of the loss of the Guadalupe, she could not resist the smirk. "Revenge really is sweet," she thought to herself. She had been waiting a long time for Blake's downfall. She would never again have nightmares about how violated she had felt by his flirtations and suggestive comments over the years. The anger and internal rage she felt was overwhelming, all the while having to be pleasant on the outside because of the benefits he promised to bring to the Guadalupe and to her father. She had to laugh at herself. Now, Maria Montoya, had finally lived to see the score settled. With all of the years of plotting and planning, she could not have planned a better ending. She had felt almost delirious upon hearing the news of his demise, in spite of her grief over the fire. She knew that she was going to have to manage her public face so that she could appear to be as shocked and grieved as all of their mutual acquaintances would be. Her only regret was that she had no one with whom to share this wonderful relief she felt in response to his demise. Yes, there was a God after all.

I broke the silence. "I cannot imagine what you, and your family, must be going through. It is important to me that you know that I had no love lost for Blake either. He and Rebecca were having an affair that ultimately ended up with our divorce. Part of the reason I left town was because of the humiliation, and betrayal, I felt from the affair. Because Santa Fe is such a small town, I felt like I was always looking over my shoulder or around corners to avoid anyone who might be aware of the betrayal. It did not take long to decide that I needed to relocate to someplace where I would be anonymous and reestablish myself. My anger toward both Blake and Rebecca was immense. I only returned because I hoped that by helping

Rebecca I could finally put closure on what had been a bad, but unfinished, situation."

Jolted out of her reverie, Maria lifted her head and stared directly at me, piercing me with the intensity of her gaze, "Scott, at minimum, we have the same enemy in common. Knowing that makes it easier for me to help you. Now tell me how I can help."

I told Maria about my background as a psychologist and the change I had made from providing therapy to individuals to consulting with businesses. I briefed her on the issues about which I worked with organizations, including executive selection, leadership development, succession planning, strategy development, and Board of Directors facilitation. I mentioned some of the industries with which I had experience. Understanding that Santa Fe is not a hub of large companies, I made certain that Maria knew that I worked with small and medium sized businesses and those that were privately held. In fact, a large amount of my work had been with entrepreneurs and business founders as their companies grew and required a more professional approach to management. Knowing I had limited time, I decided to give her only the headlines about my work and let her ask for more information as she needed it.

After my brief overview, Maria responded, "Based on what you have told me, there are a number of businesses in both Santa Fe and Albuquerque with whom we have contacts. I am very active in our local economic development commission, and I would be pleased to offer you some personal introductions once we get through all of the legal and insurance issues related to the Guadalupe fire."

Then, Maria walked to a file cabinet and pulled out a small file titled "Area Businesses." She handed it to me and said, "On your way out, have Marcy make a copy of these for you. Take a look at them and decide which of these you would like to pursue. Give me a few days, and once you are more specific about the businesses you want to approach, set up a time with Marcy to meet again and we can discuss in more detail."

"This is most generous," I gratefully replied. "Thank you. I will study the list and get back to Marcy in a few days." Recognizing the meeting was coming to an end, I got up to leave.

"You are most welcome." Maria said graciously, "The next visit, I will be able to give you more undivided attention. There is one thing you should be aware of as you begin meeting others in the community. I would encourage you to downplay your relationship with Rebecca. There are many people in the community whom Blake had offended, manipulated, or had taken advantage of. That included not only business associates but extended to customers of his businesses. In fact, the last time Blake was in the Guadalupe was for an invitation-only exclusive art showing. A rowdy, uninvited, guest appeared at the front door asking for Blake. If my father had not been trained in diplomacy, it could have become very ugly, and very quickly. The man turned out to have been one of Blake's gallery customers who was accusing Blake of swindling him by selling him a six-figure painting that was not authentic. He even commented that he wanted to strangle Blake. We were able to appease the gentlemen, but it took all of the peace keeping we could muster to avert a disaster. All this is to say, proceed with caution."

I thought Maria's warning was not only sage, but very kind, given that I was asking her for assistance, had nothing to offer in return, and had an affiliation with Rebecca. Upon hearing of the conflict, I knew he was the individual about whom Anna Pacheco was referring and whose name I needed to get to follow up with.

I responded, "Maria, you have been most kind and helpful. I heard about Blake's altercation with one of his gallery customers at the Guadalupe from Anna. Do you happen to recall his name?"

"Tyler King," Maria quickly responded. "He is a Houston oilman who has a second home here at Las Vistas. He was a bit inebriated and that only made the situation tenser. But eventually we were able to manage it. I really need to go now, Scott. Check with Marcy and I will see you again in a few days."

"Again, thank you," I said emphatically and appreciatively.

As I left I checked in with Marcy who obligingly copied the file for me and promised to call me to set up a new appointment with Maria once she knew her schedule given all of the meetings to come.

Leaving, I realized again, how much I had to process.

38

As I reflected on my conversation with Maria, I was taken with how understandably angry she was with Blake Martin and how both Maria and Roberto considered Blake to be a logical suspect for the fire of the Guadalupe.

I was also curious about having met Julio Gonzales and the relationship he had with the Montoya family. I was particularly interested in the fact that he had high-level military training and wore tennis shoes like Miguel had referenced from the cell phone video. Could this make him a suspect in Blake's murder, I wondered.

Finally, as Miguel and I had discussed, I had not only gotten the name of the gallery customer who had been upset with Blake, but having consulted in the oil industry myself, I began thinking of a way to meet with him. Maria's description of the intensity of his anger along with both the cost and the humiliation of feeling swindled, seemed to make him a possible suspect.

It was still early in the day when I left the meeting with Maria. As I rolled through all of the directions I could take, I decided that there were three things I needed to do: I needed to bring Miguel up to date; I needed to find a way to meet with Tyler King; and lastly I needed to call Rebecca. While I did not want to call Rebecca, I knew that if I called her, and was prepared with what I wanted to tell her, I could control the conversation and reduce any chances of revealing any information that was really critical to the case.

As I walked back to the hotel, I once again took the route along the Santa Fe Riverwalk. At this time in the morning, it was still relatively free of traffic and I could talk on my mobile phone without the scrutiny of others. I dialed Miguel's number and after the second ring, he picked up. "Hey Scott, what's up?"

"Hi Miguel," I answered. "I just met with Maria and want to bring you up to speed on what I know."

I then reported to Miguel about my meeting with Maria, the anger the Montoyas felt for Blake, meeting Julio Gonzales, and getting the name of Tyler King. I also gave him my plan for getting in front of Tyler King. I also mentioned my plan to contact Rebecca to manage her anxiety.

"Good work," Miguel said, sounding a bit astonished that I had progressed so fast in acquiring information. "This information definitely helps in sorting out our POIs. You should know that we have contacted Rebecca and asked her to come to the station tomorrow morning so that we can interview her further about Blake's murder. She said that she would be bringing her attorney, Charles Kahn, with her. I imagine the interview will be on her mind when you talk with her. Proceed very cautiously. Also, Scott, once we have had the interview with Rebecca tomorrow morning, you may need to make another decision. If we cannot eliminate her as a POI and you continue to work underground with me, you will need to further distance yourself from Rebecca. If you do not, it could compromise the investigation. If she is eliminated as a POI, you can continue to have a relationship with her given the boundaries you set up earlier. Let's talk again after we interview her."

Knowing that this was likely coming, and after hearing about Maria's counsel not to seem too involved with Rebecca given all of Blake's potential enemies, I was prepared to further distance myself from her.

"I understand and I will wait on your guidance following the interview this afternoon," I said.

After a few more comments, we hung up and I dialed Rebecca's number.

"Oh Scott, I am so glad you called," Rebecca said foregoing any greeting. "I have just received some really bad news and I need your help in putting things in perspective. I was concerned after our last conversation that you would be abandoning me."

I responded in the most empathic voice I could, "Really, Rebecca. What has happened?"

"I got a call this morning from detective Montez's office asking me to come in for an interview tomorrow morning," she said sounding either angry or frantic. "Why do they keep hounding me instead of going out to look for Blake's murderer? They are treating me like a suspect."

"Rebecca," I interrupted, "I am sure this is all part of standard police protocol. They want to be sure that they fully understand all of the circumstances surrounding Blake's murder, including his enemies and others whom he may have offended over the years. All you can do is be open and forthcoming," I said the last sentence realizing that she had not been that way with me.

"I am sure you are right, Scott. I just needed to hear it coming from someone I trusted. I also am going to take my attorney, Charles, with me. You met him briefly the other day," she replied.

I winced when she mentioned that I was someone she trusted. While I was not against her, I was not being totally forthcoming myself. I rationalized this behavior by thinking that while I was acting for the greater good of finding Blake's murderer, I could not always be forthcoming in the short-term.

"I always think it is important to take your attorney with you when discussing legal issues," I confirmed. "I am sure that the interview is routine and simply part of police procedure. I just wanted to call to let you know that I am still working to try to identify anyone who may have had cause to hurt Blake. I will keep you posted as I come up with something definite."

"Thank you so much for calling, Scott. I do not think I could get through this without you," Rebecca said plaintively, "I know you are in my corner, I just needed some reassurance."

We continued for another minute or so and hung up with my suggestion that I would call her in a couple of days.

Now, I needed to turn my attention to getting an interview with Tyler King. Having previously consulted in the oil and gas business, I knew of a couple of CEO contacts I could lean on as a means of getting a meeting with King. One of the larger, and ongoing, projects I have worked on was with MontCo Oil and Gas. MontCo was a multi-state oil and gas exploration company with sites as far south as the Wattenberg oil field in Colorado to as far north and east as the Bakken oil fields in North Dakota. Having begun in Montana, MontCo maintained its headquarters in Billings. I had worked with the CEO, "Rambling" Jack Wilbanks, for the past five years. He had gotten the nick name "Rambling" because he was always looking far and wide for opportunities, not content to focus on a single area. This had been a very successful strategy for the business. Initially, I had done work evaluating executives for hiring and development. The work had quickly expanded to succession planning and helping leaders develop high-performing teams. I knew that Jack appreciated the work I had done for him and would be a good reference. He was well known in the Oil and Gas industry. I would start by putting in a call to him.

39

I had the direct number of Jack's executive assistant, Deborah Millsaps. Like my assistant, Dorothy Weston, Deborah was very efficient with a wicked sense of humor. I dialed her and she picked up on the first ring.

"Jack Wilbanks office, this is Deborah," she answered formally and professionally.

"Hi Deborah, this is Scott Hunter. How are you doing? Are you still running the place?" I said in the comfortable bantering way Deborah and I had developed.

"Well, if it isn't the infamous Doctor Hunter. Of course, I am still running the place, I just need to make sure Jack knows," she teased back. "What may I do for you today?"

I went on to explain to Deborah my interest in making contact with Tyler King and whether or not Jack knew him.

"Know him," Deborah exclaimed astonished. "They go pheasant hunting together every year together as a part of the annual Western Oil and Gas Association conference. I would say he knows him!"

"Do you think Jack would be willing to serve as a reference for me to get an introduction to Mr. King?" I asked confidently.

"I am sure he would," she said. "But, why, may I ask do you want an introduction? His company is based in Houston."

I explained that I am expanding and that, after all, Houston was only a plane ride away. We talked a bit more and she suggested I talk to Jack directly. She went ahead and put me through to him.

"Scott," Jack opened in his animated style. "Where the hell are you and why aren't you here tending to my flock?"

"Hi Jack," I continued matching his bantering tone. "I am taking a few days of vacation. The way you and your people ride me, I need a break every now and then."

"Deborah mentioned you wanted to use me as a reference for Tyler King. Please feel free to use my name, as long as you let him know two things. First, tell him that I said he couldn't hit a pheasant if it landed on the tip of his rifle. Second, I have first dibs on your time. What do you think?"

It was a compliment to the relationship we had developed for Jack to have the level of comfort with me that he had to banter. I was delighted that he would be willing to help.

"Thank you, Jack. I will pass the sentiment on to him. Now that I know you will serve as a reference, I will call his office today. You may get a call from him confirming that I am a reputable consultant," I said pleased to have the reference.

"No problem, Scott. Now let me get back to making some money so I can pay you your outrageous fees! You may need his direct number, so I will transfer you back to Deborah."

As he transferred me back to Deborah, it felt good to have the confidence of one of my largest clients. Now to turn Jack's reference into a meeting with Tyler King.

I called the Houston number that Deborah had given me as a direct line to his office. A friendly voice answered, "Tyler King's office, this is Anita. How may I assist you?"

"Good afternoon," I replied. "My name is Scott Hunter and I was referred to Mr. King by Jack Wilbanks, the CEO of MontCo Oil and Gas. Is Mr. King available?"

Before I could get the final word out, Anita said with a chuckle, "If Jack is referring you, I can probably get you through to Tyler. Jack and Tyler are old friends. By the way, has Jack figured out yet that Deborah is running that outfit up there?"

"Yes, I think Jack knows the score," I kidded back.

"Well," Anita began again, "we may have to wait another couple of weeks or so for me to schedule anything with Tyler. He and his family are at their vacation home in Santa Fe at the moment and not expected back until the end of the month."

"What a coincidence," I said feigning surprise. "I am in Santa Fe myself taking a couple of weeks of vacation here. Any chance I could see him here?

Anita answered with a bit of skepticism in her voice, "That is a coincidence, what are the odds? I tell you what, give me your mobile number and I will pass it on to Tyler. If he wants to interrupt his vacation to see you, he can call you. If not, call me back and I can set something up early next month. Will that work?"

"Absolutely, Anita. You are most kind," I replied, giving her my contact information. "Thank you so much for your assistance."

From my history in consulting, I knew that Executive Assistants hold the keys to the Executive's calendar. I always treat them respectfully and as a peer. There is no faster route to being written off than to underestimate the power of a good Executive Assistant.

We wished each other a good day and hung up. I now waited for a call from Tyler King.

40

It had already been a productive morning and was approaching lunch time. I knew I had to wait on Tyler King's call before I could talk with him face-to-face. I decided to walk to a small restaurant across from the river and get a salad and some tea. I could sit on the restaurant patio, collect my thoughts, and think about next steps.

I had only walked about half the distance to the restaurant when my mobile rang. I could tell by the caller ID that it was a Houston area code. It was either Anita calling me back, or Tyler King.

I answered as I always do to unfamiliar calls, "Hello, this is Scott Hunter."

"Hi Scott," Tyler King began. "This is Tyler King, I understand that Jack Wilbanks suggested you get in touch with me."

I explained to King my work with Jack Wilbanks and MontCo and that I was familiar with the industry. I also mentioned that I was expanding and Jack suggested I call.

At the end of my brief description King replied, "So you are one of those shrinks that looks under the hood to see what makes a CEO tick. Well, Jack certainly needs that kind of work," he jokingly said. "Actually, we at King Oil may need some of that kind of work ourselves. I know this is short notice, but Anita mentioned that you are here in Santa Fe yourself. If you can come out here to Las Vistas, I will buy you lunch and we can chat. We are about twenty minutes from the Plaza."

Delighted and somewhat startled by the quick lunch offer, I replied affirmatively. We hung up and I texted for an Uber. Within two minutes I was sitting in the Uber and the driver, Marcus, and I were off to Las Vistas. Knowing I would need a ride back, I got Marcus's direct number, asked him to stay nearby once we arrived, and slipped him a twenty-dollar bill.

As King mentioned, Las Vistas is about twenty minutes southwest of the plaza. It is a luxury guard-gated golf community. While it had been in existence when I had previously lived in Sana Fe, I had never been there. It was known by Santa Feans as an enclave of the wealthy separated from the rest of the community. Having come from a working-class family, living in such a complex was beyond our means or ability. I was curious to see what it was like.

As the Uber driver pulled up to the gate house, I rolled down my window to speak to the attendant. "Hi. I am Scott Hunter and have a meeting at the clubhouse with Tyler King."

"Yes sir," he replied. "Mr. King is expecting you."

The attendant gave my driver the directions and we drove through what was a much larger, and more sparsely settled, reserve than I would have imagined. The 360-degree views were expansive with the mountains to the north and west and the desert plains to the south. The sight was truly remarkable. The clubhouse was designed in the traditional Santa Fe adobe style with porches, round wooden columns, and Vigas extending from above the porches. It was much larger than I had anticipated. As we pulled up to the clubhouse, we were greeted by yet another attendant who had obviously been called by the gatehouse guard. He came to the back door of the Uber, opened it and like the gatehouse guard said, "Good day Mr. Hunter. Mr. King is expecting you."

I thanked the Uber driver and he departed. The clubhouse attendant escorted me through the lobby and the restaurant to an outside patio. At a more remote part of the patio there sat Tyler King with a cold beer in hand waiting to greet me.

As I approached the table, King held out his hand to greet me. I gave him a firm handshake and thanked him for both meeting me on short notice and inviting me to lunch.

King appeared to be the consummate Texas oil man. He projected an overly familiar presence, appeared to be very confident, and was on the flamboyant side. He wore a cowboy hat, expensive cowboy boots that had not seen much wear, a loud print shirt and a big silver belt buckle. He had money and wanted to project that fact to those whom he met. At the outset, my psychological antennae were up and I suspected that there was a lot of Tyler King in Tyler King.

It had been my experience in working with executives, that those who were really at home with themselves did not have the need to announce their success through ostentatious behavior or attire. Self-assured executives were typically humble, demonstrated a genuine concern for others, and needed little in the way of public adoration. They had a deep appreciation for all of the help and assistance they had received for their success. They never came across as entitled or as smarter than their audience. I was hoping that my initial impression of Tyler King was inaccurate, particularly since he seemed to be a friend of Jack Wilbanks.

I began by thanking King for being willing to meet and some introductory chit-chat about his relationship with Jack Wilbanks. We then ordered lunch prior to proceeding. I noticed that King asked for another beer before his first one was completed. He tended to treat the wait staff somewhat abruptly and demanding. They clearly anticipated his behavior, and their response was always somewhat obsequious with a "Yes Mr. King," or "My pleasure Mr. King," or "Great choice, Mr. King." While their remarks were not far off from what you would expect in good wait staff behavior, there was always an overly deferential tone, as if they were King's personal servants. Interesting, I thought.

Once our order was in, I asked King about himself, his business, and his success. This lit him up and he talked non-stop for the next fifteen minutes about his favorite topic, Tyler King. I got a lesson in how smart he was, what a good dealmaker he was, and how well others thought of him. He also talked about times that he had manipulated or out-flanked others to get oil leases and other business deals. He did not grasp that by talking about his business behavior, he was also revealing his values—win at any cost and no means were too outrageous to reach the goal he wanted. His bellicose discourse increased in volume and scope after the second beer.

Finally, he asked about me and the work I had done for Jack Wilbanks. I knew that people who thought that highly of themselves really wanted to talk more than listen, so I only gave him the headlines of my consulting with MontCo Oil and Gas. I was already thinking to myself that working with King would be a consultant's nightmare, King would always know best and if you raised any suggestions that varied from his, you would be history. These kinds of narcissists are always wanting to negotiate fees, pay late, and sometimes stiff you altogether. I had to remind myself that the real reason I was here was to determine if King may have been a legitimate suspect in Blake Martin's murder. I was not really seeking to work with him as a client, thank God!

I had an opening to talk when King asked what brought me to Santa Fe. I told him about growing up here, leaving for Bozeman, and thinking about returning. I was careful not to mention my relationship to either Rebecca or Blake. I mentioned that I had begun making inquiries into the business community and had met with several business leaders including Anna Pacheco and Roberto Montoya.

At the mention of Roberto Montoya's name, King put his beer down firmly on the table and said, "Are you talking about the guy who owned the restaurant that burned down?"

I nodded my head.

King went on saying, "I saw him just before the fire. I had gone to his restaurant to find some asshole who was trying to cheat me out of a boatload of money. Lucky for him that Montoya was there to calm me down. Otherwise, I would have strangled the son of a bitch on the spot."

As he spoke, I could see King's face turning red and the veins on his neck begin to throb. This had obviously struck a nerve.

"Who was the person who was trying to cheat you?" I asked faking naivete.

King, face still red, said, "He was a gallery owner and a real shyster named Blake Martin. He sold me a very expensive painting that he said was an original. When I had my art estimator examine the painting, he said it was a forgery. I knew he was going to be at Montoya's restaurant that night. They were having an invitation-only art show and many of my Las Vistas neighbors were invited. Think about this, I had just paid him two hundred fifty grand for a goddamn forgery, and he does not even invite me to his fucking art show. Really! I wanted to kill the bastard."

He paused and I asked, "What happened then?"

King jumped back in with, "He was supposed to meet me to settle the issue and in the meantime, someone knocked him off!"

"Knocked him off?" I queried.

"Get this, he was murdered in his own studio. I heard he had been hit on the head. Probably someone else he had fucked over got to him before I did," King said with a sneer.

"What happened to your painting?" I asked further.

"I have my attorneys on it. We will be filing a lawsuit against his estate. Believe me, no one cheats Tyler King and gets away with it," he finished.

I was struck at how raw, and how deep, King's anger was. I was seeing narcissistic injury unfold before my eyes. Granted, he was on his second beer, at least that I knew about, but I wondered if this kind of rage could have elicited a homicidal response from him. In my mind, King's behavior did make him a suspect. He clearly would have had motive, and the obelisk was the means, the question was whether or not he had the opportunity. I also remembered that when they can, narcissist will get others to do their dirty work so that they can have plausible deniability. He would undoubtedly have had someone else do the dirty deed.

By this time, others were drifting into the restaurant and King was beginning to attract the attention of these guests. I had the information I had wanted, and I was anxious for the conversation to be over. I needed to find a graceful way to end it.

Typically, when I have an initial meeting with a potential client, I probe for areas where they may need help in ways that align to my services. The goal is always to further the discussion to begin the process of putting together a proposal for work at a subsequent meeting. In this case, I had no interest in further meetings, so I began the process of concluding the meeting.

I began, "Tyler, I hope your attorneys can get to the bottom of this and you are able to get all of your money back. It sounds like this guy was a real con artist."

"Believe me, my attorneys will be as ruthless as I would have been, over-turning every stone until we get the money back," King snapped.

I continued closing down the conversation with, "Now you know a bit about what I do, and you know Jack and can ask him about the work I have done with him. I really do not want to take up any more of your vacation time, you have been most generous. What if you think about what you may need and, when you are ready to discuss further, let me know?"

With a bit of a slur in his speech, he said, "That sounds like a plan, Scott. I will contact you once I have thought more about how you might help."

I thanked him for lunch, got up, reached out my hand to shake his, and departed. I have rarely been as glad to leave a meeting as I was this one. I texted Marcus to bring his Uber back to the clubhouse and we left heading back to the hotel.

I really needed some time by myself to put all of the information I had into perspective. I needed to be alone and not interrupted. I knew that there was a rooftop bar at the La Fonda. Hopefully, I could find a quiet corner and put my thoughts together to determine next steps.

41

As I arrived at the hotel, it occurred to me that Rebecca and her attorney, Charles Kahn, were probably talking now, creating a strategy for their interview in the morning with Miguel. I wished I could have been a fly on the wall for that interview! I went up to my room to freshen up, got my notebook and pen, and headed up to the Bell Tower bar on the fifth story rooftop.

Because buildings in Santa Fe are limited by code to five stories, the view from the Bell Tower bar is unobstructed and breath taking. It is possible to see the Sandia mountains to the southwest, the Sangre de Cristo mountains to the northeast and everything in between. It is the perfect place for a romantic date. Unfortunately, not for me. I had work to do. The bar was not yet crowded, so I found a private table in a shady corner. Since it was still just mid-afternoon, and I had to be clear-headed, I ordered chips and guacamole with a virgin Bloody Mary. At the rate I was eating, I knew I would have to get back to my exercise routine soon or I would be paying a price!

I got out my notebook and begin making some notes about what I had learned over the past couple of days. As I often did, I reflected first about what I knew to be true and then I tried to understand the why or who.

First, there was Blake's murder. I knew he had died of a heart attack due to an intravenous drug overdose delivered to him sometime close to the hit on the head, indicating that the murder had to have been premeditated. This definitely took the murder out of the realm of a crime of passion, or a spur-of-the-moment argument. While being hit from behind could have suggested some level of pre-meditation, the delivery of the dirty cocaine made it clear. I had also heard of rumors of the possibility that Blake was into drug trafficking.

Second, the police forensics team had few real clues except for the presence of latex traces on the murder obelisk, tennis shoe prints at the scene, bicycle tracks in the parking lot, and a fuzzy cell phone video of a large child or small adult on a bicycle, wearing tennis shoes.

Third, I had heard from various sources that Blake had many enemies, myself included. I knew by descriptions of his business practices, that he was not above manipulating, or even lying, to get what he wanted. This had been confirmed by Anna Pacheco, the Montoyas, and Tyler King.

Finally, but lower on the list in my mind, Rebecca and Blake's marriage had become one of convenience rather than one of passion. The rewriting of the pre-nup could be somewhat suspicious.

As I reviewed what I knew, I began thinking through what kind of person would have had a sufficient motive to actually kill Blake. From all of the great training I had received in detective work from Dateline and 48 Hours, I knew that murders fell into one, two, or all three, of these categories: money, love, or revenge. I knew as a psychologist that there are times when everyone can feel so angry as to want to injure someone who may have betrayed them. I also knew that it was the rare person that followed through on such criminal urges.

I also had learned that the initial, and often primary, suspects of murders were those closest to the victim—family or friends. I knew that Miguel would be interviewing Rebecca for that very reason or, as Miguel said, to eliminate her as a POI. It did not compute that Rebecca would have wanted me to be assisting her in finding the killer if she herself had been involved. I thought it was unlikely that she was a serious suspect. However, I also knew that Blake and Rebecca's relationship had become contentious because Blake had begun to cut Rebecca off financially.

Having worked for the last several years consulting to business executives, I thought about business partnerships that have gone poorly. In my experience, when there is a desire to injure the perpetrator, the drama is typically played out in court. It is not unusual to see high levels of bravado, lots of testosterone, and back biting with heated exchanges between two dueling parties trying to determine who has the biggest balls. However, it is unusual for the bluster to get beyond the posturing stage. When it does, it is almost always settled by the attorneys.

164

However, both the Montoyas' loss of their livelihood and the destruction of their long-revered Santa Fe legacy could rise to the level of anger in which murder could be an option. Considering Roberto's connection to the legislators and to law enforcement, and the degree with which the community admired him, who knows? Having briefly met Julio at Maria's office elevated my suspicions a bit.

With regard to Tyler King, narcissists have been known to be highly vindictive. But wealthy narcissists never do their own dirty work. The hallmark of narcissists is to never be seen as having made any kind of mistake, and certainly not one that is criminal. Narcissists work to create plausible deniability by distancing themselves from a crime, even if they believe it to be justified. If King were the culprit, his money could have bought the muscle needed to murder Blake. To have been publicly humiliated into purchasing a forged painting for two hundred fifty thousand dollars would be sufficient reason to want revenge. In addition, the narcissistic rage I saw indicated that King was not the least bit dismayed by Blake's demise.

The rumors about Blake's involvement in drug trafficking were interesting, but uncorroborated. While rare, it is not uncommon for people of wealth and influence to want to have more of both. Sometimes after these high-flyers have experienced the vapidness of having everything they thought they wanted, they turn to something riskier to heighten their adrenaline rush. Both the use of drugs, and the involvement in the drug underworld by wealthy and prominent people is widespread. The deaths of several prominent singers, actors, and celebrities by drug overdose has been well documented. It has also been noted that a few business executives, both in the United States and Canada, have been the financiers of sophisticated drug trafficking.

Because the illicit drug world is a very shady one, the individuals with whom you associate are typically not fine, upstanding citizens. Could Blake have gotten crosswise with the wrong crowd, I wondered. If so, this would have broadened the scope of suspects well beyond my willingness to get involved. I did not want to have inquiries lead to my kneecaps being shattered by a hooded man in a dark alley some night when I least suspected it. I may be adventuresome, but I am not reckless.

As I looked up from my rooftop location, I could not help but be struck by the contrast between the darkness of the world about which I was reflecting and the incredible beauty of the view I was absorbing. There was an other-worldly feeling to the moment as I observed the depth of the New Mexico blue sky against the still snow-covered peaks of the distant mountains. Was this paradise, I smiled and asked myself? I also noticed that the high altitude left me thirstier than a virgin Bloody Mary could quench. I caught the eye of my waiter and asked for a tonic water with ice and lime. I spent a few more minutes reviewing my notes considering my next move.

42

By now, I believed that the Montoyas, Tyler King, other deceived business associates, and some drug lords might have reason to want Blake dead. While there may have been several who also wanted him dead, the level of injury inflicted on the Montoya family and King rose to the level of high interest. Money and revenge were two possible motives in all cases. I was puzzled, that I had not identified anyone who might have wanted Blake dead for love. Maybe his libido had waned as he aged. Or maybe this was another avenue that had not come to my attention. Given the fact that the murder scene did not have any signs of a struggle, along with the post-concussion administration of cocaine, his murder seemed clearly pre-meditated. It was obvious that some kind of pre-planning was involved. This was not an in-the-moment crime of passion.

Just then, my mobile phone rang. I could see by caller ID that it was MontCo Oil and Gas. This had to be either Jack Wilbanks checking in, or his assistant Deborah.

"Scott Hunter," I answered.

"Scott," I heard in a loud man's voice. "It's Jack Wilbanks. How did you get on with Tyler King?"

I was actually glad that Jack called. After having met King, I could not really understand Jack's affinity for him.

"Hi Jack, good to hear your voice again," I replied and then asked quizzically, "Tell me again why the two of you are friends."

"Well, Scott, we are not actually friends," Jack said mildly defensively. "Why did you ask it that way?"

Without giving him the real reason I wanted to meet with King, I went on to explain to him our conversation. I told him about King being somewhat inebriated, loud, boisterous, and particularly elevated in his speech when he told me about being conned by a local gallery owner.

Surprisingly, Jack laughed saying, "Sounds like King. The reason I mentioned to you that he could not shoot a pheasant if it was at the end of his rifle, is that he was often inebriated on our pheasant hunts. In fact, we gave him the nickname 'Dick' after Dick Cheney's hunting calamity shooting another hunter. We always knew to stay behind King on our hunts, not in front of him."

Jack chuckled, then continued. "Another habit of King's was to always complain about how someone had screwed him out of a deal. He was always bellyaching about someone or something. He was also an incessant bragger about how influential he was, how much money he had, and how he was so much smarter than all of his competitors. We all saw King as more of a character than a serious businessman. He inherited the company from his father. King is the ultimate rich kid who thought he hit a triple but was really born on third base. We knew to divide anything he told us by at least two, because of his tendency to embellish."

Shocked, I replied "I thought you were good friends. Why didn't you tell me this? I was feeling a little odd that after meeting him, I did not want to do pursue him as a client."

"I wanted you to experience King without any pre-conceived notions. If you had thought of him as a sophisticated executive and one you wanted to work with, I would have questioned your judgment. Hell, I would have probably fired your ass on the spot," Jack said with deep laughter.

I was actually relieved to hear Jack's assessment of Tyler King. It aligned with mine. It also made me begin to question if King was a real suspect in Blake's murder or just another loud, boisterous, and annoying trust fund baby who was full of himself. Narcissists are notorious for drawing attention to themselves by telling the world how great they are and by debasing, humiliating, or outright lying about their perceived enemies. Narcissists try to intimidate by bullying, but their bark is often worse than their bite.

"One more thing," Jack said with a bit of caution in his voice, "be careful of King. Even though he is regarded by his peers as a buffoon, he is not above doing something nefarious for his own self-interest."

"What do you mean," I asked.

Jack continued, "Our business is one where we all know, or know about, each other. King has a reputation for having literally stolen oil rights from unsuspecting, and usually elderly, property owners. In fact, when he has had a few whiskey sours under his belt, he brags about just how devious he has been, thinking the rest of us would see his trickery as brilliant rather than ruthless. In any case, be careful."

I was a bit stunned to hear this, thinking that I could simply think of King as a spoiled, ineffectual, entitled, trust fund baby. This information again raised my doubts. Jack and I completed our conversation with a commitment to get together for lunch when I returned to Bozeman.

I was no longer questioning whether King was a bona fide suspect and worthy of more attention, or someone I should scratch off the list. I had to consider him in play. The Montoyas' loss was also cause for revenge. Now that the Fire Inspector had determined that the Guadalupe was arson, it added more fuel to the fire. I smiled to myself at my own metaphor. The Montoyas would have had ample reason to get back at Blake Martin for the fire and King continued to have reason for being publicly duped into purchasing a fake painting for six figures.

It was now early evening, and I had used up this full day. I decided to go to the Concierge lounge on my hotel floor, pick up a beer and some hors d'oeuvres and call it a day. I took the elevator down to the lobby, waved to Christina at the front desk, and headed to my room. As I crossed the lobby, I could hear my phone ping, indicating I was getting a text message.

The text was from Miguel. It simply said, "Are you available now?"

I texted back, "Yes."

Miguel texted, "Come to the south entrance of the station. I will be waiting outside for you."

So much for that beer and hors d'oeuvres. I was a bit perplexed about where he wanted us to meet, since he was particularly wanting my involvement with him to be on the q.t. I walked out of the hotel toward the plaza, crossed the plaza and walked two blocks up Lincoln Street and toward the police station.

As I approached the south entrance, I could see Miguel waiting for me. We shook hands and, opening the side door, he said, "There is something I want you to see."

43

The hall was dimly lit as we made our way through the corridor. The station was quiet with most of the staff either having left for the day or out on patrol. Miguel was particularly cautious and walked slightly in front of me, checking to see if there was anyone who might see me with him and raise suspicion. At the end of a long corridor, Miguel placed his name tag against a reader that unlocked a door. He opened the windowless door and invited me to step in. Only after he closed the door did he turn on the light. The room was dimly lit and had what appeared to be shelves of boxes along with a couple of small televisions. It must have been the evidence room with limited access. Miguel invited me to sit down in one of two chairs in front of the television. At the same time, he retrieved a USB flash drive from an evidence box that simply said, "Martin homicide."

"I just received this flash drive from forensics this afternoon. The video is from a CCTV tape and, because of a lower resolution quality, forensics had to send it off to a lab in Denver for more sophisticated analysis Once I saw it, I thought that you needed to see it as well. It may well be the break in the case we are looking for."

I sat down curious and, surprisingly, a bit anxious, about what I was about to see. Miguel turned on the television, inserted the flash drive and clicked the Play arrow.

The video was obviously taken at night and with a low-resolution CCTV camera. The image in the video was an adobe building. The only light in the video came from a streetlight that appeared to be about a block from the camera.

"Keep watching," Miguel instructed. "You will see something of interest momentarily."

After about thirty seconds of the video of the building, smoke began to emerge from what appeared to be the back side of the building.

Then flames were visible, first only slightly licking up over the back of the building, and then more fully engulfing the edifice. It was then that something caught my eye in the upper right-hand corner of the video. There was some movement, but initially hard to decipher. It was only on the screen for a few seconds, but even though the image was murky, there was a person on a bicycle! The video continued for another thirty seconds with the building fully consumed and the bicyclist out of the frame. It then stopped abruptly.

"What the hell," I thought to myself as I tried to interpret what I was watching.

"What am I watching, Miguel," I asked.

"You are watching the torching of the Guadalupe," Miguel said with emphasis in his voice. "Let me show you the same video again in slower motion."

I sat through the same video, but this time with renewed interest at what I was seeing. At the point in the video where the movement in the upper right-hand corner began, Miguel stopped the video and enlarged the image. There was a blurry, but obvious, image of an individual riding a bicycle for which the individual was oversized. In addition, you could make out that the individual had on what appeared to be high top sneakers!

"I think this is the same individual that we saw riding away from the Martin Blake Gallery on the cell phone video image provided us by the tourist," Miguel explained. "If that is so," he went on, "then we have a stronger motive for the Montoyas wanting Blake to pay a price for having the Guadalupe burn down."

"I am not sure I fully understand," I said lamely.

"Let's get out of here and get discuss this over a drink. I need to get checked out here, so I will meet you in fifteen minutes at the bar at El Meson over on Washington Avenue," Miguel directed.

With that, he carefully led back down the dark corridor to the door to the street.

the Martin

44

I made the short walk to El Meson and found a quiet high-top table in the back of the bar and waited for Miguel. El Meson is a restaurant and tapas bar. There was regular entertainment in the bar area, but being a weeknight, it was fairly quiet.

A lovely waitress named Raquel attended me. I did not wait for Miguel to arrive. I was thirsty and hungry. I ordered an Estrella Damm, an imported beer from Spain, and a Plato de Quesos Artesanales, a cheese platter.

In relatively short order, Miguel arrived, ordered the same beer, and dove into my artisanal cheese platter. I should have ordered two!

"Well," I began, "what do you think all of this means?"

Miguel went on to explain that, if the bicyclist on the CCTV was the same bicyclist as on the cell phone video, then the arson at the Guadalupe and the Blake Martin homicide were somehow connected. It also suggested that, if they were tied together, our search definitely needed to focus on finding the bicyclist. He indicated that he would be sending the new video down back down to the forensic video experts to get a more positive determination about whether the two videos did indeed have the same bicyclist in them.

These videos did raise a host of new questions. Why would the same person who was bicycling away from Blake's gallery be torching the Guadalupe? What do the videos imply in terms of motive? Who, in addition to the bicyclist, does the video implicate? Or was this all a ruse to throw off the police and the investigation altogether? How could the burning of the Guadalupe and Blake's homicide be connected?

All of these questions needed answering and quickly. The longer the investigation proceeded, the more difficult it would be to solve. Another gem I had picked up from watching Dateline, 20/20, and 48 Hours!

With a greater sense of urgency, Miguel explained, "Look, if this bicyclist is the same person, we desperately need to find him. Also, if it is the same person and he is, also, in the drug scene, he will be going underground soon. He will smell the police a mile away. In any case, we cannot afford to have him get away, so we need to act quickly. As I told you before, we are short on resources and do not have any undercover police, nor do we have informants we can trust. I need to ask a big favor and get you involved with this."

Suddenly, I felt my face flush, a churning in my stomach, and slightly nauseous.

"Look, Miguel," I said tentatively. "This is out of my area of expertise and comfort zone. It is very different from trying to get information from people, especially in a public venue. In fact, getting people to talk is my bread and butter. It is quite another thing for me to associate with those in the drug underworld. I am neither trained nor prepared for this kind of dangerous work. I need to stick to what I am good at."

"I thought that would be your response," Miguel said smilingly as he took another date from the cheese plate. "But, Hunter, I am confident that you are up to the task. I remember when I was a field officer for the Bureau, we found that those junior officers who were less experienced were often even more effective at getting difficult information from suspects than those of us that had been around a while. They had not been over-trained and were not yet jaded. They were much less likely to be suspected of being with the Bureau because of their apparent naïveté. They were able to see people, and information, with fresh eyes that longer-term agents overlooked. I actually think your lack of knowledge would be to your advantage."

Miguel was obvious in his attempt to sell me on the idea and his reasoning did beckon me back to graduate school research with which I was familiar. Apparently, much to the chagrin of experienced psychotherapists, the research determined that those recently graduated therapists, earlier in their career, had similar effectiveness as those who have been in practice for some time. In addition, newer therapists were likely to be more attentive and to ask more probing questions than those therapists who had been around for a while. The research was controversial but had been successfully replicated on several occasions. I wasn't sure this line of thinking justified my getting involved in what could be a dicey operation. Also, while I did have graduate school courses in both addiction and in criminal behavior, that had been over twenty years ago, and it was all theory. I was dubious, at best.

"I don't know, Miguel," I replied haltingly. "This seems to be out of my wheelhouse. What do you think would be involved and would I come out of this alive?," I said with a slight grin.

Taking yet another slice of cheese from the platter, Miguel ignored my uneasiness and responded, "Now that I have your attention, we are going to need a little time to discuss it all more thoroughly." Having said that, Miguel beckoned Raquel to our table and was obviously familiar with her when he said, "Raquel, you look lovely as always!" as he reached out to give her hand a friendly squeeze.

"Oh, Miguel," Raquel said both a bit embarrassed, but appreciative, "you say that to all the ladies."

"Not at all, Raquel, only to you," he smiled. "Raquel, we are going to need the full menu. My friend, Hunter, and I are going to have dinner. Do you have a more private table in the back-dining room?"

Raquel led us to a very private alcove in the rear of the adjacent dining room, brought us menus and took our drink orders. The menu reflects food from Spain, not northern New Mexico. It was replete with various kinds of paella, as well as Spain's version of fish, fowl, beef, and vegetables. I was surprised at how hungry I was, even after the cheese platter. I ordered the salmon with blue crab and brandy cream sauce. Miguel went for the grilled beef tenderloin filet over mushroom, shallot, and Tempranillo wine ragout. We both ordered another Estrella Damm beer.

Seeing Miguel's friendliness with Raquel, I was no longer surprised by his seemingly knowing everyone saw in Santa Fe. This was the third occasion we had been together in different restaurants in which he had a cordial knowledge of the wait staff. These acquaintances spoke both to how Santa Fe is a small town and to Miguel's attentiveness to those with whom he came into contact. He took no relationship for granted. A good example for me!

"Now that we have ordered, lets talk about logistics," Miguel began, assuming that I had already accepted his offer to look for this potentially dangerous bicyclist.

Fortunately, the Estrella Damm had soothed my nerves somewhat, but with some apprehension, I could only wonder what Miguel was going to say next.

45

"Hunter, I always believe in starting with getting clarity on what we are trying to accomplish," Miguel began.

I noticed he said we. I thought to myself that this inclusion was either a high complement or part of Miguel's sales pitch, and possibly it was both. In any case, I knew to take the "we" reference with a grain of salt. This was certainly Miguel's case and my interest continued to be of some assistance to my ex-wife, Rebecca. Nonetheless, I knew that this most recent video development could play an important role in solving the case. Also, I knew that I had to continually push myself out of my comfort zone and become more adventurous. So, I was all ears.

Miguel continued, "Unbeknownst to you, and by design, I have been doing some investigating on my own. Given the new information and the urgency in trying to get this case solved, I think now is the time for me to bring you fully into my confidence."

I was both pleased, and surprised, by Miguel's frankness and willingness to fully include me. It had only been a couple of days since we had initially met at Java Joe's. Things had transpired rapidly. I noted that the time since Hunter's homicide was into the second week. Miguel was right, no time to waste.

Miguel continued, "I began researching the possibility that some kind of insurance fraud could be involved as I thought about Blake's murder, and especially because there had been artwork involved, including the missing Bierstadt painting at Martin's gallery; the fire at the Guadalupe, where artwork from Martin's gallery was being showcased; and the complaints of Tyler King about Martin's representation of the value of artwork. Who could benefit from insurance on the art if Blake Martin was dead?

"When you think about all of the connections to the artwork, it makes sense," I confirmed.

Miguel went on, "When I began understanding the potential value of all of the art involved, including all of the art on display at the Guadalupe, the stolen Bierstadt painting at the gallery, and the disputed artwork being held by Tyler King, the value came to millions of dollars. At the Guadalupe alone, there were twenty paintings and another six sculptures on loan from Martin's gallery. The value of those was close to an additional million dollars."

"But who could profit with Blake dead?" I challenged,

"Well," Miguel said in his best imitation of Keith Morrison on Dateline, "that is the question, isn't it?"

The master sleuth continued, "I found out that Tyler King, Roberto Montoya, Blake Martin and, surprisingly, your ex, Rebecca, had all either taken out insurance policies on a number of pieces of the art consigned to the gallery or, in Roberto's case, he had increased the insurance on the building. Shortly before Blake's murder, Rebecca added her name to the insurance policy that Blake had purchased on the art. It makes sense that Blake would have insurance, given the value of the art in the gallery. But why would Roberto have significantly increased the insurance policy for the Guadalupe? And why would Rebecca have added her name to the insurance policy that Blake already had in place? It made some sense for Tyler King to have insurance because of the very expensive, but questionable Blumenschein painting he had purchased."

"How did you dig up all of this information? It must have taken hours of research," I asked.

"We had a little luck finding the insurance information," Miguel said with a chuckle. "It seems that insuring fine art, collectibles, and antiquities is a particular product that only some of the larger or specialized insurers provide. I snooped around with some local gallery owners whom I know and found that many of them have the same insurer, Antiquities Assurance, Inc. of New York. Fortunately, they have an agent who concentrates on the Santa Fe art market, Robin Goldstein. I contacted Robin, secured the legal waivers allowing her to talk with me, and what she said was quite interesting."

"Please," I pleaded, "tell me!"

At that moment, Raquel arrived with our orders. The sight, smell, and presentation of the dishes were magnificent and served to amplify my hunger! Raquel suggested Spanish wines she thought would complement our meals, to which we eagerly agreed. Without waiting for a response from Miguel, I took my first bite of the salmon deliciously covered with the crab and brandy cream sauce. OMG, I was temporarily transported to another place by the incredible tastes and textures of the dish. It took me a moment to recoup and refocus on Miguel.

"Oh, yes," I said, recovering, "please tell me what Ms. Goldstein had to say."

Smiling at the voraciousness by which I attacked my meal, Miguel continued. "Robin informed me that insurers are not at liberty to disclose details of an insurance policy except to those who have had it underwritten. Of course, because we had the legal documentation in place, she was able to disclose information to us. She also said that she thought it was unusual to add other names on insurance policies but that she allowed it because Blake and Rebecca were married. These issues are usually taken care of in a person's will. She also noted that in Tyler King's case, it was common for high end art buyers to take out policies to protect the value of their purchase. It appears that neither of the policy holders knew of any of the other policies. In fact, she said that both Rebecca and Tyler repeated to her that their policies needed to be confidential, even though she had assured them that they would be."

After a pause for me to absorb what Miguel had just said, he resumed. "In Roberto's case, my cousin, Rueben Montez, manages the local office of the commercial insurance carrier from which Roberto bought his insurance. He willingly gave me the information that Roberto had significantly raised the value of the policy and noted that the appraisers suggested that his request was at the very top end of the value of the building and contents. Roberto argued persuasively that, since the Guadalupe was now in possession of several high-end art pieces they should be considered as contents related to the restaurant. In the end, the underwriters allowed the increased valuation, given that Roberto had been a long-term client and because of his good standing in the community.

I was struggling trying to get my mind around all of this new information, including the CCTV video of the bicyclist cycling away from the burning Guadalupe and the various insurance policies. All of this, in addition to the knowledge that Blake Martin had seriously pissed off any number of people, suggested that several people may have been involved in Blake's murder and all wanted to profit from it! I smiled to myself at the incredulousness of this hypothesis. Nevertheless, there seemed to be multiple motives increasingly possible for Blake's murder.

"Here is what I do not understand, Miguel," I queried. "I thought that no insurance would be paid on any of the items or property insured if arson is involved. Am I missing something?"

"Well, like many legal issues, that is subject to interpretation," Miguel answered. "There is no question that arson is a criminal offense. And, when an individual or corporate policy holder is involved in the crime, either through conducting the arson themselves or hiring it to be done, then insurance companies are not responsible for covering any claims. However, when arson is confirmed as the cause of a fire, and the fire is set by a person either unknown, or unbeknownst to the policy holder, the insurer may be responsible for paying the claim. It is a very tricky set of legal questions."

"Wow," I exclaimed, "just when I thought things could not get more complicated, all of this new information comes in."

Miguel replied, "More complex, but also narrowing the field."

"So," I queried, "where do we go from here?"

I noticed as I asked the questions that I said we, not you. I took this to mean that I was all in!

Miguel smiled at my saying we and continued, "As I see it, we have narrowed the motives down to that age-old cause, money. The art insurance policies, and the increased valuation of the Guadalupe all suggest that Blake's homicide was related to three suspects: Tyler King, Roberto Montoya, and Rebecca Martin. The nature of the homicide, the injection of a lethal dose of liquid cocaine, as well as Anna Pacheco's reference to Blake's possible involvement in selling cocaine also suggest some kind of drug connection. Finally, we have identified what could be the same person on a bicycle leaving both Blake's gallery on the day of the homicide and leaving the arson at the Guadalupe. Agreed?"

"Agreed," I responded.

Miguel continued, "Here is how I think we should proceed. I have asked Robin Goldstein and Rueben Montez to keep me informed, should anyone contact either about an insurance claim. I have a second interview set up with Rebecca tomorrow morning. You have already had initial discussions with King and the Montoyas. In the short term, they will not be going anywhere, but they will both warrant further investigation. In the short-term, I think we need to find out who this person on the bicycle is and question him. Assuming forensics believes it is the same person in both videos, and I think they will, he could be a vital piece of the puzzle. I think that if he thought the police wanted to talk with him, he would become a ghost-gone with the wind. He may be on that trajectory already. I think the smart move is for you to begin trying to identify this person."

"How do I even begin?" I contested.

"We have two avenues to pursue," Miguel responded. "First, because Blake died of a drug overdose, we have to believe that our killer had a reasonably good familiarity with drugs, and specifically cocaine. We have a list of suspected drug dealers and drug users in our data base. Assuming it is the same person in both videos, we are likely looking at a "hood for hire" that is related to be drug usage. Typically drug dealers are more involved in the sale and transportation of drugs than they are committing other crimes, so I think we are more likely to be looking for a user. I have been granted permission for you to be able to review that list with one of our homicide detectives as someone helping with the investigation. Hopefully forensics can identify more definitively information on the bicyclist's gender, approximate age, height and, maybe, ethnicity. This information will help you narrow down the suspects. We are looking for someone who is likely a user and has a criminal record including theft, assault, and possibly arson."

"Okay," I sighed, "what is the second avenue?"

Miguel quickly replied, "the second avenue is through the identification of the bicycle. If forensics can identify what kind of bicycle the individual is using, and we have the bicycle tire tracks from the gallery parking lot, we may be able to find out where the bicycle was purchased and cross-reference those purchasers with our data base of drug users. In addition, we have that tennis shoe print from the back step of the gallery. This may lead to the shoe brand and possible local stores. Again, we may get lucky and be able to use this source of information to help us identify our killer and our arsonist who may be one in the same."

While the process was full of detailed research and hypotheses creation, I found it to be much like my clinical training as a psychologist. When making a psychological diagnosis, the therapist uses multiple data sources to confirm or rule out hypotheses about an individual's pathology. While the intent of this homicide research was different, the process was similar. By researching multiple sources, referencing, and cross-referencing, I could hopefully narrow the list of suspects down to our bicyclist.

"When do I get started?" I asked with my enthusiasm surprising me.

"In the morning, come to the station. Ask for me and I will put you in touch with Sergeant Apodaca. He will assist you. Hopefully, we will have the forensics evidence for you by then," Miguel concluded.

We finished our meal and drinks, shook hands, and left El Meson, walking in different directions. It was getting close to nine o'clock and I was ready to call it a day. I began walking the four blocks back to the hotel when my phone buzzed. The caller ID was that of my ex-wife, Rebecca.

Having already spoken with her earlier in the day, I was not eager to talk to Rebecca again. I almost declined the call, but my conscience got the better of me.

Reluctantly I answered, "Good evening, Rebecca. What's up?"

"Oh, Scott, I am so sorry to bother you again. I am having a meltdown and just needed to hear your voice," Rebecca said plaintively.

I braced myself for what was to come next.

Rebecca continued in an almost desperate manner, "Scott, would you please come over. I feel like my world is falling apart?"

Aware that Miguel was going to interview Rebecca in the morning, I was cautious about agreeing to her request. I feebly protested, "Rebecca, it has been a long day and I am really beat. Could we do this sometime tomorrow?"

Sobbing, Rebecca pleaded, sounding like she had been drinking, "It would mean so much to me if you could come over, just for a few minutes. I need your perspective and rationality to calm my nerves. Please."

During the time we were married, I knew that Rebecca would tug on both my sense of responsibility, and any guilt, to maneuver my emotions. Back then, I had regularly yielded to her lamenting, believing that it was my duty as a "good husband." Even though through therapy, I had become cognizant of my tendency to please, I was reluctant to refuse her request.

Tiredly, I said, "Okay, Rebecca, but just for a little while. I will get a taxi and be there in a few minutes."

We said our goodbyes, and I caught a taxi at the hotel for the ten-minute ride to Rebecca's house.

46

The taxi quickly maneuvered the slight nighttime traffic, and we were at Rebecca's house sooner than I was expected. She buzzed us into the gated drive, my driver gave me his contact information for the ride back, and I knocked on her door.

Rebecca quickly answered and almost lunged at me, giving me a firm hug saying, "Oh, Scott, you cannot imagine how much it means to me that you came."

She kept her arms around me, and I found myself slowly sinking, smelling her hair, the faint odor of my favorite perfume, and her body pressed to mine. I began noticing a slight twitching between my thighs. I knew I was beginning to think with the wrong head. Catching myself, I took a deep breath and recovered.

I nudged both of us through the door frame and closed the door behind me. It was then I noticed that she had on a low-cut red silk blouse, black tight jeans and she was barefoot. I could smell the whiff of alcohol on her breath and her eyes were bloodshot. Under other circumstances, I would be eager to consummate the evening. But I was not tonight, and not with Rebecca.

She grabbed my hand and led us both to the couch, beginning with, "What can I get you to drink?"

Maybe it was the Spanish wine and beer I had at El Meson, but I was already feeling mellow. "How about just a tonic water with lime?" I asked.

Rebecca obliged and sitting next to me with her own glass of Chardonnay, began, "I told you that I am to be interviewed tomorrow at the police station. When I called you earlier, you helped me to gain some perspective. I have been such a fool. I only wished that I could have been a better, more mature, person years ago. I should have never gotten involved with Blake. You had been perfect for me-stable, predictable, honest, transparent. And I know you loved me for who I was. If I would have faced myself and my own craziness back then, none of this would have happened. You and I would still be married, maybe with a couple of kids, and a house in the foothills like we dreamed of. I need you to know that even though my love for you was far from perfect, and I was far from perfect, you were the best thing that ever happened to me. All of the drama with Blake was just my pitiful way of running from my own problems and trying to be someone else. It worked for a while, but facades never last for long."

Hearing Rebecca, I wondered where all of this was coming from and where it was going. Some of her monologue was what she had told me before. Was this just the alcohol talking? Was this a sincere attempt at some kind of repentance or was this yet another form of deceptive manipulation now that she was in the market for another breadwinner. I knew I needed to keep my emotions, and testosterone, under control.

"Why are you telling me this, Rebecca? And what was the meltdown you alluded to on the phone," I tactfully challenged.

Rebecca sighed, took another sip of her wine, and continued, her voice becoming quieter and less dramatic, "There are times since Blake's death that I seem to be holding it together. While we had developed a marriage more of convenience than commitment, I was well taken care of and had adjusted to living what most people would consider to be an extravagant life. Periodically, I did fantasize about what life without Blake would be like, but I never wanted him to die."

As she was talking, I was thinking about Rebecca having a meeting with Miguel tomorrow and was not sure just how deep I wanted this conversation to go. I did not want to sabotage that meeting by Rebecca revealing too much to me, rather than to Miguel. However, I was interested in what she had to say.

Cautiously, I responded perfunctorily, "Rebecca, you wouldn't have asked me to be here if you thought I believed that you were a part of Blake's death. What is bothering you tonight?"

After a long silence, Rebecca continued, "This afternoon, my attorney, Charles Kahn, and I were reviewing how we wanted to respond to Detective Montez' interview tomorrow. Our conversation brought up all sorts of feelings, going back years-the good times and the bad, the lies, partial truths, and maneuvering to be in the spotlight. For me, the review was like looking into the mirror of my life. It was a long and penetrating look into who I am and who I have been."

Rebecca paused, trying to collect her thoughts. Intrigued, I asked, "Tell me more about what you discovered."

Setting her wine glass down on the coffee table in front of the couch, Rebecca ran her fingers through her long dark hair, took a deep breath, and continued. "The image I got of myself wasn't pretty. I realized that I have led a totally selfish life, from turning my back on my parents to turning my back on you and distancing myself from Blake. I was not even honest with my therapist, always working to shape her view of me in a way that she would see me favorably before I finally left her! My entire life has been one big sham. For the first time, I am really ashamed of myself for all of the hurt I have caused."

While there was some satisfaction in hearing what Rebecca was saying about her revelations, I remained unconvinced. I remembered the saying, "Fool me once, shame on you, fool me twice, shame on me."

Rebecca continued, "All of this coming at me at once had an impact on me like nothing else has—not therapy, not leaving you, not realizing I was a fool for Blake. Nothing before has painted such a powerful revealing picture as the review this afternoon. I felt like I was in one of those surreal MC Escher drawings with all of the staircases leading to different levels and floors, but all of them connecting in some unusual way. The forcefulness of all of these streams of my life and my multiple undoings sent me reeling. After Charles left, I began sobbing unconsolably. That is when I called you."

Confused, I asked, "But why call me, Rebecca?"

She answered quickly, "I remembered that when you were doing therapy with couples you would say that being fully honest with yourself, accepting your flaws and owning your behaviors, is the first step to healing. I also recalled that you would often talk to them about openly, honestly, and completely, asking the other for forgiveness for behaviors that had been hurtful. In fact, you often said that redemption cannot happen without repentance. This came to me in the midst of the realization of the harm I had done to you and to others. When I asked you to come here to help me, I thought it was to help apprehend Blake's murderer. I did not realize that I needed help myself."

I was struck by what seemed to be Rebecca's vulnerability and candor. I also found myself to be strangely guarded.

I replied, almost clinically, "Rebecca, if your time with Charles and your review of your past will help you become more the person you want to be, than I applaud your efforts. I would recommend that you make the decision to find a therapist and commit to the kind of honest work required to make the changes you want to make."

I did not want to get pulled into any deep psychological discussions with Rebecca, especially while I needed to remain unbiased in order to help Miguel find Blake's murderer. That was neither my interest, nor my intent, in being here in Santa Fe. We talked for a few more minutes and I could feel the weight of fatigue begin to settle over me. It was approaching eleven o'clock and I was anxious for a good night's sleep, knowing that I would have another busy day tomorrow.

Rebecca, much calmer now, thanked me for coming over to "calm her nerves."

I called my taxi driver, we said our goodbyes, and I went back to the hotel for what I hoped would be a good night's sleep.

47

The alarm on my cell phone wakened me well before I was ready to climb out of bed. The evening before, I had barely enough energy to brush my teeth and put on my night clothes before falling into bed into a deep sleep. The early sunlight was peeking through my blinds alerting me that another full day lay ahead. I showered, got dressed, grabbed a quick breakfast and latte in the lounge and was off. Per Miguel's instructions, I made my way to the police station and asked the officer in reception for Miguel.

The officer asked my name and said, handing me an envelope, Miguel left this note for you. I opened the envelope and read the note. "Good morning, Scott. I have a meeting prior to interviewing Rebecca, so I will not be able to join you. Sergeant Apodaca knows you are coming. Ask the officer in charge to see Sergeant Apodaca and he will come to get you. We can catch up later. Miguel"

After reading the note, I asked the officer in charge to speak to Sergeant Apodaca.

In a very short time, I was face-to-face with a rotund, affable officer who approached me with a smile and his hand extended saying, "Good morning, Scott. I am Sergeant Edward Apodaca. Please call me Ed."

I introduced myself and followed him to a small conference room with a table, two chairs, a file folder, note pads, a couple of pens, and a computer. I was invited to sit at the seat adjacent to the seat that was in front of the computer. I let Sergeant Apodaca take the lead.

"I have been working with Miguel on the Blake Martin homicide. He informed me yesterday that you have been doing some undercover work on his behalf. As you know we are short-staffed, so we appreciate the help. Miguel told me that he has known you since high school days and to let you know all that we know about the forensics and local drug users

185

whose company we have had the privilege to enjoy," he said with a hearty laugh.

"Fortunately," he continued, "we have just received this file from our forensics team that worked late into the night to get this information. I will be seeing this for the first time with you. Hopefully, the forensics will point us in the direction of possible suspects. We will then take the relevant information to enter into our database to see if we can narrow the list."

I felt my pulse quicken as we began the process. This exercise began to feel like an episode of a mystery or crime series on television in which the team begins to examine evidence from the crime scene to determine a course of action. I was focused and ready!

Opening the file folder, there were four tabs labeled:

Video
Suspect
Shoes
Bicycle

We began reading the forensic notes.

As Miguel had mentioned, the forensics team had sent the videos to a lab in Denver for higher level analysis. The Denver lab analysis confirmed that the bicycle, and the bicycle rider, in both videos was the same individual. Even though one video came from a cell phone and one from CCTV, the analysis confirmed with a high degree of confidence that the individual and the bicycle were the same in both cases.

Miguel had suspected that the person was the same, and this confirmed some sort of link between the fire at the Guadalupe and the Blake Martin homicide.

With regard to the suspect, the forensics data was vaguer. They estimated the rider to be a male between 5'7"-5'10"; of either Anglo or Mexican descent; estimated weight between 140-160 pounds; and between 18-32 years old. The report detailed how they were able to get a 3-D 360-degree review of the tapes and match the characteristics to standard developmental data.

While this was not as specific as I had hoped, it would begin to rule out some individuals.

The information on the bicycle and tennis shoes was most interesting. I was surprised at the detail they were able to ascertain from the grainy videos. In addition, they were able to use the bicycle tire prints from the crime scene to further confirm their findings. The lab's description read:

> The bicycle is a stripped down black, lowrider bike with a 16" lowrider frame, 16" 52 spoke rear and front chrome wheels, 16" x 1.75" black, white-wall tires with "Lowrider" raised letters, extended (or ape bars) handlebars, black grips, a banana saddle, and no front or rear fenders.

The summary also indicated that these stripped-down lowrider bicycles had been seen in street gangs in smaller cities where drug dealers often had a group of "drug runners" working for them in exchange for a small fee and drugs.

The tennis shoes were also interesting. The forensics lab determined that the tennis shoes were Converse All-Star Chuck Taylor high-tops. The summary noted that, for years, gangs have been using athletic gear to represent their factions or gangs. They used the gear for recruitment and intimidation. It was a way to let the underground world know to which gangster community you belonged. The report also noted that the shoe print at the crime scene matched the brand and were between a men's size 7-9 shoe. This also helped them determine the approximate height of the suspect.

Also, a note at the bottom of the summary suggested that the suspect may have had a slight limp, as noted by the uneven pedaling as he left both premises.

After reading the summary, Ed looked over to me and said, "This forensic data could be very useful in determining our suspect. This is more information than we typically get from forensics."

"Where do we go from here," I asked.

Ed replied, now we can go to our data base to see if we may have a match. If we do not have a match locally, we can expand it. However, I believe that, because of the identity of the bicycle, the same person at both locations, and the tennis shoes, we will find our suspect locally."

"What about the tennis shoes," I pressed.

Ed continued, "Converse All-Star Chuck Taylor high-tops are the very brand used by a local gang, the West Siders. These shoes have been their trademark for years. In the local gang world, the West Siders are at the top of the pecking order. They have drug-related charges, theft, assault, and, even, one murder on their resume. In addition, we can review those local bicycle shops that both sell, and modify, low rider bicycles to determine their clientele. But first, let's begin with the database."

48

The database being used by the police department was a state version of the National Crime Information Center of the FBI. The database allowed searches in any number of ways, including by location, gender, height, weight, type of crime, age, current address and phone number, marital status, credit card ownership, and usage. The database also had photos of every individual from their most recent arrest or incarceration. There were also additional areas that could be accessed such as "gang affiliation." As Ed pointed out, the database was updated regularly, but was only as good as the recency of the information entered. Nevertheless, it was a good place to begin.

Using the information we had received from forensics, Ed began the search with keywords of Santa Fe County, white and Hispanic males ages 18-32, arrested for either drug possession or distribution, height from 5'6" to 5'10", weighing between 140-160 pounds, and belonging to the West Siders gang. He hit the "search" icon and we waited for what seemed to be an eternity but was really only about ten seconds.

Then, the screen read in a flashing banner, "8 individuals identified." This was followed by the listing of the individuals with their last known address and phone number, their last interaction with local law enforcement officials, and the crime of their last conviction.

Ed smiled and said with satisfaction, "Now we are getting somewhere. This is a Who's Who of the West Siders." He printed the list, and we began to scroll through it.

William "Billie" Brownhouse
Juan Escobar
Max Gonzales
Marco Oliveras

Diego "Dorie" Reina
Pablo Rodriguez
Joe "Rascal" West
Lawrence "Shorty" Wilcox

Upon reviewing the names, Ed began, "I know everyone one of these characters and have either been involved in their arrests or their convictions. I know we can begin eliminating some of them and narrow our focus. Why don't we take a thirty-minute break, and I can quickly get some information about these guys? I will text you when I am ready to give you an update."

"Sounds good," I said. "I think I will run down to the coffee shop in La Fonda and get a coffee. Would you like me to pick you up one?"

Very quickly, Ed responded, "That would be great. Could you pick me up a large Chai Tea Latte?"

Smiling at Ed's coffee acumen, I said, "Sure. Be happy to."

I left the conference room and turned right to exit. Just as I was about to leave, I caught a glimpse of Rebecca and her attorney, Charles Kahn entering the building through a more remote door. I had temporarily forgotten her interview with Miguel. I knew that Miguel was also taking a DNA sample and Rebecca's fingerprints. I quickly ducked into the shadows. I did not want Rebecca to know how closely I was working with Miguel. I departed the building and headed for the plaza to get our coffees and await Ed's text.

49

I had just picked up our coffees and my phone alerted me that I had received a text that Ed was ready to review his finding.

Rushing back to the police station, I mused to myself that I was actually having fun with this process. I was helping solve a puzzle, much like trying to get a definitive diagnosis with patients. It was always gratifying in my former work as a therapist to land on a diagnosis from all of the data points collected and begin putting together a treatment plan. This was eerily similar.

Upon returning to the conference room, and giving Ed his Chai Tea Latte, he excitedly let me know that he had narrowed the list of suspects. He showed me the list with his notation to the side of their names.

William "Billie" Brownhouse – living in a half-way house in Albuquerque since last year.

Juan Escobar – currently incarcerated in Lovington, suspected of drug trafficking

Max Gonzales – deceased. Died under suspicious circumstances in Taos four months ago.

Marco Oliveras – whereabouts unknown. Last previous sighting was in El Paso, Texas.

Pablo Rodriguez – living in Santa Fe and working for High Desert Landscaping company.

Diego "Dorie" Reina –working in a local motorcycle shop, Mikes Bikes and Repair.

Joe "Rascal" West – working at a local car repair shop for two months, Johnny's Motors.

Lawrence "Shorty" Wilcox – living with his mother and working with a local construction company for six months, Zia Home Building and Renovation.

After reviewing the list, Ed added, "There are four suspects on this list, and I can eliminate Joe West. After speaking with West's parole officer, he had permission to attend his father's funeral in California the days surrounding Blake Martin's murder. That leaves us with Pablo Rodriguez, Lawrence Wilcox, and Diego Reina as suspects we need to eliminate. These are the three for you to focus on in your inquiries."

As Ed directed my attention, I began to realize the seriousness of the work to which I had committed to with Miguel. I began to feel anxious, hoping Ed would not be able to see my nerves fraying.

"Can you tell me more about these three?" I asked.

"Sure," Ed responded. "First, it is important to know that the drug world was only one of the West Siders' criminal activities. They have also been suspected of fencing stolen goods, human trafficking, the prostitution business, and a systematic focus on terrorizing local businesses for 'protection services.' The leaders of the gang are smart and have been very difficult to actually pin down for certain crimes."

He continued, "Two of the three suspects have been lower-level operatives in the gang's hierarchy. However, each one of them has been arrested for drug usage, but not drug dealing, also petty theft, and, in the case of Pablo Rodriguez, assault. Rodriguez has spent time in the penitentiary for assault with intent to kill, but the charges were subsequently reduced to just assault. In the gang world, the way to move up in the gang's hierarchy, is to become bolder in the crimes you commit. This can include things like taking greater risks with large thefts or even killing members of rival gangs. If we determine that one of these suspects has been involved in either the burning of the Guadalupe or the homicide of Blake Martin, the crime would qualify for their 'promotion' in the gang."

I sat astonished at how much was known about each of these criminals and how relatively quickly, through forensics and the data base, Ed was able to narrow down the list. Hearing about their previous crimes and, especially, how gang members got "promoted," I realized that I was not dealing with your average business owner, like Tyler King. I did not want any of these criminals to get promoted on the basis of have "offed" a certain psychologist, namely me!

"So," Ed continued, "I think you should focus your efforts to determine which of these characters might be our main suspect. Once your

192

investigation has uncovered 'the one,' I know that Miguel will be interested in having a discussion with him."

I was beginning to have second thoughts about the entire commitment I had made when Ed gave me three files labeled Wilcox, Rodriguez, and Reina.

"Read through these," Ed continued, "and we can discuss your approach to each one. Because they are all well-known to the police here, and because they know who we are, having you conduct some surveillance and investigation will keep their suspicions in check. I will leave you here to read the files and we can discuss, maybe over lunch."

Nodding, I thanked him, he left the conference room, and I began immersing myself in the files or our three suspects.

50

Opening each file, there were clear photographs of the three individuals. These had all been mug shots and their faces would be easily identifiable. As I read the files, I noted similarities of the three men. All of the men, now in their late twenties, had started getting into trouble with the law in their early teens. In the case of Pablo Rodriguez, he was known to juvenile authorities at the age of ten when he had stabbed a school mate on the playground with a pair of scissors. Apparently that wasn't his first assault, nor his last. In addition, two of the three, Rodriguez and Wilcox, had been raised by a single mother with the fathers nowhere in sight. Diego Reina was the product of the state foster home system, the New Mexico Children, Youth and Families Department (CYFD). He had gone from foster home to foster home, dropped out of school at the age of sixteen, and had apparently lived on his own ever since.

Also similar in the files was the progression of crimes from small incidences of petty theft and assault to more serious crimes, including drug usage and acting as a pimp. In many of their cases, the charges failed to stick, often on technicalities and occasionally because the victim decided not to press charges. Each of the suspects had been incarcerated and none of them had been able to hold down steady jobs. According to the files, they had all become members of the West Siders in their mid-teens. There was no record of any of them having been married, but Reina had apparently fathered a child for whom he was supposed to provide child support. He had been picked up on a couple of occasions for failing to make child support payments, but he was released each time and no further charges had been filed.

I took copious notes as I read their files. I noted how I could determine which of the suspects was most likely to fit the description that forensics had gathered from the videos. Did they have the signature Converse tennis shoes? Did one of them own a lowrider bicycle like the one in the video? Did one of them have a limp as noted by forensics? Assuming that the crimes were done for either money or drugs, did one of them demonstrate a recent influx of cash? Finally, with no formal authority or link to the police, how was I going to finesse getting this information without raising suspicions? I needed Ed and Miguel's guidance with that last question.

It was at that moment that Ed poked his head into the room and declared, "Why don't we get away from here for a bite of lunch. We can discuss the cases and next steps. What do you say?"

I suspected that Ed had not missed too many meals in his career and that, like Miguel, he would know some good places to eat. I found that the little I had for breakfast did not keep me sated. I was ready to eat and develop a plan.

I was correct that Ed's knowledge of good places to eat was spot on. We went to an established restaurant in Santa Fe that had been there even when I lived there, Maria's Mexican Kitchen, about a ten-minute drive from the plaza. The food and ambience were the same as I had remembered. We sat in a corner booth and strategized our next move.

I was both surprised and delighted at Ed's knowledge of police work and working undercover. Because of his affable nature, he was easy to underestimate, but he was a goldmine of knowledge.

As we reviewed our observations of the three suspects, Ed suggested that the best approach was for me to present myself to the three businesses employing our suspects on the pretense that I was moving back to Santa Fe and needed some counsel on the move. Because I was considering relocating, this made the ruse seem plausible. In the case of the construction company and the landscape business, I would be inquiring about building a house and would like to visit one of their sites where they were currently working to get a sense of the kind of work they do. Hopefully, I would be able to see their crews and make some early observations. In the case of the motorcycle shop, I would enquire as to the purchase of a used motorcycle and try to make similar observations about our suspect. Fortunately, I was familiar with motorcycles having owned one in Bozeman. Once I had been able to narrow down the suspects to a single individual, Ed indicated that Miguel would have him brought into the station for further questioning as a person of interest.

We reviewed what I had already determined to be critical characteristics for me to consider. Ed suggested I get started immediately after lunch. He was able to find a car from the police motor pool that I could use for the project. I had to smile to myself as I thought of the drama it all and, with a mixture of excitement and apprehension, I was on to my undercover assignment!

51

We finished our lunch and drove to the motor pool. As Ed had requested, the motor pool had already prepared a 2018 black Dodge Charger with a Hemi engine that had never been used in any police activities. It was a muscle car and would look the part of someone with a little money for relocating. I signed for the car and was off for my first surveillance.

Because it was close, I began with Mike's Bikes and Repair. The shop was located on a side street off of St. Michael's Drive about fifteen minutes south of the plaza. While it was hard to see at first, there was a sign indicating I was at the right place. The building was small and older with a large sliding metal door that served as the entrance. The shop area also served as the "showroom" where older, motorbikes were for sale near the area where other motorbikes were being repaired. It appeared that there were only a couple of mechanics in the shop adjacent to a small, disheveled, office. I went into the office and the heavily tattooed and bearded man behind the desk looked up and, having noted my car, began with "nice wheels."

Knowing I was off to a good start because of the Dodge Charger, I extended my hand, introduced myself and my interest, and he took me to the adjacent shop to show me the "inventory." The inventory consisted of two older and refurbished motorcycles which he assured me were in top condition and came with his personal guarantee for three months.

Looking over the shop, I spotted Diego Reina busy repairing one of the motorcycles. At that moment, Mike called for "Dorie" to join us, indicating it was him who had done the repair work on the two bikes for sale. Mike introduced us saying, "Dorie is our top mechanic. He can tell you anything you need to know about the bike." As Dorie joined us, Mike elaborated that Dorie had been with him now for almost a year and was incredibly reliable, the first to show up and the last to leave. Mike indicated that Dorie was his hardest working mechanic and about to buy a house and get married. I noticed that Dorie was not wearing the Converse high-top sneakers, but a pair of leather work boots. After a few more minutes of discussing the merits of the bike, I asked Mike for his contact information and assured him I would be in touch.

Upon leaving the shop, I noticed that Dorie did not have a limp and that there was no lowrider bicycle in sight to indicate his method of transportation. Just as I was about to pull out, Dorie navigated by me on a motorcycle headed for the highway. My initial feeling was that Dorie was not our man. Why would someone with a steady job, about to get married, and buy his first house, put it all at risk by both murdering Blake and burning the Guadalupe for money? At first glance, there did not seem to be the connection for which I was looking. So, I was on to Zia Home Building and Renovation.

52

The office for Zia Home Building and Renovation was farther south in a small industrial area. The sign above the office was wrought iron crafted in the symbol of a Zia, a round sun with groups of three rays in each of the four directions. The Zia has been the symbol of the state of New Mexico flag and is on the license plates. The office and several trucks with the Zia logo on the side were located on a larger lot. On the outside, this appeared to be a successful home-building business.

The office was quite different from that of Mike's Bikes. Walking into the office, the receptionist sat behind an attractive desk and the office was clean and fresh looking. The walls were decorated with photos of previous houses that Zia had built, all appearing to be high end homes. There was a small conference room to the right of the front door with several samples of countertop material, flooring, paint color swatches, and floorplan drawings. The door at the back of the main office seemed to go to a larger garage area holding what I suspected were supplies.

Smiling and enthusiastic, I was met with, "Good morning. How can I help you?"

I told the receptionist, Gloria, about my interest in moving to Santa Fe, finding a home builder, and visiting a site where actual building was taking place. Wanting to oblige, Gloria excused herself and went to an office with the sign above the door "Tate Newcomb, President." In short order, a tall thin man with pressed black jeans, black cowboy boots, a belt with a turquoise buckle, and a pressed white shirt walked out of the office. Smiling confidently and warmly, he extended his hand and with, "Good afternoon. I am Tate Newcomb. How can I be of service?"

I introduced myself and was invited into his office. I was actually looking forward to the conversation since moving to Santa Fe was more clearly in my future plans and I might well want to build a house. Tate and

I talked about my possible move, looking for a home builder, and wanting to see for myself the work he and his group were conducting.

He asked me how I found out about him, and without even thinking, I replied that Anna Pacheco having mentioned Zia Homes to me as a possibility. I knew that I was going to have to get in touch with Anna to cover my tracks, but I also knew that she was good currency in the area.

With the mention of Anna Pacheco, Tate's eyes lit up and his smile broadened, and he said, "Well, if you know Anna Pacheco, you are in good company! Anna and I have been good friends for years! In fact, I built her current home in Tesuque."

At that point, I knew that even if this meeting did not lead to our suspect, I had made a contact that would be beneficial in the future.

Tate was eager to show me around the premises and then on to one of their building sites. We walked through the shop where several craftsmen were working, doing some pre-fabrication on cabinets. He pointed out that they wanted to be the builder of choice in Santa Fe and worked hard to customize the interior of the homes they built, with no "off the shelf" solutions. He took me out to the yard where there were several trucks and some specialty machinery used for onsite construction.

He also said that he wanted Zia to be the best employer of choice, noting how difficult it was to get good craftsmen. Tate noted that they began every workday with the entire team starting at the office with a "morning huddle," reviewing what was under construction that day. They began with a "safety minute" exercise and encouragement to work safely. After the morning huddle, everyone rode out to the various construction sites in Zia vehicles, leaving their own vehicles at the office.

He directed me to one of the trucks to drive us out to one of their construction sites on the west side of town. As I got into the truck, I noticed that, near the employees' parking lot, there was a black lowrider bicycle with black, white-wall tires with "Lowrider" raised letters, handlebars, black grips, a banana saddle, and no front or rear fenders, exactly like forensics had identified in the videos! Stunned, I took a second look to confirm what I had seen.

Not wanting to play my hand just yet, I got into the Zia truck with Tate, and we drove out to the construction site. I was anxious to see if I could identify Lawrence Wilcox at this site. If I could, we may have our suspect.

53

The drive to the construction site took about fifteen minutes. Tate regaled me with stories of homes they had built, celebrity customers, and awards that Zia had won. As we approached the area where they were building, it was clear it was in Las Vistas, the high-end golf club community where I had previously met with Tyler King.

As we approached the guard house, it was clear that Tate was a regular and the guard opened the gate to let us in. The property was expansive with 360-degree views of mountains to the north, west, and south, and high desert to the east. The property was subdivided into neighborhoods with all sites having generous land for building. We arrived at a site where the house was, as Tate indicated, about half finished. The walls were up, the roofing on, and most of the work was now concentrated inside where all of the finishing work needing to be done. There were about twelve craftsmen working on putting up drywall, hooking up the plumbing, and installing the windows and doors.

Tate walked me through the construction, pointing out all of the special features the house had that set Zia apart from the competition. He was clearly proud of the work. As we walked through, I recognized Lawrence Wilcox working with another craftsman installing a large window with a view that would overlook one of the golf course fairways. Wilcox seemed to be struggling a bit with the window, noticeably limping on his left side. He was wearing the Converse high-top sneakers and appeared to be a bit disheveled, but unmistakably looked like his photo. I was conscious of staring at Wilcox and worked to keep up with Tate. I was sure Wilcox was our man.

Upon finishing the tour of the construction, we drove back to the office where Tate and I shared our contact information. I promised to follow up when I was ready to build and I got back into the Dodge Charger, hoping I would be able to contain my excitement. I texted both Ed and Miguel that I thought we needed to meet soon to discuss my observations. Remembering that I had used Anna's name as an introduction to Tate, I quickly called her leaving her a voice mail and letting her know that I appreciated using her as a reference when checking out home builders in the event that I would move to Santa Fe. I abandoned the idea of going to High Desert landscape company, certain that Lawrence Wilcox was likely the man on whom we needed to focus.

At that moment, my phone buzzed and indicated I had received a text. Miguel, texting both Ed and me, suggested that we reconvene at the police station to share our notes. I sent him a thumbs up and got in the Dodge Charger for what I suspected would be the last time. It was approaching five o'clock and I knew that the main thoroughfare, Cerrillos Road, would be crowded. So, I drove west to Agua Fria Street and headed back to the station. My adrenaline was pumping, and, for the first time, I was really feeling like I was a serious part of this investigation. I was back at the station and anxious to bring Miguel and Ed up to speed.

54

Miguel met me at the side door by the lot where I had parked the Charger. He shook my hand and quickly led me down a different hall from where I had been before. The station was eerily quiet with most of the administrative help having already left for the day. Miguel walked ahead of me with purpose in his stride and I followed Miguel to a conference room where Ed had already taken as seat at a small conference table. All of the chairs at the table were facing a wall with a whiteboard.

On the white board was the handwritten title at the top "Blake Martin homicide." Directly under the title, there was a timeline of events detailing, in order: Tyler King's visit to the Guadalupe; the destruction of the Guadalupe by arson; Blake Martin's homicide; the crime scene discovery of the bicycle tire and shoe print; the initial tourist cell-phone video; the CCTV video of the Guadalupe fire. As I looked at the timeline, I noted that it had been four weeks since the Guadalupe fire and only ten days since Blake Martin's murder. There was a double-pointed arrow between the Guadalupe fire and Blake's homicide, indicating a link. There was a sense of urgency among us to solve this.

Under the timeline, there was the moniker, "Suspects." Over the top of the suspects list was a photo of Blake Martin, with the description "homicide victim." Under Suspects, there were photos taped across the whiteboard of Tyler King, Roberto Montoya, Rebecca Martin, Diego Reina, Lawrence Wilcox, and Pablo Rodriquez. Each photo had the suspects name above it and a space under it for notes. It was clear that Miguel and Ed had been busy.

Miguel began the discussion saying, "We have made some good progress over the past several days and I believe we are getting closer to making an arrest. The Chief is really putting pressure on me to get this solved and the reporters are breathing down his neck. We need to move quickly to determine whom we can eliminate and on whom we need to focus. As you can see, we are about ten days out from the murder. It would be great to have an arrest by the two-week mark. So, Scott, tell us what you have discovered in your investigating this afternoon."

I recounted in detail my meeting at Mike's Bikes and shared my belief that we could eliminate Diego Reina as a suspect. Then I revealed the details of my meeting at Zia Home Builders and Renovation. I mentioned seeing the lowrider bicycle matching the description given to us from forensics; the Converse tennis shoes on Lawrence Wilcox; and the limp Wilcox had as he was working. Based on these observations, I told them that I believed Wilcox was the man in the videos. Also, I mentioned that, based on my conviction regarding Wilcox, I did not see the need to check out Pablo Rodriguez at High Desert Landscape.

At the end of my report, Ed nodded and agreed that we should focus on Wilcox. With that information, Miguel drew a large X through the photos of Reina and Rodriguez. He also made notes under Wilcox's photo regarding the bicycle, tennis shoes, and limp.

Miguel was up next. He described his meeting with Rebecca Martin and her attorney, Charles Kahn. Miguel had done a deep dive into the relationship between Rebecca and Blake including any extramarital affairs, debt, drug usage, enemies, and business associates. In addition, armed with a court order, Miguel had been given access to bank accounts, mortgage loans, life insurance policies, home equity loans, lines of credit, tax records, phone records, and information on other personal and business assets.

Miguel summarized by saying, "As you can imagine, Rebecca and Blake Martin had a very complicated financial situation. The interview took over three hours. I had requested that they bring pertinent information to the meeting, and I brought information with me had been gathered previously. It is all very convoluted, to say the least. Keep in mind that Martin had numerous investments in, and outside of, Santa Fe—including retail stores, a jewelry store, some land holdings, their home, and the gallery. They had over twenty different bank accounts and involvement in six different Limited Liability Corporations."

Ed and I both shook our heads, understanding just how much work Miguel must have been putting into the research.

Miguel continued, "We already knew that Martin had made many enemies, both in the business world and in his personal life such as people like you, Scott, whom Martin had personally injured. We fully expected to find Martin's finances to reflect significant debt that could lead us to additional suspects. However, what we found was that, with the exception of the gallery, his home, and some small land parcels, he had partners in every other case, and he was the minority investor. It seems that Martin's tendency to boast about his wealth was only partially true, but highly exaggerated."

After a pause to let this soak in, Miguel continued, "All of the holdings in which he had a minority interest were financially solvent, but his investment in them was very small. However, on both the gallery and on the house, he carried significant mortgages and had been delinquent on the past several payments on both properties. He had stopped making payments on the security system for the gallery and his home; was making only the minimum payment on several credit cards; and was even delinquent on his car payments. He had been a master at moving money from one account to another, but he was draining all of his accounts. It appeared that he was going to have to make some serious decisions about liquidating his small land holdings and his minority interest in some of the other businesses in order to stay afloat. Martin had overextended himself in both New York and in Los Angeles, trying to set up galleries in those locations. Because the art world has not made a full recovery in a bad economy, he had not been able to sell his art to cover his expenses. We believe this is why he pushed the deal with Roberto Montoya to begin displaying art in the Guadalupe restaurant, in hopes of getting some quick sales to high-end locals and tourists. Unfortunately for him, after the initial hoopla and the selling of a few pieces of art, interest died down quickly."

Ed had already been partially briefed, but this was all new information to me. I sat back trying to make sense of it all.

I wondered out loud, "Would that suggest that Martin was involved in the arson at the Guadalupe, with the possibility of collecting insurance money on the art to help offset some of his debt?"

"That is one conclusion I came to also," Miguel responded. "I had a look at the finances of Roberto Montoya and the Guadalupe to see if there was any motive for Montoya to have his own restaurant burned down—again for insurance money. However, Montoya's finances appeared to be squeaky clean. There is no mortgage on the Guadalupe building and the restaurant's net margins were regularly in the realm of twenty percent, which is really good for the restaurant business. Typical net margins for high-end restaurants are between five and eight percent. It looked like Martin's idea of displaying art at the Guadalupe had not yielded the bonanza for which he had hoped in terms of actual sales. Food and beverage sales volumes of the long-term loyal following of Guadalupe customers continued to be steady and, with a couple of exceptions, displaying the art did not seem to increase restaurant attendance or revenue."

Wanting to tie together some missing links, I queried, "If Martin was involved in the Guadalupe arson, does that keep Roberto Montoya in the frame as a suspect for his murder? If he suspected that Martin's great idea turned into Martin's folly and resulted in the destruction of the restaurant and the art for insurance purposes, wouldn't he have revenge as a motive?"

Miguel quickly replied, "Yes. It does keep Roberto in the frame but, first, I think we need to get Wilcox down here to begin interrogating him. If forensics can match the tennis shoe and bicycle tire prints found at the gallery with those of Wilcox, and if is a close match on the video tape, we definitely have grounds to bring him in. I believe we have reason to arrest him on suspicion of at least committing negligent arson. In New Mexico, this is grounds for a fourth-degree felony and carries with it the possibility of up to ten years in prison or more because of Wilcox's prior convictions. I think we have some leverage in working with Wilcox to begin connecting the dots."

Miguel continued, "We have also determined that it does not appear that either Blake or Rebecca were having any extramarital dalliances. We determined this from credit card receipts, phone records, and GPS phone tracking. Also, because of the pre-nuptial agreement and all of the debt, it appears that Rebecca will not fare as well as Blake's widow as she may have hoped. Additionally, Rebecca has confided that Martin periodically used cocaine and would make it available to guests when they had parties at the house. He seemed to be discrete in his usage of it and offered it to only a few, close, acquaintances. This could also be a link to Wilcox, given his background in the drug underworld. Ed, I will get an arrest warrant for Wilcox and a court order to search his, or I should say his mother's, premises. Will you put together a team for arresting Wilcox and I will get the necessary legal paperwork processed. Depending on what judge is available to sign-off on the search warrant, we could have this all ready to go within two hours. It may be a late night."

Ed nodded in agreement and was about to stand up to leave when Miguel smiled and said, "Great work, both of you! This would not have come about without your diligence, creativity, and attention to detail!

Scott, I think you should call it a night. The rest of the tonight's effort is a combination of police and forensics work. I will check with you in the morning. I think we should see what we get from Wilcox before proceeding with additional interviews."

"Sounds good," I replied as I got up and let myself out. "I'll wait to hear back from you in the morning."

"Oh, one more thing, I almost forgot," Miguel quickly said. "Do you remember the missing Bierstadt painting we discovered the night of the murder? Well, in going through all of the gallery invoices, we discovered that Martin had apparently sold that painting to some New Yorker over a year ago and, for some reason, it was just now being shipped to her by way of UPS. Interestingly, Rebecca had no recollection of it being sold and assumed it had been stolen by Martin's killer. The UPS office received the painting for shipment the day of Martin's homicide. Apparently, Martin had not had time to replace the Bierstadt on the gallery wall with another painting, leaving a space where it had hung. The gallery invoice had not been coded correctly and was initially overlooked. So, it does not appear that it was a theft. That is one lead that we do not have to pursue!"

As I left the police station to walk back to the hotel, the air was cool and crisp, and I could smell piñon firewood burning in hotel fireplaces and chimeneas. I was feeling good, almost heady, after all of my sleuthing activities of the day. It had been a day in which I felt like I had contributed to the case and could go to sleep satisfied with having a day well lived. I had not given any consideration to my work in Bozeman, so I was looking forward to catching up on some emails and identifying my business clients that had any questions or issues I needed to address.

I arrived at the hotel after a ten-minute walk and, as I was crossing the lobby, Christina at the front desk caught my attention, "Good evening, Doctor Hunter. Before you go to your room, I have a message for you." Smiling, Christina handed me a small envelope with "Doctor Scott Hunter" written on the front.

The envelope had the La Fonda logo on it, so I assumed it was local. I thanked her and sat down in the foyer to open the envelope. In a woman's lovely handwriting, the note said, "If you are going to use my name, the least you can do is buy me a drink! Let the front desk know your availability tonight and we can meet on the rooftop bar." It was signed, Anna Pacheco.

Unlike my dread at having to spend time with Rebecca the previous evening, I enjoyed and looked forward Anna's company. I let Christina know to make Anna aware that I would be at the rooftop bar in one hour. I went to my room, quickly checked my emails, answered the more urgent ones, and cleaned up. I was on the rooftop bar in just under one hour, feeling curious about what was on Anna's mind.

55

Unlike our previous meetings held more clandestinely at the Inn of the Anasazi and La Posada, Anna was in her own territory this time. As I arrived at the bar, Anna was seated at a corner table and had already ordered her gin and tonic. She called over the waiter to take my order. I asked for whatever local beer they had on tap.

Anna began the conversation warmly by saying, "Good to see you again Scott. I understand you met with Tate Newcomb today and used my name to make the introduction. You sound like you are really considering become one of us."

"Well," I began slowly, "I am definitely thinking about it. I understand from Tate that he actually built the house you occupy in Tesuque. He must be a good builder if you used him!"

Anna went on to tell me about her business relationship with Tate and the house he built for her. She concluded with how highly she would recommend him should I move here.

Then she asked, "Tell me how your work is going looking into Blake's murder?"

Knowing what was about to happen with Wilcox and what I knew following the debrief with Miguel, I knew I had to be cautious.

"Anna, what I can tell you is that there have been some very promising leads. That is about all I can say."

Wanting to change the conversation, I said, "I am really preoccupied with the idea of moving back. Being here again has brought back so many good memories and having been away for so long has given me a fresh perspective. I appreciate your encouragement and willingness for me to use your name in introductions."

"Well," Anna responded, "this has all happened fairly fast. How do you feel about living here with Rebecca here as well? Will that be odd? You know Santa Fe is a small town."

Anna asked a question that I, myself, had been pondering. "Anna," I responded, "I do not know how to handle the awkward relationship with Rebecca, but I know that I would find my way and develop a circle of friends that I could trust and enjoy. I hope you will be in that circle."

She smiled and said, "Gladly."

We chatted for a few more minutes before I excused myself, noting that I needed a good rest for what tomorrow would bring. We hugged and said our farewells. I left feeling that I was making a friend of Anna.

I was more tired than I realized. I retired to my room and got ready for a good night's rest knowing tomorrow would be another big day!

56

I heard my cell phone buzz. Sleepily, I looked at the time, five-thirty. Why was I getting called this early? From the caller ID I could see that it was Miguel.

I answered slowly, "Good morning, Miguel."

"Good morning, Scott. Time to rise and shine," Miguel chuckled. "We have had a very productive night. Can you meet me at the station? I will have coffee and bagels waiting."

Since I had not been able to sleep as long as I had wanted, I replied a bit grudgingly, "Sure, Miguel. I will be there in forty-five minutes."

We hung up and, even as tired as I was, I was anxious to hear what Miguel and Ed's team had discovered.

As promised, I got to the police station in forty-five minutes. As Miguel promised, he had picked up fresh bagels, flavored cream cheese, and a liter of Starbucks coffee.

Seeing me, Miguel directed, "Hey Scott, get some breakfast and meet us in the conference room."

I did as instructed and took my coffee and two blueberry bagels, heaped with strawberry cream cheese, to the conference room and took a seat. The only other person in the room was Ed, looking tired and a bit disheveled, clutching his fresh bagels and coffee.

On the white board we used last night, there had been some additional writing under Wilcox's photo. In addition, there had been a number of lines drawn between various photos.

Miguel began, "We had a very busy night. After I secured both the arrest warrant and the search warrant from Judge Gonzales, Ed and his team went to work. Ed, would you fill Scott in on what your team did?"

"Sure," Ed responded. "It took about two hours from the time we last saw you until we had the team in place and the warrants secured. We proceeded to the house of Wilcox's mother in a neighborhood off of Agua Fria. When we arrived, we made sure to have all of the exits of the house covered in the event that Wilcox might run. Wilcox mother answered the door and we served her with the search warrant. We found Wilcox in the back of the house, showed him the arrest warrant, read him his Miranda rights, and arrested him on suspicion of arson. While he protested loudly, he did not actually resist arrest. Two of our team brought Wilcox back here, booked him, and put him in a holding cell. Meanwhile, my team conducted a thorough search of the house."

Curious, and on the edge of my seat now, I asked impatiently, "Well, tell me what you found!"

Ed obliged, saying, "We immediately identified the lowrider bicycle and impounded it. We also took his tennis shoes into evidence for forensics to match the prints found at the gallery. Wilcox's mother appeared to be handicapped. She walked with a cane and moved slowly, but she kept a clean house. She has been single for years and lived a simple life. There did not appear to be anything unusual in the house. However, Wilcox's room was cluttered. We were able to locate drug paraphernalia in the clothes closet, which we secured. Our initial screening of the room did not turn up anything major. We were about to leave when one of my officers noted a loose ceiling tile in the clothes closet. That is when we hit the jackpot. Above the ceiling, we found a box with ninety quarter-gram packets of cocaine with a street value of about twenty-seven hundred dollars. In addition, we found an envelope containing eight thousand three hundred in twenty-dollar bills. We also found a book with names and addresses of contacts. We surmised that not only was Wilcox a user, but he was also a dealer. There was also a shed in the back yard where we found cans and bottles of accelerants. We confiscated those and sent them to forensics. All in all, it was a very productive night!"

Genuinely awestruck, I said, "Wow, Ed. That is incredibly impressive. What a haul! At the very least, Wilcox will have drug charges to face."

Smiling and satisfied, Ed replied, "Yes, Scott. While you slept, some of us actually worked." He winked at me as he said that.

Miguel jumped in and said, "Ed's team laid the foundation for what was to come. We worked through the night as did our forensics team. I began interrogating Wilcox immediately after he was booked. Repeat offenders tend to fall into three categories. The first category is that, upon being arrested, they immediately lawyer-up before we can talk to them. In the second category, the offender believes he, or she, is the smartest person in the room. This kind of offender declines to have an attorney present and seems to enjoy trying to outsmart the interrogator. However, they usually fold once they determine their intelligence is not commensurate with the evidence against them. We have learned that with some offenders, the third type, we do not ask any questions that would cause them to request a lawyer. Instead, we begin with the evidence and, once they have taken in the full weight of what we have, we appeal to any common sense they may have left, asking them to consider giving us information for a lesser charge. Such agreements always involve the District Attorney's office being in the loop."

"And what type of offender was Wilcox?" I queried.

Miguel responded, "Ed's team noted that Wilcox and his mother seemed to have a particularly close relationship. Keep in mind that he had an absent father with no siblings. In a sense, he had been the man of the house. We were able to use this to our advantage in making him a deal. The most compelling argument we had was in the form of the videos. The forensics team was able to positively match the bicycle to the one in the video. They also positively matched the tire track and the tennis shoe print at the gallery. While Wilcox was being arrested for the arson charge, we were able to let him know that he would also have a drug charge facing him and, possibly, even a murder charge. We painted a picture in which the only way he would see his mother in the future would be on her monthly one-hour visits to the penitentiary. It would be pretty bleak and hard on her."

"How did he take that?" I asked excitedly.

"He did something I have rarely seen an ex-con do. He held his face in his hands and began to sob. I cannot tell you how unusual this is to see." Miguel exclaimed.

From my training as a psychologist, I knew that psychopaths have great difficulty forming attachments. In fact, one thing that sets them apart from the general population is their inability to experience empathy or concern for others, including their own family members.

They just do not seem to have the empathy chip in their emotional hardware. When psychopaths have relationships, they are always short-lived and highly exploitative. The fact that Wilcox cried at the prospect of being separated from his mother suggested that his life of crime was more of a means for survival than one of ruthless exploitation.

"How did this shape the rest of the interview?" I asked.

Miguel continued, "The prospect of a long prison sentence, due to the overwhelming evidence we had on the arson, plus the drugs he was going to distribute that we found in his mother's home, all added pressure on him to be forthcoming with information, in hopes of being treated leniently."

Miguel went on to detail Wilcox's conversation. Wilcox quickly admitted to being the arsonist at the Guadalupe. However, he adamantly denied having anything to do with the murder of Blake Martin. According to Wilcox, he heard "on the street" of an opportunity to make an easy ten thousand dollars. When pressed, Wilcox confided that an individual in the drug ring to which he was connected, let him know of a job for Wilcox in order to get a ten percent "referral fee" for himself. Wilcox said that, because of his mother's disability, he was always looking for ways to help pay the mortgage on their house and put food on the table. In a sense, he said, without his income from his job and dealing drugs, they were destitute.

He let it be known that he might be interested and was instructed to pick up a package at the base of The Cross of the Martyrs monument. He arrived at the monument early on the date requested and was there just in time to see an SUV drive off. It was still dark, and he could not tell the make or model, but the sealed package had been left for him. In the package was a fully charged burner phone with typed instructions to keep the phone handy and wait for instructions. The burner phone rang within a couple of hours, while Wilcox was on a job site for Zia Homebuilders. In a heavily disguise voice, the caller told Wilcox of the job and confirmed his willingness to do it. The job was simple. He would set fire to a particular building at a certain time and date, and he would be given more details later. Upon completion of the job, Wilcox would be instructed where to pick up the payoff. As a "goodwill gesture," the caller offered to pay Wilcox an "advance" of five hundred dollars for final acceptance of the assignment. If he took the advance and did not complete the job, the caller threatened retribution and informed Wilcox that he knew exactly where he and his mother lived. Wilcox said he readily agreed. The caller then said that he would be in touch and for Wilcox to keep the burner phone close by for further instruction.

I thought to myself that the story that Wilcox was telling had a ring of truth to it. Clearly, he would not have admitted to committing arson if he had not done it. Even with the video, he would likely take his chances with a jury hoping for a lesser sentence. And why would he have set the fire in the middle of the night for no reason? It all seemed plausible.

Miguel continued, "Wilcox received similar instructions as before. He was to pick up another package at the base of The Cross of the Martyrs monument that would have the "advance" money and additional instructions. Again, Wilcox went to the location at the time and date requested and another sealed packet was waiting for him. In the packet there was six hundred dollars in old twenty-dollar bills and type written instructions. Wilcox was told what materials he would need to purchase for the arson with the additional hundred dollars, informed that the targeted building was the Guadalupe restaurant, and was told the time and date that the arson was to be conducted. The instructions also included that, following the fire and his meeting the satisfaction of the "buyer," Wilcox would receive another burner phone message on how to receive the additional ninety-five hundred dollars."

Ed chimed in, "It looks like we have our man for the arson at the Guadalupe, but how do we get the person behind this, the person who wanted the Guadalupe burned down in the first place? And, what link, if any, does this have to Blake Martin's homicide?"

I was thinking the same thing. While we had the video evidence linking Wilcox to both the Guadalupe and the gallery, we needed to know who was behind all of this. Wilcox had only been used as a conduit. He was clearly not the main operator.

Miguel replied, "Wilcox really wants to cooperate to get as light a sentence as possible. Fortunately, he kept the typed notes he received in the packets. They were in the box with the cash that Ed's team confiscated. We hope that forensics can help us identify where the notes may have originated. We thought about going up to The Cross of the Martyrs to get tire prints, but it had rained since the drop-offs and it is a popular place for visitors, especially young lovers. There is no CCTV there, so we are hoping the forensics team can pull a rabbit out of a hat."

After a pause to let all of that sink in, Miguel continued, "Wilcox did as instructed, bought the accelerants, and he hid them near the Guadalupe the day prior to the arson. Then he went to the Guadalupe early in the morning and began the incineration process. What we saw on the CCTV video was Wilcox leaving the scene on the lowrider bicycle once he had ignited the accelerants. According to Wilcox, he waited another two days for the instructions on how to pick up the remaining payment. Then, he received another call on the burner phone."

57

The second call to Wilcox turned out to be different from the other calls in that he was instructed to pick up his remaining payment directly at Blake Martin's gallery. He was given a specific date and time to arrive at the back door of the gallery. It would be shortly after business hours. Wilcox was instructed to use the burner phone to call the number he had previously been given after he arrived in the parking lot at the rear of the building. He was further instructed not to go into the gallery, but to wait in the parking lot until he was given further instructions.

"At that time," Miguel said, "I asked Wilcox if he did not find it strange to receive his payment at the gallery instead of some hidden back alley. It was then that Wilcox volunteered that he thought it might because Blake Martin had previous dealings with one of his drug suppliers and another influential drug dealer that he knew. According to Wilcox, there was some of Martin's money behind the Santa Fe drug trafficking, but he was short on details. Wilcox told us that he guessed that some of the drugs which he had planned to distribute before they were found in his mother's house, may have been part of the local drug alliance funded, in part, by Blake Martin."

Wanting badly to receive his additional nine thousand five hundred dollars, Wilcox did as he was instructed on the given date and time. He arrived on his lowrider bicycle at the parking lot near the rear of the gallery. Wilcox commented that he had to take a circuitous route because of trying to avoid the attention of tourists. Even with the route he took, he mentioned that he had encountered a small group of tourists walking down East Marcy Street. Once he was in the parking lot, Wilcox called the number he had been given. On the third ring, a man answered in a heavily disguised voice. He told Wilcox to wait five minutes and then go to the back door of the gallery. He was told there would be a packet for him on the landing up the stairs just in front of the door. He was warned again not to try to enter the gallery. Once he had secured the packet, he was instructed to take the money out of the packet and leave the burner phone in the packet before leaving. Once again, the voice told Wilcox that he knew where his mother lived and, if he ever mentioned any detail or anything at all about the assignment for which he had been paid, his mother would be "paid a visit."

Wilcox did as instructed. He waited five minutes, carefully walked his lowrider bicycle to the back steps of the gallery and saw the packet four steps up. He went up the first two steps to retrieve the packet, opened it, took out the envelope with the money and put his burner phone in the packet. He mentioned that the back door was closed and the lights in the gallery were off when he arrived. He did not hear any noises inside the gallery. Once he had the envelope with the money, he quickly left and went back home. He added that the only other person to know of the arson was the gang member who had referred the buyer to him. That gang member was named by Wilcox as no other than Pablo Rodriguez, the West Sider on our list working at High Desert landscape and whom we had ruled out once we had evidence on Wilcox!

"Gentlemen," Miguel said with some sense of satisfaction, "we clearly have sufficient evidence to hold Wilcox for both the arson and having possession of a controlled substance with intent to distribute. We also have a link now between the arson of the Guadalupe and Martin's gallery. However, we still have only circumstantial evidence that Martin's homicide was tied to Wilcox. He explained only why both his bicycle tire print and his shoe print were at the crime scene from when he picked up his payment. We must bring in Pablo Rodriguez for questioning. Ed, will you have your men bring Rodriguez to the station? You will not be arresting him, just asking him to help us with some information on a case we are working. You may have to remind him that he is on parole and that it would be in his best interest to help. I will let the chief know that we are formally booking Lawrence Wilcox for the arson at the Guadalupe and possession of a controlled substance. Scott, I think we need to pay a visit to Roberto Montoya."

Ed quickly agreed and, although tired from working all night, he still had a lightness to his step as he walked away. Miguel and I began the trek down to Roberto's office.

58

The walk to Roberto Montoya's office only took us ten minutes. It was still early and there was the possibility that the office was not yet open. Just as we turned the corner to Roberto's office, Miguel's phone rang. I could only hear Miguel's end of the conversation. He talked for several minutes and when he got off the phone, he suggested that we detour to a nearby coffee shop to discuss the call before seeing Roberto.

We walked up to a boutique, hand-crafted coffee shop a few blocks from the plaza. It was upscale and had a high table in the corner where we could talk. We put in our order and Miguel began, "that was Robin Goldstein who called."

"The woman from Antiquities Assurance," I asked.

"Yes," Miguel replied. "She wanted to give me an update on the various insurance policies on the art we discussed. Remember that Blake had policies on the art in Martin's gallery as well as the art on display in the Guadalupe. The policies for the gallery art and the art on display at the Guadalupe had been purchased independently by Blake Martin, with Rebecca adding her name onto the policies recently. In addition, she had a small policy that Tyler King had taken out on the painting he had acquired from Blake that he thought may be fraudulent."

"I remember you having told me all of this," I said.

"Well," Miguel continued, "Robin received a request from Rebecca on how to file a claim on the art destroyed in the Guadalupe. She said she has not heard from Tyler King. Earlier, Ruben Montez let me know that Roberto had put in a similar request to file a claim for the Guadalupe."

"Wow," I exclaimed. "This puts the Guadalupe fire under even more scrutiny."

Miguel posed thoughtfully, "Here is the interesting part. When arson is involved in an insurance claim, the insurance only pays out when it can be satisfactorily determined that the claimant had no knowledge of, or association with, the arson or arsonist. As Robin explained to me, if either Blake or Rebecca had knowledge of the arson or arsonist, neither one of them would get paid. Rueben said the same holds true for Roberto Montoya. Also, if any of them had any foreknowledge of the arson, they could be candidates for being prosecuted for insurance fraud. However, if it could be satisfactorily demonstrated that neither of them, or just one of them, had no foreknowledge of the arson and no association with the arsonist, they could be the recipient of a claim payout. Another wrinkle is that even though Blake is dead, Rebecca added her name on the insurance as a recipient for payment. Needless to say, Robin and Antiquities Assurance are quite interested in what associations or foreknowledge could have existed with Rebecca, Roberto, or Blake."

"This all sounds complicated and heightens the need to figure out all of the relationships, who was responsible, and if anyone had prior knowledge," I summarized.

Miguel continued, "I was only going to discuss with Roberto that we had found the arsonist and that he was beginning to talk. I had planned to put some pressure on Roberto just to see if he would indicate whether or not he had any connection. But now, we have more to consider. Since we do not yet know who was behind the payments to Wilcox, we have to keep Roberto in the frame. Even though the restaurant was doing well, could he have had something to do with the arson in order to cash in on the insurance? While it may be unlikely, the fact that he asked about filing a claim on the destroyed art continues to make him a suspect."

We finished our coffees and proceeded to Roberto's office.

We were greeted again by the smiling receptionist, Marcy. Like just about everyone in Santa Fe, she was acquainted with Miguel, and she remembered me from my meeting just days ago with Maria. We were fortunate that Roberto was available and had not begun meetings for the day. Marcy left us to inform Roberto of our presence, and he came out immediately, greeted us warmly, and vigorously shook Miguel's hand as he welcomed us into his office.

Roberto questioned why I was accompanying Miguel since I had met with Roberto and Maria earlier about relocating. Miguel confessed that I was assisting him with the Blake Martin homicide and that, because of the shortage of officers, the cost to use me fit into their lean department budget. Roberto was still a bit puzzled, but his relationship with Miguel was such that Miguel was able to get to business in short order.

As we had discussed, Miguel laid out for Roberto that we believed we had the arsonist in our custody and that, hoping for a lighter sentence, he was anxious to cooperate.

I observed Roberto as he took in this news. A sigh of relief came over him and he sank down in his chair. He seemed genuinely pleased that we had a suspect in custody and that this could be wrapped up soon.

Miguel continued with the information Rueben Montez had given him about Roberto significantly increasing the policy on the Guadalupe and his enquiry about filing a claim.

At that point, Roberto sat up straighter and said, "Miguel, I did not trust Blake Martin as far as I could throw him. I only agreed to allowing him to display the gallery's art in the Guadalupe because he convinced me that it would be of mutual benefit. I was fearful that he had a hidden agenda, and I was very concerned about the possibility of theft of the art by either our patrons, which was unlikely, or by business associates of Blake who tired of his underhanded ways. Having the art in the Guadalupe created much more work for us. We had to keep track of the inventory, our staff had to create invoices for any art that sold, and we had to take an accounting every night of any sales and what we had remaining. Hell, I had to put additional locks on the doors and interior cameras for added security. I only wished I had extended the security cameras to the outside of the building, and we would have instantly known the identity of the arsonist."

"So," Miguel queried, "what do you intend to do with the money if you are able to collect the insurance?"

Without waiting, Roberto continued, "Because I did not trust Blake, we recorded the names of all of the artists. I wanted to make certain that they were compensated for their work in the event that it did get stolen or in some way defaced. I know how hard it is to make a living when you are doing it on the basis of your own handiwork. I wanted to make sure they were compensated. As far as the Guadalupe goes, the insurance will cover the loss once the arsonist is convicted and the insurance company knows that we had nothing to do with the fire. I have nothing to gain personally from whatever the insurance company will pay out."

We talked for a few more minutes and Miguel assured Roberto that he would keep him in the loop regarding the arsonist. Miguel and I said our goodbyes and departed. We had been there less than thirty minutes.

As we walked back to the police station, Miguel asked sardonically, "Well Doctor Hunter, what observations did you make as Roberto heard the news of the arsonist and insurance claim?"

Part of my training as a psychologist was in "deception recognition." Recognizing deception is particularly valuable in relationship counseling when being transparent and honest is crucial to the success of the therapy. I found the same skills highly valuable when interviewing candidates for senior positions in companies. We were even trained by FBI agents who would interview domestic terrorists. Over time, I had become very skilled at identifying deceptive interview answers and had often wished that I would have had that skill when I was married to Rebecca!

During interviews, deception can come in the form of failing to answer the question being asked, attacking the questioner, demonstrating an inappropriate level of concern or being overly polite, speaking with a level of certainty about an issue in order to shut down communication, and verbal/non-verbal disconnects like inappropriately smiling when talking about something serious or mournful, or shaking your head "no" while saying "yes."

In addition to how the subject answers questions, there are some behavioral "tells" that can indicate deception. These behaviors can include an increased level or pace of breathing that is inconsistent with the content of the message or signs of anxiety, including lip licking, ear pulling, nose rubbing, excessive swallowing or throat-clearing, hand-to-face activity, and hiding of mouth or eyes.

Thinking about all that I had observed of Roberto during the conversation, I commented, "I believe Roberto was telling us the truth. What I saw was congruence between what he said and how he said it. He was not trying to convince us of anything, and he was totally transparent about his feelings for Blake Martin. His breathing, sighing, and slumping indicated that he was taking in what we told him about Wilcox and that it was a relief. He did not seem to be fearful about what Wilcox might say, indicating that he did not have anything to hide. He did not demonstrate any deceptive hand or facial behaviors. I believe he was being truthful and not deceptive."

Smiling, Miguel said, "I knew you would be good for something, I just wasn't sure what. Now I know! You are a pro at recognizing liars and cheats. I should have had you in the Wilcox interview!"

I could hear Miguel's phone ping, indicating he had received a text message. He looked at the message and said, "The forensics team has some information on the instruction sheets Wilcox had kept and that they were researching. They have asked us to come back to the station."

With that, Miguel led the way and we briskly walked back to the station to meet the forensics team.

59

Miguel led us to the same conference room where we had been spending most of our time reviewing the case. The white board was still there with photographs of suspects and numerous notes. There was a new person in the room to whom Miguel introduced me.

"Scott," he began, "this is Dolores Griego. Dolores heads up our forensics team. She is an incredible scientist and sleuth and has helped up solve numerous cases."

Extending my hand to a blushing Dolores, I said, "It is a pleasure to meet you, I am Scott Hunter."

Miguel continued, "Scott is a psychologist, and an old friend who is helping us uncover evidence to solve this mystery. Tell us what you have found."

"Well," Dolores replied, "we looked at the paper on which the instructions had been typed and are lucky that the instructions were printed from a consumer grade printer. Most consumer grade printers are outfitted with what are called microdots when they print. Microdots are a nearly invisible binary code that can signify a printer's serial number, as well as the date and time the document was actually printed. These microdots are a security feature that helps law enforcement know when an individual is trying to print counterfeit money. In this case, these microdots can help us learn, with great certainty, the printer from which the instructions were printed. Now what we need to do is to match the binary code we have with documents that have come from the same printer."

"See Scott," Miguel said as he smiled, "I told you that Dolores was amazing! Where do we go from here, Dolores?"

Dolores responded, "The next step is to obtain documents printed from printers of your suspects and try to match them. I will tell you that it is hard to get a court order to do this unless you have probable cause for a search. It is better to be able to do this in a clandestine manner, and once you have a match, find probable cause to get a search warrant."

Miguel jumped in, "Our suspects include Roberto Montoya, Rebecca Martin, Tyler King, Blake Martin in absentia, and anyone that Pablo Rodriguez might reveal. Scott, what do you think?"

Remembering my visit with Maria Montoya, I replied excitedly, "I have a document from a file that was copied for me at Roberto Montoya's office. I can bring it in."

"That would be great," Dolores said. "I will wait for any documents you may have and run the comparisons when I get them.'

Dolores was about to leave when I remembered that Rebecca had given me a copy of Blake's obituary the night I was at her house. I mentioned that I would bring that also.

Dolores left the room and Miguel said, "I think we have several copies from the printer at the gallery from past receipts, invoices, and information about the paintings. We do lack anything from Tyler King, and I will leave that to you, Scott. Why don't we meet back here after lunch? Bring the documents you have for Dolores, and I will do the same. By then, Ed should have brought Pablo in for questioning."

I agreed and headed out of the conference room and back to the hotel. I decided to stop at a sandwich shop in the upstairs of a building overlooking the plaza before securing the documents in my hotel room. I ate lunch quickly, procured the documents, and was headed back to the station earlier than I had anticipated. I was anxious to see if we could find any matches.

60

By the time I returned to the station, Sergeant Ed Apodaca's team had already brought in Pablo Rodriguez for questioning. Miguel indicated to me that the interview took precedence over anything else, and he had to be in the room with Pablo. He pointed me in the direction of Dolores Griego's office to drop off the documents I had from Maria Montoya and Rebecca. I found Dolores already working on sorting through documents that she had accumulated from the gallery. Among the documents were invoices, artist biographies, shipping receipts, letters, and a number of miscellaneous paperwork.

"Hi again," I said as I walked into Dolores's office.

"Well, hi," she said smiling. "I was just about to let Miguel know that you would not have to get any printed copies from Tyler King. I found a couple of letters he sent to Blake complaining about the painting he had purchased and threatening legal action."

"Great," I exclaimed. "This should shorten the process."

Dolores said, "If you want to hang around, I will show you how we find the microdots on these documents and maybe even find a match!"

I was very interested in how the process worked and hoped we could determine who placed the notes to Wilcox that were in the two packets.

For my benefit, Dolores summarized saying, "Most consumer grade printers print an almost invisible grid of yellow dots that allow for tracking when and where documents are printed. Under normal light, they are nearly impossible to see without magnification. They can be seen under blue LED light and "read" by a computer program. These dots reveal a binary code in the grid. Once we are able to enter the dots found on the documents into the computer program, we can see what data they contain. This will tell us if any of these documents were printed by the same printer that printed the instructions Wilcox received."

As I was astonished by the technology, I asked, "Does this raise any issues about privacy? I can see the benefits of the application to identify counterfeit operations, but what if a person wants to send a note anonymously, and for a good cause? Doesn't this raise legal issues? For example, what if a corporate whistleblower wants to remain anonymous, but these microdots can be traced back to the printer used and put the whistleblower in jeopardy."

"Yes," Dolores replied. "There have been a number of privacy issues raised regarding privacy, but, for the time being, the printing manufacturers have found it in their best interest to work with the government and keep this technology active. The government's response is that this technology has the potential to identify terrorist acts before they occur, when threatening letters have been sent. This technology can also be used to identify where government leaks come from. At this point, the microdots are seen as a kind of DNA for printers and not likely to go away soon."

At that moment, Miguel poked his head in the door, "Sorry to bother you, but I need Scott to see this interview."

"No problem," Dolores responded. "I will be analyzing these documents and should be able to tell you if there is a match, once the interview is completed."

I left the office with Miguel walking toward an AV room. Miguel began, "Scott, with your expertise on deception, I would like you to see us interview Pablo Rodriguez. I cannot have you in the room with me, but I have gotten permission for you to watch the interview from our viewing room. Let me know what you think about his behavior as we question him."

Armed with a pad and pen, I sat down at the monitor to observe the interview.

61

Watching Miguel as he interviewed Pablo Rodriguez was like watching two very skilled chess players. Miguel had honed his skills at interviewing with the FBI, and seeing him spar with Pablo, who had spent his life identifying, and exploiting, the vulnerabilities of his victims, was like watching two Grand Masters. This interview room was no place for amateurs, I thought.

Miguel had shown me Rodriguez's rap sheet and he seemed to fit the criminal psychopath profile much better than Wilcox. Wilcox was a criminal of opportunity and need. Rodriguez had added the dimension of inflicting pain or humiliation to his crimes. His crimes all included assault, ostensibly as a means for getting what he wanted. But the description of them suggested that he seemed to enjoy hurting his victims. He had been in the legal system since he was eight years old when he had maliciously chopped off the legs of a puppy "just to see what would happen." He had escalated his cruel criminal behavior to include robbery, breaking and entering, and assault and battery with intent to kill, among others. He had spent most of the past ten years in and out of the penitentiary. Even now, he had been on parole for just a few months. In the West Sider's gang, he was near the top of the heap. He had reached the pinnacle of bad-ass success.

As a psychologist, I am often asked about the nature/nurture debate. Is a person's personality formed from birth or is it shaped from the environment? Research has found that both are important, and that personality can change over time. However, having studied psychopathology, I have often wondered if some personalities, like that of Rodriguez, are somehow hardwired from birth. Is there a "bad seed" explanation for some psychopaths? If so, Rodriguez would be one of them.

I believe that behaviors persist because they are incentivized and, ultimately, reward self-interest. Miguel's challenge with Rodriguez was to find the right incentives for Rodriguez to believe that he would gain something significant enough for him to give Miguel needed information. Miguel's goal was to get Rodriguez to give up more information than he may have planned. This all had to be done in such a way as to discourage the suspect from lawyering-up and shutting down altogether. When Sergeant Ed Apodaca picked up Rodriguez, it was not an official arrest. Ed had asked Rodriguez to come in on his own volition to help with another case. He was free to go in the event that the questioning became too uncomfortable.

One tactic in the interview room is to wear down the suspect sufficiently so that he would eventually tire of the ordeal and simply give in. This usually requires interviewing the suspect for several hours without a break. Another tactic is the "good cop, bad cop" sequence, with two interviewers alternating between being accusatory and supportive, hoping to get the suspect to "crack."

Miguel knew that because Rodriguez was a seasoned interviewee, neither of these tactics would work with him. Instead, Miguel took the approach of appealing to Rodriguez' intelligence and experience, requesting Rodriguez to help on a case based on his knowledge of the criminal world. Knowing that psychopaths have a grandiose sense of self-worth and are highly narcissistic, Miguel knew that by appealing to Rodriguez' ego, he was more likely to gain insight into his role in the fire than by trying to wage a war of words with him.

As Miguel laid out the fire at the Guadalupe and the murder of Blake Martin, he asked Rodriguez his thoughts about what kind of person would do such things, not who. Miguel did not want Rodriguez to become defensive or defiant. He wanted Rodriguez to begin to speculate about the motives of such a person and what would be their ultimate goal.

Rodriguez, being susceptible to the admiration of others, began to lay out a scenario that included things like insurance fraud, revenge, and even mischief as a motive for the arson. It was after about forty-five minutes of back-and-forth that Miguel finally let Rodriguez know about the CCTV tape of the individual on a lowrider bicycle pedaling away from the fire. This information stimulated Rodriguez' creativity in suggesting that the arsonist was likely someone who had planned for the event, rather than it having been a spontaneous or mischievous act. He even suggested that the bicyclist could have been hired by someone to set the fire, someone wanting to get revenge.

At that point, Miguel told Rodriguez that the police had been able to identify the individual on the bicycle. He had Rodriguez' full attention when he added that the rider had implicated Rodriguez as the middleman connecting the rider with the individual wanting the Guadalupe to be torched. Miguel reminded Rodriguez about the seriousness of being involved in criminal activity while on parole, and that it was in his best interest to cooperate.

Knowing he had been trapped and that there was no easy exit, Rodriguez began to sing.

62

Dolores had been working diligently to try to match the documents she had been given with the documents given to Wilcox in the packets. She was using the software to try and match microdots on the documents. When looking at printer microdots in previous investigations, Dolores was surprised at how most suspects seemed to go the path of least resistance by using computers and printers familiar to them. When sending threatening letters that were supposed to be anonymous, the sender typically used their home or work computer and printers, rather than going to a local Fed Ex office or internet cafe. She had become comfortable in her belief that if they found a match, it would have been from the printer commonly used by the sender.

Using special lighting to identify the microdot pattern on the Wilcox document, Dolores created a master template The template had an image of the grid found on both documents with specific microdots highlighted to show unique pattern. She was then able to overlay the microdot patterns from the other documents onto that of the Wilcox document. The process was very similar to DNA matching.

In her possession, she had documents from the Martin gallery in the form of invoices, artist biographies and inventories. These would have been from the gallery printer and could have been created by Blake Martin, Rebecca Martin, or any of their staff. When she compared these microdots to those of the Wilcox documents, there was no match.

She followed the same procedure for the Tyler King documents. Tyler King had sent Blake Martin letters threatening legal action. They had been sent via Certified Mail. In the Tyler King case, there had been two different printers used, creating two separate microdot patterns. Yet again, no match with either document.

Dolores had the documents in the copied file given to Scott Hunter from Maria Montoya, originating at the Montoya's office. Maria had these copied for Scott for future networking purposes. Still, there was no match.

A copy of Blake Martin's obituary had been given to Scott Hunter by Rebecca Martin and had been printed at the Rebecca's home. This document did not provide a match to Wilcox's document either.

Feeling discouraged, Dolores had run into a dead end. None of the documents from any of the suspects had microdot patterns that matched those of the Wilcox document. Dolores racked her brain to think of who else may have been instrumental in sending Wilcox the documents.

Then she had an idea.

63

As I observed Miguel's interview with Pablo Rodriguez, I could not identify any deceptive answers from Rodriguez in the first part of the interview. The questions that Miguel served up were "softball" questions, easy to answer and not creating any anxiety or defensiveness on the part of Rodriguez. His answers were typically quick, straightforward, and I did not detect any of the behaviors associated with deception.

However, once Miguel introduced the videotape information from the CCTV tape, it was apparent that Rodriguez was beginning to feel uncomfortable. I could see behaviors like nose flaring, excessive movement in his chair, and increased leg and foot twitching, that all indicated an increased level of anxiety on the part of Rodriguez as Miguel began laying out what he knew about the Guadalupe fire and the involvement of Wilcox as the arsonist.

As expected, Rodriguez initially denied that he had any involvement in the plan. However, when reminded again of the conditions of his parole and the possible consequences if he were to lie, Rodriguez admitted to his involvement in the plan.

According to Rodriguez, he had a history with Blake Martin in the drug business. Martin had provided funds for Rodriguez to buy high quality cocaine for Martin to have at his parties and for some of his personal friends. The deal was that Rodriguez would find a source for the cocaine, ask Martin how much he wanted and then get cash from him to secure the cocaine. They would have the drop at the gallery in the evening at closing time. Rodriquez would call Martin ahead of time to make sure no one was around to witness the drop. Initially, it was set up that Martin would have cash for these transactions.

However, in the past year, Martin had asked Rodriguez to put the cocaine on his "tab" to be paid later. The payments became later and later until they finally stopped altogether. According to Rodriguez, Martin owed him in the neighborhood of twenty-five thousand dollars. In addition, Rodriguez said that Martin was becoming more belligerent and dismissive in their conversations. Rodriguez even started going to the gallery during business hours to try to collect, but Martin would either be out or unavailable. Rodriguez began to get annoyed, and even aggressive, in his conversations with Martin. Rodriguez said that, because Martin was such a high-profile person in the community, he was reluctant to push so hard that Martin would retaliate. He had heard rumors that Martin "owned" the police department.

Rodriguez went on to say that he had received a call a month ago from what he suspected was a burner phone. In a heavily disguised voice, a man asked him if he was interested in getting payment for the transactions with Martin that he had already delivered. Rodriguez thought the request was strange, but he had spent twenty-five thousand of his own money to cover the cocaine for Martin. When Rodriguez said he was interested, he was told he would receive more information in a packet that would be placed at the statue at Tommy Macaione Park, about six blocks from the Plaza. He was given the specific time and date of the pick-up and told that instructions would be inside the packet.

Rodriguez indicated that he did as instructed and picked up a sealed envelope on a certain day and time. In the packet there was a burner phone, already charged, along with typed instructions that he was to only use the burner phone when talking with the individual wanting the work done. To this point, the process had very much the same sequence to it as that of Wilcox job.

Rodriguez went on to tell Miguel that he received a call when he was at work later that day. The caller outlined to Rodriguez that there were two jobs to be done, a small one and a big one. For the small job, Rodriguez was to find someone else to carry it out. The big job was for Rodriguez to do himself. For the small job, there was a ten-thousand-dollars payment and for the larger job, there was a fifty-thousand-dollar payment. The buyer asked Rodriguez if he was still interested and told him that, once he accepted, there was no turning back. He also told him that if he were to back out, it would be the end of Rodriguez. He was told that he would be called in two days and that he needed to have someone lined up for the smaller job. He was also told that the bigger job would happen very soon after the smaller job, so to be ready. The caller reassured Rodriguez that the chances of getting caught were negligible if this was all done according to plan.

Rodriguez told Miguel that he had never before agreed to conduct transactions unless they were face-fo-face. However, he explained that Martin had put him in a bind, and he was desperate for money. The job at High Desert Landscape paid minimum wages and was a condition of his parole. He said that he could not see how to get out of the situation he was in, and that he owed money to others "upstream." Unless Martin paid him off he believed that he would be forced to engage in more dubious practices. Rodriguez portrayed himself as a victim of his own illegal conduct, thus justifying additional risky, illegal endeavors.

As I witnessed this part of the interview, I remembered from my training that victimization is a common stance among psychopaths and criminals. They report that they do the things they do because they have been victimized by the police, the government, the "system," or the rich and powerful. They view themselves as having had "no choice" in their illicit behaviors. They are masters at spinning the truth and pointing fingers. Sometimes this practice actually works. They can be very charming, engaging, cunning, and believable. I thought about Ted Bundy.

Rodriguez told Miguel that he then reached out to Wilcox for the smaller job.

When asked, "Why Wilcox?" Miguel noted that he had always seen Wilcox as a weaker, desperate, and even fearful individual who would be compliant and remain confidential. He saw Wilcox as more of a "small time" crook than a hardened criminal. He obviously did not think that Wilcox would get caught!

Miguel suggested they take a short break. Appealing to Rodriguez' sense of self-importance, Miguel indicated that they would not be able to crack this case without Rodriguez' help, and that this information would bode well with his parole officer.

Miguel did not let him know what was to come next.

64

Miguel came back to the video viewing room to confer with me about what I had observed. I told Miguel that, surprisingly, I thought Rodriguez was being truthful for the most part. I mentioned his increased anxiety when Miguel mentioned the CCTV videos and the deceptive behaviors when he described himself as a victim to Martin. Rodriguez had also flared his nose and touched his face when talking about receiving the call on what he said was a burner phone. Other than those instances, I told Miguel that I thought Rodriguez was not going to show great deception until, and if, discussing Martin's homicide. At this point, Rodriguez was not under arrest, and had only engaged in relatively small-time drug dealing. Miguel assured him that the history he had with Martin would not go against him.

Rodriguez' description of Wilcox also matched up with mine as a criminal of desperation and opportunity, rather than the typical psychopath. I actually felt a bit sorry for Wilcox. With a lack of education and training, and being the "bread winner" for his mother, turning to crime seemed like his only alternative. Wilcox was an easy mark to undertake what seemed like a low-risk arson for a big payoff.

At that moment, Dolores knocked and entered the room.

"Sorry to bother you," she said. "I wanted to update you on my research into the documents."

"Please come in," Miguel replied. "We are anxious to hear what you have found."

"Well," Dolores said a bit deflated, "I have some not-so-good news. I have tried to match the microdot patterns to all of the documents from Tyler King, Maria Montoya, Rebecca Martin, and the gallery. I conducted multiple scans of the documents and, sadly to say, none of them match those of Lawrence Wilcox.

Miguel said, surprised, "None of them?"

"Not a single one," Dolores replied. "

"What a disappointment," Miguel continued. "I thought we would get a hit on one of them and would be able to wrap this case up."

Dolores responded, "Although none of them matched, I did have another idea. I wondered if there were people, or opportunities, close to these people that may have had printers from which they could have printed the documents. Maybe we could do some research in that direction."

"What do you mean, Dolores?" Miguel queried.

"For instance," Dolores replied, "what if there is a business center at Las Vistas that Tyler King could have used? Is there a local internet café or Fed Ex office that could have been used? It would not be hard, nor take long, to explore these options. What do you think?"

Miguel sighed and replied, "We have nothing to lose. Let's generate a short list to research. I can get Sergeant Apodaca on these today. Your idea about the business center at Las Vistas is a good one. I am also familiar with the two Fed Ex offices. I know we could get samples from them. As far as internet cafes are concerned, I think there is only one now with a printer. I will call Ed and see if he can get something from them soon. It is possible that either Blake Martin or Rebecca could have used the office of their attorney, Charles Kahn. I will have Ed check that out, too."

We all stood up and Dolores was about to leave the video viewing room when Miguel said, "I think I have some legal documents from Charles Kahn from when we questioned Rebecca. We had to sign off on some issues related to confidentiality. Dolores, they should be in the file with notes from the Rebecca Martin interview. This will save some time."

"Great," Dolores replied as she left the room. "I will check out those documents and wait on Ed for the rest."

Once Dolores had left the room, I turned to Miguel and asked, "What is your strategy now with Rodriguez? Where do you go from here?"

Miguel summarized, "Rodriguez acknowledged that he was the go-between for the buyer and Wilcox. Before we heard from Dolores, I was operating on the assumption that Blake Martin was behind the Guadalupe fire to get revenge on Roberto Montoya for Montoya's unwillingness to allow Martin to become a partner at the Guadalupe. I was also assuming that Montoya would have suspected that Martin was behind the fire and may have found a way to get back at Martin, perhaps by using one of his workers like Julio Gonzales. You met him at the Montoya's office. He is former military and would do anything for Roberto."

"That is the direction in which I was going also. I thought that with Wilcox picking up payment at Martin's gallery for the torching of the Guadalupe, it made sense that Blake Martin was behind the torching. I suspected that Dolores would find a match to the printer at the gallery or at the Martin's home. No match puts a different light on the situation. Now, I am not sure what to think," I reflected. "I am also curious as to this larger job. The modus operandi for both Wilcox and Rodriguez has been the same. They were told to pick up packets with instructions and burner phones. They were given specific times and locations for picking up the packets and, in Wilcox's situation, to set the fire at the Guadalupe and then pick up the final payment. It now seems to all point to the same person, but who? And what was the larger job?"

Miguel resumed, "I need to put pressure on Rodriguez now to determine who is behind all of this, what the bigger job was, and Rodriguez' role in it. Keep observing, Scott, I do not want to miss anything in this interview."

"Will do," I answered dutifully.

We both got up to leave when Dolores again barged into the room with a smile on her face and said, "We have a match."

238

65

Stunned, Miguel and I sat back down.

"Scott," Miguel started with a smile and excitement in his voice, "I told you Dolores was our magician. She uncovers details in minutes that it would take others months to do! What do you have for us?"

Dolores replied in enthusiastically, "Because I had already pulled up the Wilcox microdot grid on my computer, all I had to do was simply input a microdot grid from any new documents and the comparison was easy. So, I found the documents that Charles Kahn had provided for us to review prior to the interview with Rebecca Martin. It turned out that there were two sets of documents from Kahn on two different occasions. When I compared the first document to that of Wilcox's, there was not a match."

She paused to let that sink in, and then continued, "When I compared the second, and most recent document, it matched perfectly! After so many previous documents did not match, I was surprised so I checked it a second time and then asked a colleague to check it again. There is no doubt that the microdot grid on the documents we have from Wilcox perfectly match those of the second Kahn documents."

Naïvely, I asked, "Does this mean that the documents from Wilcox came from Kahn's printer?"

"That is my conclusion," Dolores replied with a smile.

Miguel, who had been quiet and taking this all in finally said, "This is a twist I really did not expect. When I threw out that Rebecca or Blake could have used Kahn's office to print the documents, I was just throwing a "Hail Mary," because all other leads seemed to have vanished. Now I can use this information in my interview with Rodriguez. Hopefully, it can help us dig deeper and get to the bottom of this. Thank you Dolores! Would you make sure to treat this information as evidence, log it and make sure it is stored correctly. The last thing we need is to screw this up."

"I will make sure it is all catalogued and put in the evidence file but remember Miguel, that the document we have from Khan's office cannot be entered into evidence yet. Actually, you will have to get a search warrant to get the printer in order for this to stand up in court," Dolores said as she got up and left the room.

Miguel said as he reflected on Dolores' parting comment, "I can use this information as leverage when I talk with Rodriguez. Then we can do a 'work around' later to get a search warrant showing cause. At this point we are still focusing on the Guadalupe arson. I need to see if I can use this information to put the squeeze on Rodriguez. Keep watching, Scott, and noting any behaviors you believe to be deceptive or unusual. I will take a break about every forty-five minutes to confer with you. I need to be careful so that Rodriguez will stay willingly and not walk out, since he is not under arrest. I would really like to get this done without making an arrest until we have all of the information. If I have to make an arrest prematurely, Rodriguez may ask for an attorney and then it will take weeks. So, Scott, keep an eye on me as well. Observe any behaviors on my part that could shut Rodriguez down."

I was adept at observing executives, especially in the merger and acquisition world. I had often been hired by company executives to be on the due diligence team to lookout for behaviors indicating deceit or devious intent. Part of my work had been to try and spot inconsistencies in executives wanting to sell their companies. The motives for wanting to sell, or merge, a company were typically complicated to really understand. Common merger themes included increasing shareholder value; increasing market share; and diversifying products or customers. Yet, more often than not, there were other motives that were often related to executive greed. When I worked on these projects, it was in order to identify when executives were being straight forward and when they were being misleading. However, this was my first work with identified criminals who had made a business out of being deceptive. I had to check myself to realize that the executives with whom I had worked in the past were novices when it came to criminal deception. Actual criminals presented an entirely new challenge.

"I will keep an eye on both of you," I replied.

66

This new information about the match of Kahn's printer with that of the Wilcox document served to embolden Miguel. Noting the importance of keeping Rodriguez engaged, Miguel took a cold soft drink for Rodriguez to the interview. Rodriguez had taken a bio break and had returned to the conference room indicating an ongoing willingness to cooperate.

Miguel began, "Pablo, your insights have been exceedingly helpful. You have been forthcoming about your situation, and I know the pressure you must feel not receiving the money you were owed and ending up in debt to someone else. I imagine that the folks you are dealing with mean business."

Pablo was quiet but seemed to be appreciative of the affirmation.

Then Miguel began the interview in earnest. He explained to Pablo about his knowledge that the documents for Wilcox, and likely Rodriguez, came from a printer in Charles Khan's office. He described that the modus operandi used for Wilcox and Rodriguez were the same regarding burner phones and documents in packets. Miguel exaggerated and said that he knew who the person behind all of this was and stressed that person was the real subject of interest. He further said to Rodriguez that he could play a major role in bringing this person down.

Rodriguez began to fidget and squirm. His knee tapping increased, and his breathing deepened. This is unusual for a psychopathic personality. Typically, the more intense a situation becomes, the calmer a psychopath becomes. Because their emotional wiring is the opposite of most people, when psychopaths are in crisis, they usually become focused. Rodriguez' behavior was counter to what would have been expected. It indicated that Rodriguez wanted to go against his usual urges but was conflicted. His anxiety suggested the internal struggle he was having with himself.

He burst out emphatically, "God damnit! Kahn said he had covered all of his tracks! I should have known he would fuck-up! Anyway, that asshole Martin got exactly what he deserved!"

Momentarily speechless, and not expecting this response, Miguel had to regroup. The fact that Rodriguez confirmed Kahn as the mastermind of the operation opened the door for Miguel to get a search warrant for Kahn's office and make Dolores' findings legitimate.

"What do you mean, Pablo?" By Miguel calling Rodriguez by his first name, it made him more of a person and strengthened the alliance between Rodriguez and Miguel.

Rodriguez continued, "Fucking Martin thought his shit didn't stink. He treated everyone like he was the king of the fucking world. Well, you see how smart he is now!"

"How did this all go down, Pablo?" urged Miguel.

There ensued a long silence. Miguel knew not to push, not wanting Pablo to shut down.

After what seemed like an eternity but was only about two minutes, Pablo asked, "If I give you information you need to bring Kahn down, what do I get out of it since I have been involved?"

Having worked with the District Attorney's office in the past, Miguel knew that the DA had a point of view about plea bargaining. The DA was a very clever woman, Maxine Barbaros. She was a fifth generation New Mexican with a law degree from Georgetown. She always believed in doing what was necessary to get to the origin of the problem. She termed this her "loss leader" strategy. You give up proximate opportunities for ultimate goals. In other words, she believed in using plea bargains if there was assurance that, by doing so, she would "land the big one," as she was prone to say.

Miguel asked Rodriguez permission to make a quick call. That being granted, he called Maxine and explained the situation. Maxine had great confidence in Miguel because of his FBI experience and stellar detective work. Miguel briefly brought Maxine up to date on the events, explained that Rodriguez had not been formally charged, and asked for direction. As expected, Maxine gave him the thumbs up sign and Miguel was 'off to the races.'

67

Miguel returned to the meeting room with Rodriguez with another soft drink in hand.

"Pablo," Miguel began, "I have been instructed that I can offer you the best plea deal under the law. I do not know what you are going to tell me but, if what you tell me leads us to make an arrest, I can assure you the best deal you can get. Obviously, I cannot guarantee you that you will not have prison time, but I can guarantee that what you tell me will carry great weight in your sentencing."

Taking this all in, Pablo sat still for a moment. Except for his jitteriness when Miguel presented him with the earlier information about securing information about the origin of Wilcox's documents, I had not seen any deceptive behaviors in Rodriguez. In fact, I continued to observe Rodriguez when Miguel left the interview room to call the DA. During that time, I continued to see Rodriguez experience some anguish. I knew that psychopaths typically feel invincible and think they can outwit any opponent. Because of this, they rarely display anxiety. But Rodriguez was pacing the room, clearly grappling with what he was going to tell Miguel and considering the lesser of two evils—coming clean and hoping for a "deal," or lying and deceiving while knowing that a "deal" would be off of the table. I was as curious as Miguel as to what direction Rodriguez would take.

Finally, Rodriguez began, "Let me begin again. I lied to you when I said that a disguised voice called me on a burner phone. What really happened was that I got a call from Kahn saying he wanted to meet me to talk about a job."

"How did Kahn know who you were and how to get a hold of you?" Miguel asked.

"On one occasion, when I was making a drop to Martin at the gallery after hours, Kahn was also there. That was the only time I met him. I guess he got my cell number from Martin," Rodriguez replied.

"That makes sense," Miguel responded. "Tell me more."

"Well, Kahn said to meet him late one evening in the parking lot where I worked at High Desert Landscape. Everyone leaves work by six o'clock and the security system they have is on the very front of the building. There are no security cameras on the side parking lot, so I suggested meeting there," Rodriguez stopped to take a drink and a deep breath, another sign of his internal anguish.

Beginning again, he said, "Kahn told me he had two jobs. The smaller one I mentioned earlier was the burning of the Guadalupe restaurant. That was the one he wanted me to recruit someone for and the pay was ten thousand dollars. He suggested that I could get a 'finder's fee' from whomever I could recruit. He said once I gave him the person's name and phone number, he would take it from there. That is when I recruited Wilcox. Wilcox was eager to get the work, always talking about helping his mother. Really pathetic."

Watching from the viewing room, I saw no behaviors that Rodriguez was lying. In fact, I was so intrigued by him that my heart was probably racing faster than his as he revealed this information.

Miguel questioned, "Why would you get involved with this? You know you are on parole, and it was only a matter of time that you would get off and be a free man."

Rodriguez snickered saying, "Kahn knew about the cocaine I was providing Martin. He told me that this was a 'win-win' situation. Not only could I make some "easy money" and get out of debt, but Kahn said he would not have to tell my parole officer about my drug dealing. He warned me that, because of my previous felons, he knew I could automatically get a stiffer sentence if he "spilled the frijoles" to my parole officer. He added that he did not want to have to do that. I felt like I was in a 'lose-lose' situation, damned if I do and damned if I don't."

I noted the return of the sense of victimization often seen with psychopaths. Rodriguez was presenting himself as a victim of Kahn's wicked request, rather than taking responsibility for having put himself in this predicament in the first place!

Miguel cleverly played to Rodriguez' predicament, sympathizing saying, "Pablo, he put you in a hell of a bind. You must have felt that Kahn had you by the short hairs."

"Exactly," Rodriguez continued. "I had to do whatever that prick said."

"Tell me," Miguel asked, "why was the payoff for Wilcox set to be at the gallery instead of somewhere more private?"

Disdainfully, Rodriguez responded, "That was another one of Kahn's big ideas. He thought that if Wilcox got caught and told the cops where he got the payoff, it would point to Martin as the person behind the Guadalupe fire. Actually, with Kahn having a key to the gallery he arranged the pick-up, Wilcox would also think it was Martin behind the idea. Kahn called this his 'fail safe' plan. Big fucking plan, right?"

Miguel, pushing slightly asked, "What was the bigger job?"

During a brief silence, Rodriguez sighed, took a couple of swigs from his soda, and stretched, which were all indications of both delay and preparation for talking about the next level of information.

Finally, Rodriguez began again, "Kahn suspected that Martin owed me money for drugs. He guessed that I had no love lost for that jackass. Knowing that, Kahn said he would give me fifty-thousand to "off" Martin. I was fucking shocked at the request, the amount of money, and that his target was Martin. I thought he and Martin were big buddies. Kahn told me that Martin had stiffed him, too, and that Martin threatened to tell the state bar that Kahn was involved with using illegal drugs if he pushed him too hard. Turns out that Kahn was a victim just like me. We both had a common enemy. What a fucking joke!"

"So, Kahn was trying to solve a problem you both had," Miguel summarized.

"Yeah," Rodriguez replied. "Funny isn't it?"

"Tell me more," Miguel requested.

"Get me a cigarette, and I'll tell you the plan," Rodriguez demanded.

68

Miguel and Rodriguez both took a short bio break and Miguel brought Rodriguez the cigarette he wanted. Miguel was astounded and shaking his head at what he was hearing. He could not believe how quickly this house-of-cards was falling just by noting a high-top tennis shoe rider on a lowrider bicycle on two separate, but grainy, video tapes.

Returning to the conference room and taking their seats, Miguel began, "Tell me the plan, Pablo."

After another long sip of his soda, Rodriguez began, "Kahn knew that Martin liked his cocaine. He suggested I offer Martin an "olive branch," whatever the hell that is. It just sounded like a favor to me. He knew that I'd always provided top notch product to Martin and that he would trust me. Anyway, Kahn's idea was for me to offer Martin some really good coke but, this time, in liquid form in a syringe with a needle. Kahn said that I should cut the cocaine with enough fentanyl to be lethal. Kahn believed that when Martin died, it would be ruled a suicide as the result of a drug overdose because of all of the debt he was facing. Kahn believed that this was a fool proof-way for me to get even with Martin and get a big payoff from Kahn. This was Kahn's "win-win" proposal. Kahn knew that I fucking hated Martin."

"Sounds like a fool proof plan. What went wrong?" Miguel asked.

Rodriguez continued, "Kahn told me to contact Martin and let him know that I understood that he would pay me what he owed me in the future. He told me to act like I was sorry for having doubted Martin and that I had a special gift to bring him, meaning the cut liquid cocaine. I would bring it to him when the gallery was closed so as not to be seen."

Rodriguez took another drag from his cigarette and continued, "Martin and I set up a time for me to arrive at the gallery. I made a mixture of the liquid cocaine and the fentanyl in the syringe and took it with me.

Anytime I handle product, I use latex gloves. This was no exception. I had the gloves on as I entered through the side door, not the back door, of the gallery. The side door went directly into Martin's office and was more hidden then either the front or back doors. When I arrived, Martin let me in. Instead of being grateful, he began talking some shit about how I should be grateful that he was my 'client.' I started to get pissed but kept myself in check. I gave Martin the "gift." He accepted it but did not look like he was going to take it then. He said he was going to meet his wife for dinner at Geronimo's and wanted to be clear headed. I told him that this mix was so fine that he would only feel good and feel even more like fucking. I told him he would only need about fifteen minutes after injecting it before he could drive. I also told him that the mixture loses its potency overnight. He decided to take it then. He rolled up his sleeve, found the vein in his arm, and injected it. He gave me the syringe and needle to take with me."

"What happened next," Miguel asked.

"I was about to leave," Rodriguez continued, "when Martin started acting all aggressive and paranoid. The drugs were kicking in sooner than I had anticipated. He started talking more shit and accusing me of not trusting him to pay his debt. We were near the main gallery. The door was closed, and it was beginning to get dark outside. Martin stood between me and the side door, so I started walking toward the front of the gallery. I told him I was leaving and he tried to stop me. I was pissed by now. Martin turned his back for a moment, and I grabbed some kind of heavy art from the shelf. I hit him on the head once and he fell. I still had on the latex gloves, so I did not worry about fingerprints. I put the heavy art object back on the floor and I left. That was the last I saw of him, but I lost no sleep over hitting him. Someone needed to teach that prick a lesson."

As Rodriquez made the last statement, it was with great pride that he had dealt with an adversary. For the moment, the victim was the victor. He could only hold onto the façade of being a decent collaborator for so long before the reemergence of the real Pablo Rodriguez.

Rodriguez continued, "I met up again with Kahn in the High Desert parking lot and told him the job was finished. Kahn gave me a large, sealed envelope with twenty-five thousand dollars in small bills. I protested that he had promised me fifty thousand. He said I would get the rest of the cash in two weeks and that he would call me with details. Normally, I would have pressed him harder, but twenty-five thousand would get me out of trouble for a while."

"When did you hear about Martin's death?" Miguel asked.

"The next morning, I heard on the news that he'd been found dead in the gallery, but the police were holding back any information pending an investigation," Rodriguez replied, with some pride that he was behind killing an enemy.

"One more thing, Pablo," Miguel inquired. "Who paid off Wilcox? He said he was instructed to go to the gallery to get his payoff. Why was that?"

"Kahn had a key to the gallery, and he was behind it. He thought that, if the payoff was at the gallery and the police found out about Wilcox, then Martin would get blamed for hiring Wilcox to set the fire at the Guadalupe. Kahn said there was bad blood between Martin and Roberto Montoya. Kahn also added that Martin was treating his wife like shit, and he needed someone to teach him a lesson. I stayed out of all that and focused on getting Wilcox involved. I only heard about the fire on the news."

"Great, Pablo. You have been exceedingly helpful. Are you willing to testify to this in court if necessary?" Miguel asked hopefully.

"I know you have to arrest me now. If you keep your promise that my testimony will help reduce my sentencing then, yes. I will testify to this. If you fuck it up though, no way," said Rodriguez testily.

"I will keep my end of the deal and you keep yours," Miguel responded.

Before he left the interview room, Rodriguez uncharacteristically offered Miguel a fist bump and said, "I'm counting on you."

Miguel replied, "Thanks for everything, Pablo. You have helped immensely, and I will do my part to help you out." With that closing remark, Miguel sent in Sergeant Apodaca to arrest Rodriguez and read him his Miranda rights.

Miguel came back to the viewing room, "What do you think, Scott?"

I was almost as wrung out as Miguel. It had been a riveting interview. "First, Miguel I am amazed and humbled by all of the information you got from Rodriguez. Your approach to him was genius, treating him initially as a co-collaborator, calling him by his first name to encourage a bond, and treating him like a colleague and not a criminal. You could have been a psychologist in your former life. With the exception of Rodriguez taking some psychopathic pride in dealing with Martin, his behavior was uncharacteristically non-psychopathic. My assessment is that he knew he was cornered and that, because you were treating him civilly, he believed he could trust you as much as a psychopath can trust anyone. He was posturing for the best deal he could get before too many other people got involved. Outstanding work, Miguel."

Miguel responded, "Thanks, Scott. Your help and your partnership have been invaluable. I need to fill in the Chief and the DA here and then let's go get a beer to celebrate."

"Sounds like a plan," I replied.

Miguel brought Chief Trujillo and District Attorney Barbaros up to speed. He secured a warrant to search the office of Charles Kahn as well as an arrest warrant for Kahn. Because Kahn had been the attorney for Rebecca and there could well be a collaboration between the two of them, Miguel secured a warrant for her house as well.

Miguel and I met at the bar at Inn of the Anasazi for a beer. Miguel had invited Dolores and Sergeant Apodaca to join us and the four of us took a few moments to relish the successes of the day. It had been a team effort and it was good to begin to see some closure. Privately, I was taking no joy in all that I had heard. It was clear that Kahn was implicated. I was somewhat discouraged that Rebecca could have also had a hand in the plan to kill Blake. I was not sure if my dysphoria was because someone I had loved could be involved in a horrible crime or because of my personal failure in not having seen her deceptive pattern years ago. I knew I had to do some further exploration. However, my feelings were mixed. Knowing that Rebecca had probably been involved both saddened me and confirmed what I had sensed for some time. Her motivations were of self-interest, and she was as exploitive as Rodriguez, just more sophisticated. After a couple of beers, the earlier exhilaration subsided and fatigue began to settle over all of us, so we called it a night.

Miguel noticed my muted excitement and, after Dolores and Sergeant Apodaca were on their way out, he stopped me and asked, "What's up, Scott? It is clear to me that you are not as excited as the rest of us about bringing this case to a close. What's going on?"

"Think about it, Miguel," I said somewhat defensively. "I originally came here to help Rebecca find who might have been involved in Blake's murder. Now, I have learned that her attorney is probably behind it, and she could have also had a hand in this crime. In spite of all that happened between Rebecca and me, I am still disheartened that I may have been deceived, once again, and even used to muddy up the suspect pool. Miguel,

I need to get some kind of closure with her for my own piece of mind. I am going to see if she is available tonight. Obviously, I will not say a word about anything I have heard today or at any other time in the investigation. I have so many questions and I will let you know if I learn any new information."

I could tell by the stern look on his face that Miguel was not thrilled with the idea of me seeing Rebecca the night before her house was to be searched. He refuted, "Look Scott, this could queer the entire investigation if you screw this up. Why not just let things play out and talk to her once this all gets resolved?"

I knew Miguel had a point, but things were moving too quickly. It seemed that it is now or never for me to get some answers from Rebecca because, once the search warrant for her home is executed, she may never want to talk with me again. I replied just as certainly, "Miguel, I understand your concerns, and I will not do anything to interfere with the search or the investigation. But I feel compelled to see her tonight and I would really like your support and understanding."

At that point, Miguel shrugged, put his hand on my shoulder and said, "I understand. Go with my blessing."

At that point, we shook hands, and I was on my way. I called Rebecca and requested to see her at her house. I decided to walk the twenty minutes to her house to clarify to myself what I hoped to get from the conversation.

69

They say there are five stages to any grief process: denial, anger, bargaining, depression, and acceptance which includes forgiveness. Grief can be the result of losing someone you love, the loss of a dream, or the accepting the reality of a situation that you had been trying to avoid or deny. In my own therapy, I had gone through this grief process with the dissolution of my marriage to Rebecca. I had to systematically move through the anger stage of the betrayal, the subsequent sadness of the finality of the divorce, and finally to acceptance. When I arrived in Santa Fe in response to Rebecca's call, I had come to terms with all of the deception and no longer had feelings of loathing for Rebecca or Blake. It had only taken me three years of therapy!

As I reflected on the entire set of circumstances of the past week, it occurred to me that, in some respects, I was going through a similar, albeit less personal, grief process now as I had eleven years ago. I came back to Santa Fe with the expectation that I could, in some strange way, help Rebecca determine who Blake's murderer was. The process began with the belief that Rebecca's intentions were sincere and transparent, although I did have an ongoing nagging concern about my own intentions and why I had accepted her offer. Once I decided to stay and help her, I had taken Rebecca at her word.

By sorting through the puzzle, piece by piece, over the course of the week, I had come to terms with a renewed sense of denial, anger, and hopefulness that what I was learning about Rebecca and Charles Kahn must have an alternate explanation. In fact, I still had a glimmer of hope that Kahn had masterminded the entire plot on his own and that Rebecca was more of a bystander than a co-conspirator. The fact that Rebecca had taken some ownership of her past bad behavior, had sought out counseling, and had seemed clear-eyed about her treatment of me and subsequent affirmation of me, helped flame the embers of hope. However, those embers were dying. It was time for me to face reality.

I knew I had to be cautious about not revealing anything to her that I had learned from various sources during the week.

I got to Rebecca's gate and she buzzed me in. She opened the door of her house, wine glass in hand, and said with a friendly hug, "Oh, Scott, what a pleasant surprise. You are a dear to come over and I am so pleased to see you."

It was clear that Rebecca was dressed to impress with a black velvet blouse with round silver buttons, garnished with a silver necklace and matching silver earrings. She had on tight black pants with a Concho belt worn loosely around the untucked blouse. She wore no shoes. As before, she had the scent of the perfume she knew I had liked. She had clearly prepared to persuade.

"Can I get you a drink?" Rebecca asked.

Feeling tired after having downed a couple of beers already, I requested tonic water with lime. As Rebecca retrieved my drink, I walked around the room again, wishing I could have been a fly on the wall when Rebecca and Charles Kahn were talking. Throughout all that had happened, I still wanted Rebecca to be innocent of anything that could have happened to Blake. I decided to let Rebecca take the lead. I wanted to form my own impression of her without revealing anything I had discovered.

As I walked around the room, I could see the home office where I suspected Rebecca's computer and printer were. I was walking toward it when Rebecca returned and said, pointing to the couch, "Shall we sit?"

"Tell me, Scott," Rebecca began. "What led you to call me? I am delighted that you are here, but I must say that I was not expecting you to reach out so soon."

Taking a page from Miguel's playbook with Rodriguez, I sought to engage Rebecca and not to confront her, at least not yet. I began, "Rebecca, since I have been here, you have worked to be transparent and open about yourself, Blake, and the murder as you have seen it. Yes, you did have to correct yourself when you were initially not forthcoming, but you did own up eventually and I appreciate it."

Rebecca blushed uncharacteristically. In all of our previous meetings, I had been careful not to be complementary or affirming, not wanting to send her any mixed messages. Now, I wanted to be honest, but with a feigned softer edge than I had in past meetings.

I continued, "I was initially shocked when I received your call to come and help you. I was more than a little skeptical and had to figure out why I would agree to come to Santa Fe. Yet, if I can be of help I am glad I came."

Smiling, Rebecca responded, "I am glad you came too, Scott. It has meant the world to me to know that you are helping get to the bottom of this."

"There are some things that would be helpful if we could go over them again. I have a couple of questions if you are up to it," I stated.

Rebecca quickly responded, "I am happy to provide any information that will be of help."

"Fist, I would like to get some of your thoughts on the Guadalupe fire," I began.

"The Guadalupe fire," Rebecca asked almost startled. "What does that have to do with Blake's murder?"

I was struck by how quickly she seemed to challenge the question. Her knees began to twitch as she took another drink. I thought that her drinking may just loosen her defenses enough to give me some revealing information.

I continued, "You had mentioned that Blake's general mood seemed to have become more agitated after his last talk with Roberto on the night of the art showing at the Guadalupe. I am trying to figure out if there is any relationship between Blake's foul mood and the fire. I am also trying to piece together if there is any relationship between the fire and Blake's subsequent murder."

Quickly, Rebecca said, "You think that Blake had something to do with the fire? I know that Blake had a temper and could be manipulative, but I think him being involved in the fire is a real stretch. Besides, he was home with me the night of the fire, so he couldn't have been involved."

I knew that Blake was not involved in the fire, but I wanted to use this line of questioning as my own form of misdirection. I persisted, "If Blake was involved, Rebecca, he would not have done the job himself. He would have found someone to do the job for him—a lower-level person who either owed Blake a favor or who was doing it for money. You said yourself that something about Blake's last interaction with Roberto Montoya did not seem to go well."

"It did not go well, and we did not return to the Guadalupe after the night of the last party. But really Scott, I don't think Blake would have burned down the restaurant, do you?" she asked.

I could begin to see the wheels turning in Rebecca's mind. Her eyes were narrowing, and she was clearly entertaining a new idea. With her rhetorical question comment, I thought she could be formulating a way to create a revenge scenario between Blake and Roberto. A business deal gone wrong could certainly be a motive.

"I am just trying to understand the depth of loathing that a person would have to have to set the Guadalupe on fire or kill Blake," I pondered.

"Well, now that you mention it Scott, you should know that our finances were not exactly what I thought they were. While it is hard to imagine Blake being involved, I guess it could be possible." Rebecca said, changing her previous tone.

Rebecca had taken the bait and now I was ready for a bit more exploration. "Did Charles Kahn know about Blake's financial problems?"

"Charley," she said and then quickly corrected the use of her familiar name for him. "I mean Charles had managed all of Blake's business contracts and did know about his finances. In fact, he brought a large dossier of financial records to the interview I had with Detective Montez. That is how I became knowledgeable of Blake's financial woes. Unbeknownst to me, Blake had overcommitted to opening galleries in New York and Los Angeles at a time when revenue for the Santa Fe gallery was taking a serious hit. Given all of this, maybe Blake was involved somehow in the Guadalupe fire. He had insurance on all of the art there."

"Hmm," I wondered out loud. "So, if Blake was involved in the fire, the insurance on the art could have helped with his financial situation. Was Blake current on his payments to Charles Kahn for legal services? And how would you characterize Charles Kahn?"

With those questions, Rebecca stiffened, her neck reddened, her voice quivered and, then for the first time, she became a bit aggressive. "What exactly are you getting at, Scott? Charles has been a trusted advisor of ours for years. He has been absolutely wonderful throughout all of the chaos and difficulty since Blake's death. I am not sure exactly what you are getting at. It seems like you are just throwing stuff against the wall to see what sticks."

Rebecca's comment and the forcefulness with which she had responded told me everything I needed to know. It was evident that Rebecca was willing to consider Blake as the instigator of the Guadalupe fire, providing motive for Roberto Montoya to retaliate. It did not take very long for her to entertain this possibility. It was also clear that Rebecca's relationship with Charles Kahn, or "Charley" as she had affectionately referred to him, was more than simply a professional relationship.

Internally, I was feeling a deep sense of dread and disappointment. Knowing that "slips of the tongue" have real meaning, I came to the realization that Rebecca and "Charley" were likely in this together. My hope that Rebecca was simply collateral damage, or an innocent bystander, was no longer viable. Regardless of how the plan to kill Blake had been executed, Rebecca and Charles were obviously in this together. I found it revolting that Rebecca's involvement in Blake's murder confirmed that she was as much a psychopath as Blake had been. It should not have been a surprise given everything that I had learned. Nevertheless, knowing conclusively just how damaged, deceitful, and self-serving Rebecca was came as the final blow to any illusions I had entertained. I could now, without reservation, help Miguel and his team bring closure to this case.

It was also obvious that I needed to slowly back off and make my exit without demonstrating my deep disappointment. "Rebecca," I answered, "I am just trying to make sure I understand all of the relationships involved and if there is anything I may have missed. I am sorry if I have offended you."

"I'm sorry, too, Scott. My nerves are a bit frayed with all of this. Maybe we should call it a night and try to get together next week when I am not so tired," Rebecca said apologetically.

"I agree. Let's try to get together sometime next week," I said, knowing that it was an unlikely possibility.

We said good night and I used the Uber app to get a driver. I was really tired. My heart was heavy and would be for some time, knowing what tomorrow was to bring.

70

Morning came early as my phone rang at six o'clock. It was Miguel asking me to accompany him and the investigation team to search Kahn's office. I met Miguel at the police station and briefed him on the previous night's conversation with Rebecca. I told him that regarding Blake's murder and the Guadalupe fire, I was free of any conflicts I may have had before.

We arrived at Kahn's office just as his secretary was opening it up at eight o'clock. Miguel served her the warrant. She indicated that Kahn would not be arriving until later that morning and that she would need to let Kahn know that Miguel and the investigation team were at the office. The investigation team confiscated both printers and, with the help of the secretary, also confiscated all files and documents related to Blake and Rebecca Martin. The team walked out with boxes of files and miscellaneous documents that looked like they could be relevant. It was quite a haul.

Next we were off to Rebecca's house. I was not looking forward to seeing her under these conditions. Knowing that she was involved with Kahn, and that I had not completely revealed to her my role with Miguel, I suspected I would receive a very chilly reception. When the team arrived at Rebecca's house, Rosita the housekeeper answered the door. I had previously met her and, like everyone else I met in Santa Fe, Rosita knew Miguel. She greeted Miguel warmly and remembered me as well. Rosita indicated that Rebecca was not at home and had left earlier in the morning with a suitcase. She told Rosita that she was going to visit her sister. Rosita thought this was unusual because she had never visited her before. She indicated that she would be gone for a couple of weeks.

Rosita welcomed Miguel and the investigation team into the house. As the team searched the house, they found small packets of cocaine hidden in the bedroom closet. They also discovered reminder notes that Rebecca had written to herself crumpled and thrown in the trash. One note in particular was interesting. On the note written systematically was:

1. Call Robin Goldstein re: art insurance
2. Call about Blake's life insurance
3. UA 217 to Zurich
4. Withdraw from WF acct.
5. Pay Rosita
6. Call Scott

As they had at Kahn's office, the investigation team left Rebecca's house with a couple of boxes of documents and the printer, in the event that the printers in Kahn's office could have been switched.

With a renewed sense of urgency, Miguel turned to me and said, "I think we need to get down to the airport in Albuquerque. With Charles not at work and Rebecca indicating she was going to leave the area, plus these notes, it looks like they are leaving together. I am going to call the airport authorities and my friends at the Albuquerque police station to meet us at the airport."

Miguel made a couple of quick calls and said, "I think we can make it. The flight to Zurich goes through Chicago. It leaves in about two hours, and it is an hour's drive to the Albuquerque airport. The police will meet us there."

With that pronouncement, Miguel and I got in his car and, with sirens blaring, we headed down Interstate 25 to the Albuquerque airport.

Along the way, Miguel explained that, since we had Pablo Rodriguez' information, Charles Kahn could be arrested for suspicion of solicitation of murder. On the other hand, Miguel also suspected Rebecca was part of the murder plan, but more evidence was needed. In the meantime, she could be arrested for possession of a controlled substance. That would give the investigation team time to look at text messages, computer searches, and emails to see if a case could be built to charge her with solicitation of murder as well.

We made the hour-long trip to the Albuquerque airport mostly in silence. I had that time for the reality of all that was happening to set in. It had been only a week ago that I met Rebecca at the Santa Fe airport and she made her plea for me to help her find Blake's killer. Now, I was with the chief detective of the Santa Fe police who was about to arrest her. It was

257

dizzying, to say the least. Memories flooded my mind of being married to Rebecca years ago, her betrayal, my recovery, and now this sad conclusion. I felt a sense of sadness: sadness for Rebecca's parents and siblings; sadness for her friends, like Anna Pacheco, who had also been betrayed; and sadness for Rebecca making the choices she had made. I did not feel sadness for myself. I was somber, but eager for this chapter to be over.

The airport was now in sight and my stomach was knotted for what was to come.

71

Miguel and I conferred with the Albuquerque police and found a perch behind a column to watch the events unfold. Right on time, there was Rebecca and her attorney, Charles Kahn, entering the Albuquerque Sunport, toting their roller board suitcases headed for the United desk to check-in. From the vantage point that I had with Miguel Montez, we could see the events begin to unfold without either Rebecca or Charles seeing us.

As they got in line to check-in, three uniformed police, two men and a woman, came up to them and asked them to please step to the side so they could talk. The police were trying to avoid a public confrontation to the degree possible. However, Charles protested, letting them know that he was an attorney of some importance.

Miguel and I could see the police, acting as professionally as possible, insist that Rebecca and Charles step to the side. Once Rebecca and Charles stepped out of line with their suitcases behind them, the female officer asked Rebecca to come with her while the two male officers escorted Charles in a different direction. The male officers took Charles to a room at the end of the check-in corridor that was labeled Albuquerque Police Department. They showed Charles into the room and closed the door.

At the same time, the female officer was coming our way with Rebecca. It was at that time when Miguel and I came out from behind the large column from which we were hidden. When Rebecca saw us, she immediately turned pale and collapsed to the floor like strings being cut on a marionette. The female officer comforted her momentarily, helped her to her feet, and continued toward us.

As Rebecca came directly in front of us, Miguel said, "Rebecca Martin, I am arresting you for possession of a controlled substance. You have the right to remain silent. Anything you say can be used against you in court. You have the right to talk to a lawyer for advice before we ask you any questions. You have the right to have a lawyer with you during questioning. If you cannot afford a lawyer, one will be appointed for you before any questioning if you wish. If you decide to answer questions now without a lawyer present, you have the right to stop answering at any time. Do you understand?"

At the same moment as Rebecca said, "I understand," she flashed a look to me that was a combination of pure contempt along with a plea for pity. Miguel then handcuffed her while the female officer took possession of her suitcase.

"Scott," Rebecca said tearfully, and with some confusion. "What is this all about? I thought you were here to help find Blake's murderer. Why am I being arrested? What about last night?"

I did not answer and let the process unfold. All I could think of was the sense of vindication I felt for not having seen Rebecca's character initially. She had fooled everybody, as psychopaths often do. The reason her marriage to Blake lasted as long as it had was that they were "birds of a feather." Typical or malignant narcissists, when a relationship is no longer useful, they leave them behind easily. In extreme situations, they even kill them, or in Rebecca's instance, have them killed. Charles Kahn may have been a psychopath or, as I had been, simply manipulated by the charms of Rebecca. I suspected a combination of the two.

Miguel and the female officer led Rebecca to a police van for the drive back to Santa Fe. In a separate vehicle, police were escorting Charles Kahn into custody. Their fates would now be determined by the courts.

EPILOGUE

It had been six months since the trials of Rebecca and Charles. Through subsequent reviews of her computer, texts, emails, and financial maneuvering, it had become clear that Rebecca and Charles had been in this whole plot together. During their respective trials, Rebecca and Charles Kahn pointed fingers at each other, blaming the other for the scheme to kill Blake and walk away with the insurance money. In the end, it came clear that they had both colluded in the plans. Just as Rebecca had deceived me by having an affair with Blake, she had deceived Blake by having an affair with their attorney, Charles Kahn, for over two years. Kahn had taken a serious disliking to Blake Martin and was also in the queue waiting to get paid for services rendered, being owed over a hundred thousand dollars for legal services. I could not help but notice both the irony and the karma of the situation.

Rebecca and Charles were both found guilty of solicitation of murder, a Capital Felony. They were sentenced and could be eligible for parole in thirty years. They would be housed in the state penitentiary just south of Santa Fe. Rebecca was also found guilty of attempted insurance fraud, to the delight of Robin Goldstein.

Pablo Rodriguez was convicted of the murder of Blake Martin. True to her promise, District Attorney Maxine Barbaros took into account his assistance in bringing down Rebecca Martin and Charles Kahn by recommending a lighter sentence. Rodriguez did not actually kill Martin, but clearly beat him with the obelisk and provided the cut cocaine that Martin injected. Rodriguez was convicted on assault and the distribution of narcotics with intent to inflict harm—a Capital Felony. Rodriguez was considered a habitual criminal. Nevertheless, he was allowed to be in a special alternative incarceration program typically set aside for young felony offenders. It included training, substance abuse treatment, and counseling. If Rodriguez could successfully complete this program, he could be eligible for parole in fifteen years. While some thought the sentence was too lenient, Miguel doubted that Rodriguez would be able to effectively complete the program because of his personality and temperament, and that he would likely spend all his days behind bars.

In a total surprise to the court, Roberto Montoya decided not to press charges on Lawrence Wilcox. Knowing the full history of Wilcox's impoverished childhood, and his near destitute situation with his mother, Roberto decided to give Wilcox a second chance. In fact, he asked that once Wilcox was eligible for parole, a condition of that parole would be having Wilcox placed to work at the new Guadalupe. Always the philanthropist, Montoya would allow Wilcox the opportunity to demonstrate his abilities to learn and grow and he would be given a wage that he and his mother could live on. Roberto also provided the means for Wilcox to get training at the local technical school for a real career in the future. Montoya had a history of giving second chances and help to those less fortunate that he was. True to his word, Montoya made sure that all of the artists whose art was hanging in the Guadalupe at the time of the fire were fairly compensated for their work.

Just prior to Blake's death, Tyler King had filed a lawsuit claiming that Blake had fraudulently misrepresented a painting as a Blumenschein when it was, in fact, a fake. The court required an art expert to examine the painting and the expert determined that the painting was definitely a counterfeit. Subsequently, the court ruled in King's favor. King was now one of many in the queue to receive damages from the Blake Martin estate—damages he was unlikely to ever recover.

I had not attended the trial. However, my time back in Santa Fe, and with people I had connected, or reconnected, made the place where I had grown up seem to beckon me to return. Considering my friendship with Miguel and others in the community, I had decided to come back "home."

I traveled to Bozeman, transferred my local clients to my other colleagues, and said my goodbyes. Dorothy and I had a farewell dinner full of laughter, and some tears. I was beginning a new chapter in an old and familiar place. I was reminded of the T.S. Eliot Poem:

"We shall not cease from exploration

And the end of all our exploring
Will be to arrive where we started
And know the place for the first time."

I was ready for the next adventure.

READERS GUIDE

1. Why did the author include several scenes not related to the detective work: scenes such as the airport reunion with Rebecca; and the dinners at several Santa Fe restaurants and bars?

2. What were the biggest differences between Scott and his ex-wife Rebecca? How did Scott, being a psychologist, not see Rebecca's deception?

3. If you had been betrayed by your partner or spouse would you help them solve the murder of the person with whom they cheated?

4. Marriages of convenience are not unusual. However, plotting the murder of your spouse for money is uncommon. What would you have done if you had been in a loveless marriage like Rebecca?

5. Scott's parents encouraged his education and his values. How did your parents influence yours? How has that been a factor in your life?

6. Roberto held steadfast in not wanting to expand the Guadalupe with Blake because of family loyalty. Would you have done the same thing? Why or why not?

7. Why did Miguel return to Santa Fe from a successful career with the FBI? Have you given up opportunity for family or relationships? How did that turn out? Would you do it again?

8. Tyler King, a smart and successful businessman, was totally duped by Blake into buying a very expensive, but fraudulent, art piece? Have you experienced trusting someone only to have been disappointed, or even deceived?

9. Roberto kept his business relationship with Blake, in spite some of his concerns. Have you maintained a relationship, business or personal, with someone that was not in your best interest because you had difficulty ending it? What were the implications for you?

10. Scott used his psychological training to identify deception and interpersonal manipulation. What means do you use every day to understand others? How does this help you?

11. Scott took a risk to help Miguel, venturing into some areas that were unfamiliar and could have been dangerous. Have you taken risks before that were "out of your comfort zone?" How did they turn out? In retrospect, are there times you wish you would have taken a risk and did not?

12. Technology helped solve this mystery. The use of microdots to be able to identify printers is real. Do you ever worry that there is too much of your information available either through social media or "in the cloud" that could be used against you? What concerns do you have? What are you doing about it?

13. Part of Blake's downfall was his drug usage. Given the rampant availability of drugs across the country (like oxycodone), many people have found themselves unwittingly addicted. If you were told that your use of pain medication was excessive, what would you do?

CPSIA information can be obtained
at www.ICGtesting.com
Printed in the USA
BVHW081055260722
643031BV00010B/665

9 781632 933775